BARGAIN WITH THE DEVIL

WILLIAM CHRISTIE

ROUGH
EDGES
PRESS

Bargain with the Devil
Paperback Edition
© Copyright 2022 (As Revised) William Christie

Rough Edges Press
An Imprint of Wolfpack Publishing
5130 S. Fort Apache Rd. 215-380
Las Vegas, NV 89148

roughedgespress.com

Paperback ISBN 978-1-68549-115-4

For all my friends

Acknowledgments

My profound thanks to all those in Africa who helped me out. The responsibility for what is written here is mine, not theirs.

As always, to my agent, Richard Curtis of Richard Curtis Associates. The best in the business.

UNDERSHAFT: [*with a touch of brutality*] The government of your country! I am the government of your country: I, and Lazarus. Do you suppose that you and half a dozen amateurs like you, sitting in a row in that foolish gabble shop, can govern Undershaft and Lazarus? No, my friend: you will do what pays us. You will make war when it suits us, and keep peace when it doesn't. You will find out that trade requires certain measures when we have decided on those measures. When I want anything to keep my dividends up, you will discover that my want is a national need. When other people want something to keep my dividends down, you will call out the police and military. And in return you shall have the support and applause of my newspapers, and the delight of imagining that you are a great statesman. Government of your country! Be off with you, my boy, and play with your caucuses and leading articles and historic parties and great leaders and burning questions and the rest of your toys. *I* am going back to my counting house to pay the piper and call the tune.

George Bernard Shaw. **Major Barbara**. 1907.

BARGAIN WITH THE DEVIL

Chapter One

THE OFFICES of the Nigerian Energy Ministry were not as opulent as, say, their Arab counterparts in the Persian Gulf Emirates. Though no longer number one on the list of the most corrupt nations on earth, Nigeria definitely hadn't fallen off the charts. And that put them in a no-win position. Too sumptuous and everyone would be shaking their heads knowingly. Too Spartan and they'd be wondering whose Swiss bank account the ministry decorating budget got siphoned into. Unlike other colonial subjects the Nigerians couldn't even blame it on the British, since they'd built their capital, Abuja, out of the empty savannah beginning in the 1970's.

Abuja had supposedly been situated in the center of the country as a symbol of religious and ethnic neutrality between the Muslim north and Christian south, but most thought there were two real reasons. From the Roman aqueducts to the American interstate highway system, there was no surer source of graft than big public works projects. Build a capital city from scratch and the opportunities to skim were endless. Coupled to that was the popular Nigerian belief that their politicians had up and decided to build themselves a whole new city because the old capital of Lagos had become just too squalid and dangerous for them.

All that oil wealth still had to be displayed, however, so there were the tropical hardwoods and traditional artwork contrasting with the usual worshipful representations of that source of all good things: oil derricks and offshore platforms. Just like the Persian Gulf, there was that same nagging element of insecurity, as if the Nigerians felt they had to show the people they did business with that they weren't just a bunch of spear-carrying natives.

And they might not be wrong, Peter Avakian thought. At least based on the way his own client talked about them. He was about to return to the paperback on his lap when one of the Nigerian members of his detail caught his eye.

In the security business most of your day was spent waiting around for the principal you were protecting to do his or her business. Some people took to this better than others.

Avakian was consulting with Safoil, the South African Energy Corporation, on ways to streamline their security procedures for executive travel outside the country. One of their vice presidents was negotiating far-offshore drilling leases with the Nigerians, and Avakian had taken this trip to get a ground-floor view of what was required. It was a long time since he'd been on an actual detail, but it hadn't taken long to recall why he'd never liked doing them. It wasn't only traveling with a snotty South African who didn't like Americans.

Because most countries frowned upon armed foreigners running around on their soil, it was customary in these cases to hire local security licensed to carry firearms. Avakian had a pair with him there on the 4th floor of the Federal Secretariat Complex, and another two driving the brace of armored SUVs outside.

And Sani had been looking nervous all morning. Avakian had a near-religious belief in taking heed of your instincts. And his were telling him not to return to his book just yet.

Sani continued to fidget, and finally bounded up from his chair. "Coffee, Pete?"

Avakian always had his guys call him by his first name. He'd just as soon not get involved in boss or sir between white and black in Africa, and he had no trouble being friendly without inviting the intimacy that would undermine his authority. If everyone knew you were in charge, you didn't have to make an issue of it. "Sure, Sani."

Sani's partner Edmund, a man of less than few words, merely shook his head.

After Sani left the ante-room, Avakian stood up himself.

Edmund's eyes followed him.

"Better visit the restroom before I start drinking coffee," Avakian told him. "Be back in a minute."

Edmund nodded. It was why you always had more than one on a detail. Someone could run an errand, someone could visit the bathroom, and someone was still on duty.

Avakian went out the door and down the hall of

the corner suite past closed office doors and then the reception area. Ducking a head inside the secretaries' coffee mess. No Sani. He smiled at the secretaries, but he didn't ask any of them. Inevitably, one would say to Sani, "Oh, your boss was looking for you."

Leaving the office suite and into the main 4th floor hallway. No Sani. This was getting interesting. Imagining what a short stocky white guy with a shaven head looked like walking down a hallway exclusively populated by much taller black Nigerians put a smile on Avakian's face. As was his habit, he greeted everyone he passed, eliciting surprised but warm replies. Something along the lines of: a white businessman actually said hello to me. He peeked into open office doorways, but no Sani.

At the end of the hall Avakian paused before the entrance to the stairwell, putting his ear to the fireproof door. Sani's voice, carrying on a conversation. But only pauses—no reply from another party. So he was on his cell phone.

Avakian always banned cell phone use on security details. Otherwise everyone would be yakking and texting all day long. And bodyguards focused on their phones didn't see what was going on around them, and didn't hear what was going on around them.

But his guys could certainly use their phones during breaks, so there was no reason for Sani to be hiding out in the stairwell. Avakian pressed his ear tighter against the door, but he couldn't make out what Sani was saying.

The bad vibes were just coming in waves now. Avakian headed back. Passing through the office suite on the way to the ante-room, he stopped at the reception desk. Everyone treated secretaries like furniture, but they knew everything that went on in an office the same way nurses knew everything about hospitals. Always make friends with the secretaries. "Sarah, can I ask you for a favor?"

She was in her late twenties, big and bubbly. "You can ask, Peter."

Avakian thought Nigerians had the most mellifluous speaking voices of anyone on earth. "In about fifteen minutes, would you come in and whisper in my ear, as if you're telling me something. I want to play a little joke on the guys." Sensing resistance, he added, "I'm buying lunch."

"But are you *taking* me to lunch," she asked.

"Darlin', I'd love to. But you know I've got to work. Why don't you treat your girlfriends," he said, involving them all in the conspiracy. He pulled his hand from his pocket and pressed a wad of bills into her palm as he took her hand, then gently turned it over and kissed it.

The other secretaries began tittering. "What should I say?" she asked.

"Anything you like," Avakian replied. He held a finger up to his lips. "Just don't tell the guys."

"Fifteen minutes?" she said.

"Fifteen minutes," said Avakian.

When Sani returned with the two coffees Avakian stood up to take his, moving around so Edmund was in his sight line. "Where were you?"

Sani jumped a little. "Getting coffee."

"I had to step out for a second," Avakian said evenly. "You weren't at the coffee mess."

The truth always slid right out, but a lie took a

moment. "I had to make a call…my mom is bad sick, and I had to check on her."

A lie always contained too much information. "Oh, I'm sorry to hear that," said Avakian. "What's wrong with her?"

"Ah, she's poorly, but the doctors don't know what it is yet."

Avakian took a step closer and looked up. He was barely 5' 7", a half foot shorter, but Sani was the one who was intimidated. Sani's pupils were also dilated, giving him those "beady eyes," as the apt expression went. Involuntarily touching his mouth to hold the lie in. Unless you worked hard to master your body, it was hard to avoid giving away those non-verbal cues.

"Do you want to go to her?" Avakian asked, blowing on his coffee to cool it. "I can spare you."

At that Edmund, whom Avakian wouldn't have expected to care less, started looking very concerned.

"No, no," Sani exclaimed. "I don't want to leave you short-handed. She be fine."

"You sure?" said Avakian, taking a sip of coffee.

"Sure, sure," said Sani.

"Okay. If you change your mind, let me know," said Avakian, sitting back down. Not good. Not good at all.

A few minutes later Sarah came in, bent over, and whispered in Avakian's ear. "Is this what you wanted?"

Avakian nodded. "Perfect," he whispered back.

"What do we talk about?" she whispered.

"Anything you like."

"Do you like girls who wear garter belts?"

"Men always appreciate the extra effort," Avakian whispered, after a pause to work through the most appropriate responses—and not the first one he'd thought of.

"Some day I show you mine."

"My girlfriend would kill you. And then she'd kill me."

"I'm worth it," Sarah whispered, pulling away and sashaying across the room. All the bodyguards' eyes followed her.

Avakian had started shaving his head after losing the battle with male pattern baldness. His Armenian ancestors had bequeathed him a powerfully prominent nose, and the gravitational forces of age fifty-two accented the cragginess of his features. Like most members of the non-beautiful people set he was perfectly aware of the limits of his own attractiveness, and didn't doubt that being a well-to-do American had everything to do with the flirtation.

"Change in plans," he announced. "They're going to be in there longer than expected, and they're having lunch brought in. So you guys can go to lunch. Tell them downstairs, and take both cars. If there's another change I'll give you a call. Otherwise be back here at two o'clock."

"You don't want one of us to stay?" said Edmund.

"No need," said Avakian. "First rule in this business. If you get a decent chance to eat, take it. Because the last thing the principal cares about is your mealtimes."

"We bring you back something," said Sani.

"The secretaries are going to take care of me," Avakian said with a wink.

Forced chuckles from the other two.

Avakian would have expected a stampede out the

door, but Sani didn't move until Edmund cocked his head at him. "Two o'clock," said Avakian, holding up two fingers. "No later."

"Two o'clock," they echoed.

As soon as the door shut behind them, the smile fell off Avakian's face. He pulled out a cell phone, a local pre-paid one, and dialed. "Avakian," he said, once the connection was established. "I'm going to need you. Outside the Federal Secretariat, back gate. Within the hour. Yeah, I need that, too. Call me when you get there."

Avakian snapped the phone shut and thought for a minute. Then he returned to his paperback.

At eleven thirty the opposite door opened and the negotiating group filed out. Avakian's client the sole white face among a group of Nigerians. Avakian had a bet with himself that the jerk wouldn't even notice that his detail was gone. He'd already had to explain to the guy that bodyguards were there to protect his life, not be his personal valet service.

Admittedly painting with a broad brush, there were two main varieties of South African whites. Those who spoke Afrikaans, the Dutch dialect of the original settlers, as their primary language. And those who spoke English, the language of the British imperialists. Most spoke both, but Afrikaner and Englishman was how they tended to categorize themselves.

And Anthony Spencer was certainly an Englishman. A Brit once told Avakian that no one put on upper-class snob better than a colonial who'd gone to Oxford. That was definitely the case here, from the Saville Row pinstripes, school tie, and pocket square to the signet ring to the Piaget watch that cost as much as the typical family car. Another warning Avakian had issued, that had fallen on deaf ears. It was the kind of watch someone would follow you across town and chop your hand off to get ahold of. The personal package was nondescript: sandy hair, watery eyes, and a nose like a pistol sight for looking down on people. Avakian hadn't been called "my good man" yet, but that was only because Spencer didn't believe in speaking to the help any more than necessary. All of which, Avakian had no doubt, were going to combine to make what he had to do next even harder.

Soon the handshakes were completed, and Avakian led the way out the door. Going through the outer office all the secretaries trilled, "Goodbye, Peter." Avakian gave them a wave.

When the elevator door opened up on the ground floor, Avakian took Spencer's arm and made an unexpected turn. "We're going out the back door."

Predictably, the first sentence was a complaint. "*Why,* isn't the car out front?"

"We're not taking the car," said Avakian.

Halfway through the door. "Look, I don't know what…"

That statement was halted when Avakian grabbed him just above the elbow. "I'm going to need you to listen to me. Are you listening?"

"Release my arm…"

Instead, Avakian tightened his grip to hard enough to leave fingerprints on human skin. "You're still not listening. Are you listening now?"

In pain, it came out, "Yes, yes."

"Good. We're leaving the country right now."

"But I am supposed to leave tomorrow…," cut off when his bicep was squeezed hard enough to bring tears to his eyes. "My arm."

"You really need to give me your complete attention. You're leaving the country now because I'm pretty sure someone is planning on kidnapping you today."

"Kidnap? Me? What about the guards?" For the first time, Spencer looked back over his shoulder. "Where are the guards?"

Avakian put his sunglasses on with his free hand, and mentally paid himself off on his bet. "Your bodyguards were either going to do it themselves, or sit back and watch while it happened."

"But we always use that firm."

"Yeah, we're going to have to talk about that back in Johannesburg. I'm thinking someone made the guys a better offer. The worst trouble always comes from inside your own team."

The upper crust cool was gone, and Spencer was now stammering and off-balance. "What?"

"Didn't you ever see *The Godfather*?"

"But why?"

"Why would anyone want to kidnap you? You mean, besides this being Nigeria and you being an executive of one of the richest companies in South Africa?"

"I meant…"

"Yeah, I know. A nice guy like you, and all. Let's just say, for the sake of argument, that one of the Nigerian officials you're negotiating with happened to accept a larger suitcase of cash from one of your competitors than the one you offered him. You get kidnapped, the competition gets the lease, and he gets to keep both suitcases plus a piece of your ransom. Sounds like a big win for him. They must have a term for that in business school, don't they?"

Spencer was beginning to focus. "How do you know I'm about to be kidnapped?"

"I don't. The only way to know for sure is to let you be kidnapped. This way, if nothing happens then I have to listen to you bellyache for the rest of the flight home. But I save your life." Avakian glanced over at him. "Don't make me reconsider my decision."

The conversation had taken them across the large parking lot to the rear gate. The complex was circled by the inevitable Nigerian wall topped by razor wire. Being a government complex of course there were a load of armed guards, and they were all staring at them, wondering why two white men in suits were going out the service gate on foot. Avakian just waved to them. You never had any trouble leaving somewhere, only getting in.

Avakian paused at the curb to check up and down the street. "Ah, there we are." About thirty yards away was a white Kia 2700, a light 4-wheeled delivery truck. This particular one had an open back like a pickup truck, empty. A Nigerian in sunglasses and a wild afro was slouching against the hood. At Avakian's arrival he straightened up. "Peter, how goes it?"

Avakian shook hands. "Good to see you, Idris. Everything ready?"

"The little item you requested is under the front seat."

"Everything better be working, Idris. And it better be clean. I get stopped by the police, I'm going to be very put out."

"That's how I stay in business, man. Everything as promised. You don't exceed the speed limit, you don't get stopped by the police."

"Yeah, right," said Avakian. He turned to Spencer. "Get in."

Spencer's tone was incredulous. "This?"

Avakian's voice dropped two octaves. "Get in."

Spencer climbed up into the passenger's seat with the same gingerly distaste as if he'd been forced to ride a donkey bareback in his Saville Road suit.

Avakian got behind the wheel.

Idris said, "Peter…"

"Just a second, Idris." Avakian started the engine. Sounded all right. Full gas tank. He leaned over and yanked a shopping bag out from under the seat. Inside was a Glock 19 9mm pistol, two loaded magazines, and a plastic Fobus holster. Avakian stripped the slide off, examined the mechanism, and did a function check. Reassembling the weapon, he slapped in a magazine and racked the slide to chamber a round. The pistol and holster went in his waistband. When he dropped the extra magazine in the pocket of his suit coat, he removed an envelope and handed it down to Idris.

Idris thumbed through the cash.

"Okay?" Avakian said.

"Very okay, man," Idris replied.

"I'll call and tell you where to pick it up."

"You get in any trouble, don't bother."

Avakian thought that over. "I'm serious about the police, Idris."

"Don't you be worrying, my friend."

Avakian shut the door, and Idris was already gone.

"Who in God's name was that?" Spencer demanded.

"Friend of a friend," Avakian said. "Having yourself a reliable fixer in the country you're working in is a major part of the job." Spencer's expression was blank. "Guys who can come up with anything you might possibly need?" It wasn't registering. "Networking? Never mind."

Spencer looked around the inside of the delivery truck as if he'd never seen one before. "And why are we driving in…in this?"

"Perfect camouflage. No one would expect to see you in anything so down-market."

"And where are we going?"

"The airport."

"But I have a dinner with the deputy minister tonight."

This was what happened when you let them sit down, Avakian thought. By all rights he should have made the bastard run alongside the truck. "We'll send your regrets once we're in the air."

"I have to make that dinner."

Denial was such a wonderful thing. Avakian pulled over by the side of the road. "Okay, I'm going back to South Africa now. You want to go to the dinner, get out."

"What?"

"Enjoy. If you get there in one piece, my advice is to savor every course. It'll probably be your last real meal."

The door didn't open. "What about my luggage?"

Well, it finally seemed to be dawning on him. Slowly. Avakian pulled out into traffic. "I'll have the hotel send our luggage along."

"I have to go back to the hotel."

"No. Dumb idea."

A long pause. "I left my passport at the hotel."

Avakian did not approve to taking your eyes off the

road while driving. Even so, he turned to look at his passenger. "You don't have your passport with you?"

"No. It's back at the hotel."

Walking around in a foreign country without a passport. But it's your own fault, Avakian, he told himself. If you were a little more used to doing details, and a little less old and dumb, you'd be carrying the idiot's passport for him. Great. He had to make a couple of turns to head them out of the Central District, where the Federal offices were located, to the Maitama District in the northern part of the city. Very exclusive and expensive, where most of the foreign embassies were located.

Abuja was still under construction, and probably would ever be, so it was a common sight to see huge grassy lots littered with building debris spread out between shiny beige office buildings. Everything had a wall around it. Which you understood immediately when you saw that the fronts of the walls had sprouted impromptu nailed-together open-air stalls with mattresses stacked up on the sidewalks or pots and pans or boxes of pirated CD's and DVD's. Every gas station was a used car lot.

The Hilton was a whole walled compound, and the guard at the southernmost gate eyed the truck dubiously. Avakian showed him the room key and receipt, but two and two just weren't coming together. Finally, unable to come up with any alternate explanation, he let the two crazy white men pass.

Inside the hotel grounds were neatly bricked sidewalks, columns of palm trees, and manicured grass. Avakian parked in the lot nearest the southern wing, opposite the pool. He thought briefly about leaving Spencer in the truck, but that was a bad idea for a great many reasons. He'd have to come along. "Okay, let's make this quick."

They avoided the lobby, and any surveillance that might have been lounging around there, along with the always-for-sale front desk. Just a phone call away from anyone who might be paying for information.

Spencer had recovered from the initial shock of being taken out of his routine, and bitched mightily about being made to take the stairs up. Avakian ignored him. Stairwells weren't perfect, but at least you could go up or down. While an elevator was a potential deathtrap whenever the doors opened.

Avakian used the key card with his left hand. The drawn Glock was in his right, but concealed under his jacket like a portrait of Napoleon. "Stay out here until I call you," he ordered.

The lock blinked green and the card was already in his pocket. Avakian turned the latch and hit the door with his shoulder at the same time. He charged in, the Glock out in front in a tight, two-handed grip.

The bathroom door was open and the shower curtain back, so no one was in there. Sweeping into the room, pistol trained on the far side of the bed until he saw it was clear. Then quickly dropping down on one knee and lifting the bedspread with his non-shooting hand. Yes, that under the bed thing had actually happened once or twice.

After a quick poke at the curtain to be sure the balcony was unoccupied, he turned around to call Spencer in. But the door was closed, and from the hallway on the other side came a series of timid knocks. Avakian shook his head. Stuck out in the hallway, and not even enough sense to put a foot in front of the door to keep it from shutting in his face.

Avakian holstered the pistol and opened the door. "Grab your passport and let's get out of here."

With Spencer safely inside, he followed his own advice about the bathroom. He'd have to make sure Spencer did, too. More often than not being a bodyguard was like being dad on the family vacation.

While washing his hands, Avakian looked up and couldn't believe what he was seeing in the mirror. Spencer had his suitcases open on the bed and was busy packing. "What the hell are you doing?"

"I'm not leaving without my things."

"You had your passport all the time," said Avakian, walking toward him. A statement, not a question.

Spencer was smiling triumphantly, like a kid who'd gotten away with something. It was the smile that did it.

Avakian swung his arm and delivered a full-force open-handed slap to the side of Spencer's head. It wiped the smile off his face and put him on the floor. Other than trained fighters, people who are hit automatically bring their hand up to the point of impact. When Spencer did, Avakian bent down and delivered another slap to the other side of his head. The message delivered, he gave Spencer a quick frisk and relieved him of his passport and his cell phone. Grabbing a fistful of Spencer's hair encouraged him up on his feet and propelled him out the door. Spencer could piss in his pants for all Avakian cared. Probably had already.

Spencer actually had tears running down his cheeks. "I *will* report this to my firm."

Jeez, what a wimp. "Going to tell on me?" Avakian said. "Well, you've got to get back to South Africa to do that. And you might just have thrown a monkey wrench into that little plan, genius. Now, I suggest you take a deep, cleansing breath and pull yourself together."

Out through the ground level door of the south wing. Plenty of security cameras if someone had bribed the monitors to give them a call. Avakian was mentally ripping himself for all the mistakes. Getting old. Getting complacent. Getting sloppy. Not good, not good at all.

Unhealthy paranoia was one of the main pitfalls of the job, along with that deadly complacency. You either fell asleep and missed everything until the roof fell in on you, or you started pulling your gun on people reaching for their phones.

So was he jumping at shadows and slapping a client for no good reason? If every jerk client got slapped, there would be fifty thousand bodyguards competing for about six clients.

Well, there wasn't much choice now. Get the jerk home and start coming to grips with retirement for real. Still, embarrassing as hell for a last job. Everyone asking: what the hell happened to Avakian? He just lost it in Nigeria.

All this was churning through his mind when, just after they left the hotel compound, the tail showed up behind them. Avakian was definitely not pleased, since all his labors up to then had been directed toward avoiding this very thing. Yet he was not totally displeased, in the way of a paranoid who suddenly discovers that he does in fact have real enemies.

"Buckle your seatbelt," he ordered Spencer.

"What?"

"Buckle up. We're being followed." Then he

added, "And do *not* turn around and look out the rear window."

Spencer had been about to do just that. "Who is following us?"

Avakian sighed. The captains of industry. "Well, I'm just guessing, mind you, but I'd have to say your prospective kidnappers. This is what happens when you show up someplace you're expected, and the people after you are pros." Two white men in a truck was great camouflage. Two white men repeatedly getting into and out of a delivery truck wasn't. And now that they were made it was something slow and easy to follow in traffic.

Avakian took a few turns, but there was just the one car behind them.

Spencer was locked onto his side mirror. "I can't see anyone."

"Imagine that," said Avakian. "Black Mercedes, four cars back. Want to bet they're talking to someone else on the phone even as we speak?"

Avakian knew that if it went on much longer two or more cars would show up and they'd be driving into some jackpot for sure. He had no intention of letting that happen. Mainly because the first move in the kidnapping playbook was to always blow away the bodyguard in front of the victim, making them easier to handle and leaving one less piece of excess baggage to drag around.

A phone was vibrating on Avakian's belt. He had to feel around, because he was carrying three. Ironic for a man who bitterly hated mobile phones. It was his regular phone, and a familiar number. "Hi, Judy," he said cheerily. "Couldn't sleep, or did you just get out of surgery? Yeah, that's what I thought. Okay, but what kind of crash?"

Avakian laughed loudly, while Spencer looked at him as if he were a madman.

"What do I keep telling you about motorcycles?" Avakian demanded into the phone. "I know, right? Look, honey, I'm in the middle of something right now. Uh, huh. No, just the usual work stuff. Let me call you back when I have a little more time. Okay. Miss you, too. Bye." He snapped the phone shut and secured it back on his belt. "Girlfriend's an orthopedic surgeon in Denver. Like every woman in the world, her timing is immaculate. Now, what were we talking about?"

"The car following us!" Spencer burst out. Then he flinched, as if expecting to get hit again.

But Avakian was utterly calm. "Right. Black Mercedes. It's all coming back to me now."

Not getting hit emboldened Spencer. "Are you going to shoot them?"

Avakian glanced over at him. "Bloodthirsty little businessman, aren't you?" He popped the clutch, stalling the truck out in the middle of the road.

"What in God's name are you doing?"

"Stopping the truck," Avakian said. As horns began to blare, he turned on the emergency flashers and began to languidly wave for the cars behind to pass. "You see, there's at least two guys in that Mercedes, maybe more, and we've got to assume they're all armed. Problem with gunfights is that people get shot and, despite all your best efforts, it's not always the other guy."

The first three cars behind them had passed around. The Mercedes hesitated, and Avakian could imagine the debate inside. They had to pass or be blown, and could always turn around at the next block. "Brace yourself," he said to Spencer, shifting into reverse and flooring the gas pedal.

The wheels spun and shrieked, and the truck lurched backward. The rear bumper bar smashed into the front of the Mercedes but didn't go over the hood.

Avakian quickly shifted to first and floored it again. To rip them free in case the two vehicles were locked together, and to get the hell out of range before the occupants of the Mercedes recovered from the impact and started shooting out the windows.

Avakian ran through the gears as quickly as he could, which wasn't at all quickly in a Kia delivery truck. The rear tires felt all right. In the rearview mirror he watched people running toward the Mercedes, which was pumping steam from its hood. His stop had cleared out the traffic in front up to the next intersection. And he blew right through that, nearly clipping a Toyota sedan and ignoring the frantic waving of the traffic cop in his dark blue uniform and beret.

Once through and out of sight, he dropped his speed even with the surrounding traffic and turned back to Spencer and remarked, "Traffic accidents, on the other hand, happen all the time."

Spencer's face was gray from the lack of blood his body, in terror, had called back to its core. He was gripping the front of his seat so hard the tendons stood out in his neck. He managed, "Are we going to the airport, now?"

"So *now* you want to leave," said Avakian. "Problem is, there's just that one road to the airport. If we take it I've got a feeling we'd be running into some kind of problem. Kidnappers dressed as Nigerian cops, or maybe real Nigerian cops doing a little moonlighting. Nope, it's time to go to Plan C." He produced the local pre-paid cell, and when the number picked up, said, "Peter Avakian for the General." And after a long pause, "Yes, sir, how are you? Good, good. It seems that I'm going to need to take advantage of your hospitality. Yes, that's just about what happened. Yes, you know me. I can be on my way right now. Yes, I'm sure I can find it. If not, I'll call back. Excellent. Looking forward to seeing you, too."

Chucking, Avakian now began dialing a third phone, a Thuraya SG-2520 satellite model. Thuraya was a provider based in the United Arab Emirates with excellent coverage of Africa and a handset the size of a regular cell. "*Allo*? Jean Francois? Avakian here. *Oui, c'est un emergencie.* I need you to launch. Right now, damn it. Yes, the same location we discussed. And the same destination we discussed. No. Don't worry, I'll have it. What's your ETA? *D'accord.* Okay, get moving."

Avakian could feel Spencer's curiosity, but he kept his eyes on the road and offered no information. He had been heading south toward the airport but now made a rapid series of turns to clear their last location and eventually circle back to the north. He didn't see anything behind them, but felt it was no time to lose that healthy sense of paranoia. The cube-like red and white roadside crash barriers were perfect to put a rifleman behind. Every intersection seemed to be a gathering spot for crowds of people, parked cars with their hoods up, and sun-glassed Africans sitting on motorbikes. At best it was a vaguely threatening sight as you drove up and slowed down. You had to slow down, since most of the intersections had speed bumps. At worst it made every stop a possible ambush. But that was just the Third World.

He kept scanning the roadsides, mostly bare turned red earth and treeless from construction. As he turned onto the highway northwest toward Jiru the ground began to undulate into naked rock hills, each only lightly dotted with green. The savannah was now much more forested.

Twice he stopped to consult the directions on his BlackBerry.

After driving by once and doubling back, he turned onto an unmarked red dirt road that seemed to disappear into the forest.

"Don't ask," Avakian said after a half mile of weaving through the trees. "Not sure myself." He stopped where he thought the truck wouldn't get bogged down and once again checked the GPS on his phone. "Nope, this is supposed to be the way."

A quarter mile further and they came around a bend in the road onto a gate and a rickety guard shack with the paint peeling off it. Two Nigerians stepped out wearing unmarked green fatigues and wielding Nigerian Army FN FAL rifles. Avakian pulled up toward them very, very slowly. "Peter Avakian. The General is expecting me."

One of the guards got on a walkie-talkie while the other covered them. The events of the past half hour had totally shut Spencer down. Maybe because every question seemed to bring an answer he didn't want to hear. In any case, Avakian appreciated the silence.

The guards opened the gate and waved them on.

As soon as they passed through the road was paved. Soon the forest opened up into landscaped grounds. There was a horse paddock, a stable, several outbuildings. And finally the main house. It resembled nothing less than a very large safari lodge. Knowing the owner, Avakian got the joke. And he understood the setup perfectly. If you had something nice in a country like Nigeria you kept it hidden and hired your own army to defend it or else someone was going to show up and take it away from you. In this part of the world a gated community wasn't an affectation but a necessity.

As they came around the circular drive a servant wearing a blazer was waiting for them in front of the house. "Be on your best behavior," Avakian warned Spencer.

The servant didn't blink an eye as Avakian climbed down from the battered truck. "Mr. Avakian?"

"That's right. What's your name?"

Now he did blink an eye. "Joseph, sir. The General is waiting to receive you. Please follow me."

"Very nice to meet you, Joseph. You can have someone move the truck to where the General keeps his working vehicles. The keys are in the ignition."

"Very good, sir."

The sheer level of consistency from Kuala Lumpur to Buenos Aires to Abuja always led Avakian to suspect that all high-end servants were trained from a single British butler's manual that was directly sourced from the Jeeves novels of P.G. Wodehouse. Except that the irony was always lost in translation.

The house was beautifully appointed, local art and Western furnishing. They passed through double doors into a pool and patio area. Standing beside an umbrella-covered table was an imposing African man in his fifties. Close to six feet tall, with rough features that left him less than handsome except for the intelligent, wary eyes. He had the shoulders of an athlete but the abdomen of a man who'd acquired thirty pounds in middle age, and wore an immaculate white shirt whose creases could have been used as an edged weapon, tailored slacks, and handmade loafers.

He charged forward, passing the servant as if he weren't even there, and wrapped Avakian up in a bear hug. "Ah, my good friend. It has been too long."

Avakian locked his wrists and briefly lifted the man off the ground. "You're living large, Hamzah."

The black man laughed uproariously and slapped Avakian across the back. "He tells me that I have settled into the comfortable years," he said to Spencer. "While he is the same block of granite that I knew fifteen years ago."

"Just wait until I stop having to work for a living," said Avakian, smiling affectionately. "General Medani, allow me to introduce Mr. Anthony Spencer of the South African Energy Corporation. Mr. Spencer, Major General Hamzah Medani of the Nigerian Army."

Spencer had a tight little smile on his face, like that of an archbishop forced to attend a Polynesian fertility ceremony. "My pleasure, General."

Avakian watched the General take it all in. He didn't offer his hand. "The pleasure is mine, Mr. Spencer. Welcome to my home."

Spencer said, "Thank you for your hospitality."

The General was still running the rule over him. "Perhaps you would like to freshen up a bit?"

"I would, thank you."

"Joseph will show you." And with a tiny hand gesture, both the servant and Spencer were dismissed.

The General turned back to Avakian, and his

expression made them both laugh. "Wherever did you find him?"

"My client," Avakian said with a resigned shrug. "Or should I say his company is."

"Whatever did you do to him?"

"Saved his life."

"Most probably against his will."

Avakian nodded.

"This must be why he looks so terrible."

"Just a little post-traumatic stress," said Avakian. "But don't worry about it. I'm sure he has a top-notch medical plan."

"Will you tell me the story?"

"How could I refuse and insult your hospitality?"

"I have truly missed you," General Medani said. "But then it was always difficult to know when you were speaking frankly and when you were, as the British say, taking the piss out of someone." He glanced at his watch. "Will you stay for lunch?"

"I'd like to say I never argue with generals. But we both know that wouldn't be true."

"I will take that as a yes, Peter. It is a little early. Tea?"

"Tea?" said Avakian, as if he'd just been insulted. "Have you gone on the wagon, Hamzah?"

The General laughed again, and waved to another servant who appeared with a silver tray holding a bottle of Glenlivet and some glasses. "Have you begun drinking your whiskey with ice, like an American swine?"

"Oh, now that hurt," said Avakian. "Just leave the water on the side. I wouldn't want to get dehydrated."

Lunch was served on the patio, and the General was holding court, telling Spencer, "Peter and I were students together at the American Army Command and Staff College at Fort Leavenworth in Kansas. We were both young majors, and I had never seen such a place as Kansas. I do not think I have ever been as cold in my life as I was that winter. And then this strange man in a green beret introduced himself and introduced me to two very important things. Single malt scotch and hunting pheasant." He shook his head. "But young Nigerian Army majors cannot afford much single malt."

"So you drank all of mine," said Avakian.

"Unfortunately, I have never been able to introduce pheasant to Nigeria," the General said sadly to Spencer, ignoring Avakian. "And he also took me to more interesting places than Kansas. Have you ever been to the Grand Canyon?"

Unlike Avakian, Spencer had left his jacket and tie on and was sweating like a wheel of cheese. He'd also self-medicated his trauma with alcohol, and that combined with the heat had brought him to the point where it was much easier to shake his head no than speak.

"You should make a point of it," the General said. "And then years later I was a young colonel doing peacekeeping in Sierra Leone, and one day an American lieutenant colonel in a green beret walks up, lifts me from the ground just as you saw, and says to me, "Hamzah, long time no see." My staff were shocked. The coincidences of life are very strange, are they not."

"No coincidence there," said Avakian. "You teach a major to drink scotch, and he becomes a general. I've got a whole bunch of them that made it. Be smart, keep your nose clean, don't argue with generals, and you're good to go. Otherwise you retire as a colonel."

The General smiled at him affectionately, then turned back to Spencer. "You were very lucky," he said. "First of all, that you had Peter with you. All these arrangements do not just happen on a whim—they require careful planning. In advance, not when trouble strikes. And Peter is known for that, are you not, Peter?"

"Life's hard lessons," said Avakian. "The older I get, the more different exit strategies I seem to need for every country I'm visiting."

"Yes, very lucky," said the General. "It used to be a few crazy boys with pistols who would kidnap. Easy to avoid. Now these cults are very large, well armed, and well informed."

"Cults?" said Spencer.

"That's what they call gangs here," said Avakian.

"For years the politicians employ young men as thugs to intimidate voters and their political opponents," the General said with a soldier's distaste. "But when they regain office they throw these youths back onto the street. They have created whole armies in love with violence and easy money. After your company had wired the ransom to their account in some overseas bank they would most certainly have fed you to their hyena."

"Hyena?" Spencer blurted out.

"Yeah, those kinds of business contracts are hard to enforce," said Avakian.

"But you said hyena," said Spencer, to the General.

"Yes," said the General. "All these cults, they keep hyena as pets. It is a status symbol among them."

"And nature's walking garbage disposal," said

Avakian. "They even eat bones. Saves a lot of sweat digging graves, not to mention a bundle on hyena chow."

"Oh, my God," Spencer moaned. He very unsteadily rose to his feet. "Please excuse me." And disappeared into the bushes.

"He is very delicate," the General observed.

"Don't even get me started," said Avakian.

There was a drone of aircraft engines overhead, that gradually grew louder.

"That's my ride," said Avakian. "If he doesn't crash."

"I will be angry if he hits my house," said the General.

"I would be, too," said Avakian. "Now, are you sure I can't cover your expenses for this? Safoil is going to shit when they see my bill, but they'll pay."

The General shook his head. "My pleasure, my friend. But I insist that you come back and hunt birds with me before you leave Africa."

"Sounds great," said Avakian.

"Do you want me to make inquiries about these kidnappers?"

"Personally, I could care less," said Avakian. "I'll let you know if Safoil wants to pay for the information. Oh, I almost forgot. You can keep the truck. It's going to need a little fender work, and I wouldn't drive it off the ranch without changing the registration first."

"You must never change, Peter," the General ordered.

"Haven't had much luck so far," Avakian said.

The general's Range Rover brought them to the paved airstrip. A double prop Piper Navajo was parked there, the pilot masked by the fuselage. All that was visible of him were two blue-jeaned legs and a stream of urine.

"That's my boy," said Avakian. "Classy as always. We ready to go?"

"Don't you know pilots need their rest?" came a French-accented voice over the sound of a zipper being drawn up.

"I've heard that *merde* all my life," said Avakian. "Little old ladies can drive a car for ten hours, but pilots need their rest. Let's get moving." He held up a food hamper, courtesy of the General. "I've even got goodies."

"Some American shit, eh?" came the reply. "Peanut paste and jam sandwich? Those little yellow cakes made in factories and wrapped in plastic? What do you call them, Twinks?"

"Twinkies," said Avakian. "You can have what you like. I'll be eating the pâté."

The pilot appeared from around the aircraft, and he resembled nothing less than a complete stereotype of the louche Frenchman. Mid thirties, too-tight jeans, open shirt, three-day beard, collar-length hair, aviator sunglasses, cigarette dangling from the corner of his mouth.

"*Ça va*, Jean Francois," said Avakian. "Still listening to those Serge Gainsbourg albums, eh?"

"Peter, how wonderful to see you." And then without a pause for breath, "You have my money?"

Avakian handed over another envelope.

Jean Francois riffled through the banknotes. "*Bien*." Then he theatrically scanned the tree line. "Will there be people shooting at us soon?"

"Not this time," said Avakian, gesturing for

Spencer to board the aircraft. Which he did, very unsteadily.

Eyeing him carefully, Jean Francois said, "He pukes in my plane, it costs you extra."

"You know as well as I do," Avakian replied. "I agree to that and you'll honk this thing around until you *make* him puke."

The Frenchman smiled for the first time.

"Yaoundé, Cameroon," said Avakian. "And don't take the scenic route."

"You want to land at the airport?"

"Don't worry, we're legal."

"Two and a half hours," said Jean Francois. "No problem."

The propellers revved up and the Piper shot down the strip. As it went airborne it skimmed over the trees on the far side and stood on its side as Jean Francois banked hard.

Spencer had turned gray again.

"Very nice strip," Jean Francois said over the engine noise as he leveled off. "Your friend does well."

"I'm sure he does," said Avakian. "You don't get a place like this on a Nigerian general's salary. Must be a lot of stuff flying in and out of here."

"What's that building with the dome down there?" Spencer asked.

"The General has his own mosque," said Avakian.

"A Muslim?" said Spencer.

"Most of the senior officers in the Nigerian Army are Muslim," said Avakian.

"I thought Muslims didn't drink," said Spencer.

"I'm sure there are one or two Christians who don't keep the Sabbath day holy, either," said Avakian. "Now, I'm going to take a nap. Don't wake me unless we're about to land. Or crash. Oh, Jean Francois. I've got to throw a pistol out the window before we touch down. Don't let me forget."

"Pistol?" said Jean Francois.

"Yeah, a Glock."

"I could use one of those, Peter."

"I'm sure you could," said Avakian. "I could use not going to jail in Cameroon."

Chapter Two

AS A SECURITY PROFESSIONAL, Peter Avakian had little doubt about the most dangerous human beings on the planet. Soccer fans. Even Somali tribal militiamen high on khat took a close second. Yes, the Somalis were heavily armed, volatile, and dangerously unpredictable even when not stoned out of their gourds, but they didn't wake up in the morning just itching to stomp someone into the pavement. Soccer was a lethal combination of alcohol, the absolute freedom from restraint that came from being part of a crowd, and the incredible screaming frustration of watching a soccer game. Spending three hours watching a 1-1 tie made Avakian want to riot, too.

So with that in mind he was interested to see what a South African rugby crowd was like. Because South Africans—at least white South Africans—took their rugby just as seriously as Americans took football in, say, Pittsburgh or Denver.

Not that Avakian would have gone out of his way to attend a game, not with it on TV in any South

African drinking establishment. He certainly wouldn't have extended his trip, not with his consulting job done, nor flown from Johannesburg to Cape Town. But he wasn't about to say no when one of the Safoil board of directors offered up a flight in one of the corporate jets, a hotel room, and a seat in a private luxury box just to talk with him.

All of which led him to guess that the Nigerian job had made him the boutique flavor of the month, and that the director was going to spring some kind of private job offer on him. Keep the wife from getting carjacked while shopping at Prada; make sure the cokehead son didn't buy drugs. Maybe stick a listening device in the limo of one of his corporate rivals. Since Avakian had no intention of doing any of the above, his plans encompassed listening politely, watching the game, and catching the early flight back to the U.S. the next day.

A limo took him to the VIP lot and the laminated badge got him into a private elevator to the top of Green Point Stadium. Which was brand new, built for the 2010 soccer World Cup on a peninsula of the same name at the very tip of the city, looking out over the cold dark waters of the South Atlantic.

The elevator door brought Avakian face to face with what unsuccessful former players did for a living. The crew-cut Afrikaner who was stuffed into his venue security staff blazer like a sausage skin had a neck thick enough to take an ox yoke and hands so big anyone else could have used his wedding ring for a bracelet. He examined the laminate and said, "Mr. Avakian?" In English, but with the rolling tongue pop of the Dutch pronunciation .

"That's right," Avakian replied.

"Please follow the attendant, sir," the guard said, waving one of those massive paws toward a much, much smaller gray-haired black man whose professional uniform immediately made Avakian think: are you kidding me?

When confronted by a black servant wearing a short, starched white jacket and matching gloves, any white person who was actually aware of what they were seeing usually did one of two things. Choke up and act like there was no one in front of you and hope it all went away soon, or make some kind of awkward, heavy-handed, and inevitably embarrassing attempt to prove you're not prejudiced.

"This way, sir," the attendant said.

"I'm sorry, I didn't catch your name," said Avakian.

"Joseph, sir."

Avakian blinked, and for one brief fleeting moment thought about asking if he was related to the general's butler in Nigeria. Maybe there was some kind of rule for all African servants, so their employers would only have to remember a single name. "Lead the way, Joseph."

He followed the attendant around the curve of the hallway past a line of luxury box doors, finally stopping at one.

At least it wasn't decorated like an African game lodge, Avakian thought. No zebra skins, Zulu shields, or trophy heads.

"Mr. Sternkamp will be with you shortly, sir," the attendant said gravely. "May I offer you some refreshment?"

Avakian settled himself into the leather couch facing the full length window onto the field. "Well,

Joseph, since we're watching a game I think a beer is in order. What do you recommend?"

"What do you prefer, sir?"

"I'm not much for sweet beers. Have you got a good lager or pilsner that isn't mass-produced? If not, I'll take the mass-produced as long as it's cold."

"One moment, sir."

Avakian crossed his legs. He wasn't immune to hoping that he hadn't sounded like a complete jerk. A minute later Joseph returned and set a tall pilsner glass on the coffee table in front of him. Avakian took a sip of a very complex lager. "Wow, that's good. It's not pasteurized, is it?"

"No, sir. It is called Forester's Draught, made by a local brewpub."

"It's outstanding."

Joseph set down a tray of cheeses and crackers, and some bowls of cashews, macadamias, and almonds. "Would you care for anything else, sir?"

"No. Thank you very much, Joseph."

"If there is anything, sir, please ring." Before he left he showed Avakian the recessed button mounted on the arm of the couch.

Avakian glanced at his watch and left the beer sitting on the table. The rich and powerful worked according to their own clocks. They waited for no one, and everyone waited for them. Well, at least there was a game to watch.

The stadium was almost full. Since blue and white stripes were the predominant color scheme, it wasn't hard to pick out the home team. The crowd was predominately white. Everything in South Africa was racial, especially sport. Rugby was the white game, soccer black. There was a lot of singing—he could feel the vibration right through the windows—but no fights or thrown flares yet. There had been a misty rain earlier, but it was just overcast now. October was spring in the Southern Hemisphere.

Hearing the door click open, Avakian swung an arm over the back of the couch and twisted around. A tall man in his early sixties strode in with the confidence of someone who owned the joint. Unusually without entourage. Dressed expensive casual in a cashmere cardigan sweater, oxford shirt, slacks, and loafers. Bald on top and steel gray hair cut close on the sides. He had the physique of a former athlete who now had both the means to employ a personal trainer and the means to eat in a different 4-star restaurant every night.

Avakian stood up. Since it was work he was wearing a suit. Since it was a game he wasn't wearing a tie. The man came to him and put out his hand. "Mr. Avakian. I'm Willem Sternkamp."

Afrikaners didn't really tan under the African sun. They just turned varying hues of red. "Pleased to meet you, Mr. Sternkamp. Thank you for the invitation."

"Sit, sit," Sternkamp commanded, placing one hand on Avakian's shoulder and nearly pushing him back onto the couch.

Avakian didn't like people putting their hands on him under any circumstances, but concealed it well.

Sternkamp sat down beside him, just as Joseph soundlessly glided in and placed what looked to be a large gin and tonic on the table. As Avakian might have predicted, Sternkamp didn't even acknowledge his servant's existence.

"Are you good?" Sternkamp asked, gesturing toward the beer.

"Fine, thanks," Avakian replied.

Joseph left and Sternkamp raised his glass. "Cheers."

Avakian touched his against it. "Cheers."

"I wanted very much to meet you," said Sternkamp. "But I wasn't sure this would be your cup of tea."

His speech was Oxford layered over Afrikaans, so Avakian figured Rhodes Scholar. "Being a Yank?"

Undaunted at being called out, Sternkamp laughed. "Exactly."

"I played rugby at university," said Avakian, intentionally choosing the British term.

"Ach," Sternkamp exclaimed, lapsing back into the Afrikaner. "I thought you had the look of the front row."

"Props aren't made," Avakian said. "They're born." Meaning short and stocky.

"What university?"

"West Point."

"Ach," Sternkamp said again, this time quietly and thoughtfully. "Did you play any afterward?"

"In the U.S. Army," said Avakian. "When I had the time." He cocked his head toward the field. "Never thought I'd see cheerleaders at a rugby match, though."

A group of attractive young women were dancing on the midfield line, wearing cute little sailor caps and midriff-baring blue and white striped sailor tops. Tight spandex hot pants with, incongruously, Vodacom printed prominently across the buttocks. Taking sponsorship to the next level, Avakian thought.

Sternkamp let out a disapproving growl. "The sport needed to professionalize and modernize, but the commercialism has gone too far. Now you can barely make out the team colors for all the sponsorship logos."

"I miss the jerseys with collars," said Avakian. "These skintight performance t-shirts just don't do it for me."

"Ja. They make ruggers look like the modern dancers my wife is always dragging me to see."

Avakian chuckled. No one would ever mistake a few of these gorillas for modern dancers. "I guess we're old school. Who are we rooting for?"

"*Die Streeptruie*, of course," Sternkamp said indignantly.

"Pardon?"

"Your pardon," said Sternkamp, though without apology. "The striped jerseys." He motioned toward the team dressed in blue and white hoops, like the cheerleaders. "Western Province." A more dismissive wave in the direction of the opposition, in white with a red center band. "The Lions. Johannesburg. They've had our measure lately, but if we win this match we're in the Currie Cup semifinals." Then he abruptly shifted gears. "Do you know why I asked you here?"

"You mean besides watching the match?" Avakian said mischievously.

Sternkamp was totally serious when he said, "Yes."

Avakian shifted gears to meet his tone. There was always a test on the material. "You're a prominent and busy man, Mr. Sternkamp. I'm used to being fit into people's schedules when they want to talk business, so coming to the game doesn't surprise me. But this is a large box, and I don't see any friends, family, or business associates. Which leads me to assume you want to speak with me in some private place, where you're not regularly seen. So what can I do for you, sir?"

"Half my senior executives wouldn't have come to that conclusion until I told them. Tell me, how was young Spencer in Nigeria? Truthfully."

"He was out of his element, as anyone in his position might be. It was my skill set. He wasn't any trouble."

"That I doubt," said Sternkamp. "Your tact, and my experience, tell me he was at least a millstone, if not a bloody coward. No, you don't need to say anything." He abruptly stood up and began pacing as he spoke. "You did a fine job. Only a few years ago no one would have dared to try and kidnap one of our executives. It shows you how far this country's stock has fallen in the world."

Avakian guessed that Sternkamp was the type who liked to dictate on his feet. And there was also the psychological factor of looking down on his audience as he spoke.

"Spencer told me your evaluation of events," said Sternkamp. "And I agree. This was nothing less than an attempt to shoulder us out of Nigeria. And I tell you confidentially that it's a sad state of affairs when you can't even do a deal in Nigeria any more. But it's part and parcel of what's going on everywhere. We're used to being pushed out of markets by the big American firms and Royal Dutch. But now it's also the Russians and the Chinese. Even the bloody French. Do you know the only deal we've made lately? Papua New Guinea. Papua *bloody* New Guinea. And does our brilliant board of directors care? Of course not. The government has stocked it with blacks, Indians, coloreds, women, none of whom know a bloody thing about the oil business. It's disastrous. They shake the trees for any black with a degree, then send them to run companies. Panda bears."

Avakian really didn't want to further enable a rant like that, but the last part left him unable to help himself. "Excuse me. Did you say panda bears?"

"*Ja*. They know to put their fist in the air for the ANC boys, they know to tell us how much it's going to cost to put them in an executive office. Panda bears. Half black, half white—all they do is eat."

Well, every time you thought you'd heard it all from white corporate executives, they laid something new on you. The establishment of apartheid in 1948 only codified into law what had been practiced in South Africa since the first Dutch settlers landed in 1652. A system of racial segregation and discrimination so comprehensive and oppressive that it made the Jim Crow laws of the American south look like Sweden. That it lasted until black majority rule in 1994 made it unsurprising that there were only a limited number of blacks in the country with advanced degrees since the previous white governments had no interest whatsoever in spending any money on the health, welfare, or education of anyone who wasn't white. Avakian had heard the same garbage all over the world, but Sternkamp's little tirade was significant considering Safoil's history.

When the rest of the world gradually moved on from white supremacism South Africa found itself subject to embargoes and boycotts. A serious matter for a country with no crude oil of its own. So during the apartheid Safoil, as the national energy company, supplied the country's needs by using the process developed by the Germans in World War II to produce gasoline and diesel from coal and natural gas. They ran South Africa's gas stations and were also involved in mining and chemicals. Being so closely linked to white majority rule made them a prime target when the African National Congress came to power.

And based on what Avakian was hearing, the old Afrikaner elite were definitely feeling on the run. What Sternkamp said about the new racial composition of the board was true. There was even a retired French CEO on it to keep an eye on affirmative action in executive hiring. This hadn't come out of the blue, and the private meeting definitely wasn't about keeping the kids off cocaine. They hadn't even been interrupted by a cell phone call, which was unprecedented in Avakian's experience. He had a very bad feeling that he was about to hear something he definitely didn't want to. And for that reason he continued to keep his mouth shut and watch the game, though he could feel Sternkamp's eyes on him.

Once you got into rugby it was hard to go back to watching its younger brother, American football. The speed and action were so much superior. In rugby play didn't stop when the runner was tackled, only when the ball went out of bounds or the official blew the whistle for an infraction.

"What are your plans for the future?" said Sternkamp. True to character, it was more a demand than a question.

"I'll be heading back to the States shortly," said Avakian. "I have some commitments there."

"Another job?"

"Quite possibly."

"I must say, I appreciate both your competence and your discretion," said Sternkamp. "I daresay it would have cost us much more than he was worth to get young Spencer back. Would you be interested in another job?"

"Let me put it this way," said Avakian. "I'm always interested in hearing another proposal."

"Fair enough." Sternkamp flipped his shirt cuff back to look at his watch. "I'm about to introduce you to two gentlemen who will make the proposal. They both have my confidence."

"Do they?" said Avakian, amused by the terminology. "Your confidence. Are these gentlemen affiliated with you, or is this strictly an introduction?"

"I believe you may have met them before," said Sternkamp, blithely ignoring the question. He leaned down to press the button on his arm of the couch, and then stuck out his hand. "Good to have met you, Avakian."

Avakian rose to take it. "Likewise."

Sternkamp was out the door, and all Avakian's warning systems were blaring. Didn't even want to be in the same room with the gentlemen he was making the introduction for, eh? They called that deniability. Come to think of it, it would be interesting to know just whose luxury box this was. Oh, Avakian, what are you getting yourself into now? If he had any sense at all he'd make his own exit this very minute.

But those two evil twins curiosity and perversity kept him around. Two guys that he had met before. Well, he wasn't going to be pacing the room when they rolled in. He settled back down on the couch.

There was a single perfunctory knock before the door opened. Avakian came up off the couch and onto the balls of his feet. Initially he couldn't place the first man who entered the room, but the second brought it all back because he looked the same lean and hard bastard he'd been more than fifteen years before. It had been a long damn time.

HE ALWAYS LIKED to describe tropical forest as a wall of green. So green that even though you knew there had to be brown bark in there somewhere, your eyes still couldn't pick it out. It loomed over the winding clay-brown dirt road, as if threatening at any moment to take it back.

Two days earlier Lieutenant Colonel Peter Avakian had been knocking around the headquarters of European Command in Stuttgart, waiting to take command of the deployed 1st battalion of the 10th Special Forces Group in Panzer Kaserne. Now he was in Sierra Leone with orders to make an appreciation of the situation there. And the situation sucked.

The notorious Charles Taylor, who'd taken over the government of Liberia and treated it like his own personal shopping center, had turned his wandering eye to the diamonds and minerals of next door Sierra Leone. In 1991 he sponsored a rebel leader named Foday Sankoh with some seed money and a hundred or so Liberian mercenaries to start a civil war. Now four years later the rebels were on the outskirts of the capital, Freetown. Gazing into the abyss, the group of singularly incompetent military officers who were the Sierra Leone government called a South African company called Corporate Solutions to get them out of the jam.

And that was whose Land Rover Avakian was riding in. Former South African and British special forces, now mercenaries. An army for hire with a corporate logo.

The Land Rovers were also green, and someone had hurriedly taken a paint brush and slapped some lighter green blotches on them for extra camouflage. They didn't have catalytic converters, so if you were farther back in a column of vehicles, as Avakian was, you were driving through a fog of brown road dust mixed with leaded gasoline exhaust. Something most Americans hadn't smelled since the 1970's.

The British colonials had called Sierra Leone the white man's grave for a reason. The equatorial sun was brutal, and the humidity left a sheen of sweat on everyone that the road dust stuck to like glue. Avakian had discarded his hot wool green beret and was wearing a wide brim bush hat over his woodland camouflage battle dress uniform. His sleeves were rolled down. Every insect in the land carried some sort of disease vector, and there was no sense inviting them aboard.

He was sitting behind a retired sergeant major of the Special Air Service Regiment, Britain's elite special forces, who introduced himself as Fred. Originally from Fiji, he'd mentioned in passing that he'd fought everywhere from Borneo in 1964 to the Falkland Islands in 1982. The other three occupants of the Land Rover were former soldiers of the South African army's 32 Battalion. A group of black Angolans who had been on the losing side in their country's 1970's civil war against the Marxist MPLA. They were recruited by South Africa to form an elite, initially secret Portuguese-speaking battalion to fight in Namibia and occasionally across the border in Angola. Black soldiers with white officers in a segregated army.

With perfect irony their nickname, the buffalo soldiers, was the same as the black 9th and 10th cavalry regiments of the segregated U.S. Army during the Indian Wars of the 19th century. For obvious reasons this foreign legion was not favorably looked upon by the African National Congress when they took power, and 32 Battalion was immediately disbanded. All those well-trained but unemployed soldiers had been a ready source of mercenary talent ever since.

The road was littered with the burned out skeletons of Sierra Leone army vehicles that had been caught in rebel ambushes. The front line was supposed to be another ten miles down the road. But the sum of Avakian's military experience said that the only place the enemy was likely never to be found was where intelligence reports said they'd be.

Bullets always arrive before the sound of firing. Avakian saw them patter like raindrops in the dry dust of the road up ahead a beat or two before the distinctive *bap-bap-bap* of AK-47 fire arrived at his ears.

The ambush was aimed at the lead vehicle, a common mistake. And the first bursts missed. The typical teenaged African soldier usually pointed his weapon in the general vicinity of the target and fired full auto, eyes either open or shut, until the magazine was empty.

An RPG boomed from uphill and the rocket sailed over the lead Rover to explode in the road.

None of this would have mattered against the Sierra Leone army. The passengers of the vehicle would have huddled forlornly behind it until the ambushers had the chance to walk their fire onto the target. And the rest of the column would have turned around and run away.

That didn't happen this time. After the first burst the lead Rover was empty, everyone charging into the jungle with the vehicle left out in the road to attract the ambushers' fire.

Avakian's experienced ear told him that they were being shot at by about 20 AK's and a machinegun. The driver of his vehicle cut the wheel hard, driving it right into the trees and out of the kill zone.

Fred the Fijian sprang out with his Belgian Minimi light machinegun in one hand like a toy. Avakian followed, grabbing the folding stock AKMS and the bag of magazines Fred had helpfully pointed out when the drive began. Being a neutral observer was all well and good, but once you were caught in an ambush you either broke it or died.

Fred led the way up the hill with Avakian and the three black soldiers in single file behind him. Like a pro the Fijian was sliding between the thick foliage instead of crashing through it. His legs were moving like two pistons, and a much shorter Avakian was running uphill nearly flat out to keep up with him.

Fred, like Avakian, was basing his movement on the sound of the firing, which was off to their left. When they were about even with it Fred stopped and faced left. As they all followed him in turn they'd gone from moving in a single file to being on line. Avakian pointed a knife hand forward to give the direction, and Fred nodded. He whispered into the Motorola walkie-talkie on his webbing. "Fred here. I've flanked the ambush. Turn off your fire."

Avakian listened, and everyone down on the road who had been firing up at the ambush abruptly stopped. Damn but they were disciplined. The ambushers were still shooting downhill and probably didn't even notice it.

Fred moved forward slowly. Avakian and the others stayed even with him, everyone with a clear field of fire to their front.

Avakian was in a low crouch, left foot always forward and right dragging to create a more stable shooting platform. He felt the familiar pounding of his heart in his chest. He blinked to keep his vision from tunneling amid the dump of adrenaline through his system. The hormone sharpened everything to the point where he thought he could hear every insect buzzing in the jungle up ahead. The air was totally still in the thick foliage, cooler than out on the road but even more stupefyingly humid. The adrenaline had sucked all the moisture from his mouth.

They were close enough now that they could hear shouting along with the shooting. Avakian even thought he smelled marijuana. Toking in battle. Great idea.

He saw them first, bringing his AK from the high ready position up to his shoulder. Fred's eyes followed the barrel as a pointer until he saw them too.

The flank attack was perfect because the ambushers were all on line facing downhill. So the five of them could shoot straight down that line while only the ambusher on the far left had an unobstructed shot at them. And of course these minor leaguers hadn't put out flank guards for just such an eventuality.

Avakian positioned himself behind a tree for cover. In his favorite kneeling position, because it made you a smaller target but also made it easier to get up and move fast. He waited for Fred to initiate, which he did with a long burst from the Minimi that laced bullets down the line of ambushers. Not being sure of the sights of his weapon, Avakian opened up with a 5-round burst that took down an ambusher wearing a grubby red beret. The one next to him had his torso crisscrossed with belts of machinegun ammunition, which made a nice shiny aiming point. By that time the rest were up and running away, which only made them easier to shoot at.

Avakian's magazine ran out, and as he paused to reload Fred's Minimi continued to chatter from its 200 round belt.

The surviving ambushers were now all on a dead run back into the forest, and Fred shouted, "After them!"

Which wasn't as crazy as it sounded. They were still outnumbered, and keeping their adversaries running would keep them from reorganizing and realizing that.

Unfortunately the forest was too thick for grenades. Avakian knew that if anyone threw one the odds were that it would hit a tree trunk and bounce right back into their laps.

Shouting and firing, they chased the ambushers up the hill. Avakian was just rounding the trunk of an enormous tree when a man exploded from the brush right in front of him, screaming and firing.

The burst thudded into the tree trunk and filled his peripheral vision with a spray of wood splinters. His refusal to obey the pull to look at it saved his life, as did the insistence of an old special forces instructor, a grizzled Vietnam recon veteran, that the barrel of your weapon should always follow the track of your eyes. Already lined up, he squeezed the trigger and fired half a magazine into the African's chest. The range was so close that the man's momentum piled him up into the dirt right at Avakian's feet. Avakian squeezed off another short burst into his back, just to be sure. He flipped the body over with his foot. As he'd seen so many times after violent death, the mouth was open and the eyes amazed by what had occurred. The African's front teeth were filed, and he was wearing a mass of beads and amulets around his neck. So much for your bulletproof magic, Avakian thought.

He realized he'd fallen behind the others, and sprinted to catch up. They'd all stopped at the top of the ridgeline. The downhill opened up on a clear-cut slope, and they were enjoying the excellent shooting opportunity.

There probably was some kind of assembly area in the vicinity, because a lot more rebels were running away. Fred was on his radio again. One of the Land Rovers down below must have set up a mortar right out in the road because Avakian could hear the hollow metallic banging as it fired and watched the bursts as Fred kept adjusting the fall of the bombs onto the fleeing figures in the distance.

Once again the brush crashed next to Avakian, and he nearly opened fire before seeing a bearded white face poke out from the green. Both of them dropped their rifle muzzles at the same time.

Appearing behind the bearded man was a much cooler looking customer in an immaculate British DPM camouflage jacket, complete with sweat scarf tucked around his neck like an ascot. He was also speaking on a radio, and a few moments later the forest sounds were all drowned out by the beating of rotors overhead. A Russian Hind helicopter gunship popped up over the ridgeline and with a louder whooshing roar loosed off two whole pods of 57mm rockets downhill.

Watching with his fingers in his ears, Avakian knew that after all this any survivors were not going to stop running until their legs failed. Then they'd tell their friends that there was a new sheriff and it was definitely time to leave town.

As the helicopter flew off the bearded white man nudged his partner. "The Yank colonel's alive," he announced in that Afrikaans accent. "At least that's one headache we won't have to deal with."

————

AND EVEN AFTER all this time he still looked pretty much the same. Except the beard had gone salt and pepper. Now he was wearing jeans and a windbreaker instead of camouflage. His partner still looked immaculate, though it was easier to do in a tailored blazer and slacks. But he'd been harder to recognize, having fleshed out on many business lunches in the intervening years.

They were both his peers, over the cusp of fifty. "Payne-Best and De Wet," Avakian said.

"He remembers," Herbert Payne-Best said in that rich, upper-class English accent. He smiled at Avakian. Pieter De Wet didn't.

But then Avakian couldn't remember ever seeing that bastard smile anyway. Just his luck. Start a meeting with a South African industrialist and end up in a room with two of the most notorious mercenaries in Africa.

Unlike upper-class Americans, who only showed up in the military when there was a war on, and lately not even then, upper-class Englishmen had a long history of choosing military careers. The eldest son inherited, the clever went into business, the clergy, or other intellectual pursuits, and the less academically inclined and/or belligerent joined the Army or Navy depending on family tradition. Payne-Best was Eton, Sandhurst, and the Grenadier Guards. Avakian knew he'd also commanded the Guards Squadron of the Special Air Service Regiment.

De Wet was more the off-the-farm old school Afrikaner. Another career soldier who'd fought with South Africa's elite Reconnaissance Commandos in Namibia and Angola during the dirty wars of the 1980's.

Both had gone freelance with Corporate Solutions, which sprang into being to provide a mercenary army to the government of Angola to fight its homegrown rebel movement. All the more ironic that De Wet had fought against Angola with the UNITA rebels only a few years previously. But money talked, and military pensions didn't buy vacation homes.

In one of history's ironies, the father of the modern corporate mercenary movement was Nelson Mandela. The first black president of South Africa knew that all those hard-assed Afrikaner soldiers and security men who had spent their careers fighting the African National Congress would have to go, but leaving them sitting around unemployed and disgruntled might just be the start of an insurrection against him. Far better to get them out of the country. And if they were going to be fighting for money, far better to do it on behalf of black governments who were friends of the ANC.

After Angola Corporate Solutions moved on to

Sierra Leone. The flew into Freetown with about 125 mercenaries and a pair of Hind gunships flown by Ukrainian mercenary pilots. Within nine days they'd pushed the rebels back into the jungle. After that Avakian had returned to Germany. A few weeks later the diamond fields and mines were cleared and secured.

Corporate Solutions had initially figured out a way for the Sierra Leone government to charge the cost of their services to International Monetary Fund aid packages. Later they took a piece of the diamond mines in lieu of pay.

It all worked out well for all concerned. But Corporate Solutions had become so successful and so notorious that the South African government, now firmly in power, felt free to pass some draconian anti-mercenary laws that shut them down.

But where there was a will there was a way. All Payne-Best did was form a new up-market company, based in London, that did the exact same work but just subcontracted the unpleasant details to the same South Africans as before.

Avakian knew they were all roughly in the same business, but those two swam in waters he preferred to stay out of. He made a lot less money but he didn't have any trouble sleeping at night. The last he'd heard Payne-Best and De Wet had been funneling South African mercenaries into the insatiable security maw of Iraq, though that gold mine was pretty well tapped out. After all the cash they'd raked in he wondered why they weren't retired. And he wondered what they were up to now.

And he still hadn't walked out the door.

"Is Sternkamp part of this, or is he just facilitating the meeting?" Avakian asked.

"That would depend," Payne-Best replied.

"On whether or not I'm in?" said Avakian. "Okay, lay it on me."

"That's a relief," said De Wet. "We don't have to spend the next half hour fucking about."

The requirements of maintaining a professional reputation with the captains of industry meant that Avakian had to be polite with Sternkamp. He was under no such obligation with these two. And he now knew why he'd been summoned to watch the game. If any of the parties had been under surveillance then their watchers had long since been lost in the capacity crowd.

All the bluntness didn't put a strain on Payne-Best's manners. "Never believed in diving into waters until I knew how deep they were. Any chance of getting a drink?"

"Just push the button on the arm of the couch," said Avakian.

Joseph appeared and took their drink orders.

"Heard about you in China," said Payne-Best. "Dust up with Taiwan, public disorder, foreigners movements restricted. One moment Peter Avakian is in Beijing doing security work, next he's in Mongolia, like magic, with a bullet in his leg. Talk said you hadn't been all that particular about not breaking anything on your way out. Talk said you'd caused the Chinese no end of trouble."

"People talk," said Avakian.

"They do at that," Payne-Best agreed, as Joseph returned with their drinks. He only continued after the servant left again. "Any trouble with China since then?"

"They've got their own problems to deal with," said Avakian. "But to answer your question, I'm still here."

"So you are," said Payne-Best. "Though I imagine you take care to glance over your shoulder occasionally. And, as I understand, you haven't done any work in Asia since then."

De Wet, clutching his bottle of beer, sighed impatiently.

"No matter," said Payne-Best, in the only clue that he'd heard. "As our proposal only concerns this continent. But before I make it, I have a question."

"Will it take long?" Avakian inquired.

"That depends on the answer. I've read your complete curriculum vitae. I note you spent your Army career in special operations, but you never joined Delta Force. Did you fail selection?"

"I never took it," said Avakian.

"Too tough for you?" said De Wet.

"I wouldn't know," said Avakian, "since I never took it."

"Why not?" said Payne-Best.

Avakian should have expected the question. Both the British SAS and Delta were the prima donna snobs of all time. "At the time I got the invitation, every major operation they'd done was a failure. And you know what? That's still the case. Spent a ton of money, shot off tons of ammunition, did all the state of the art training in the world—starved the rest of special forces —and failed. A few little successes. The Colombians killed Pablo Escobar and Delta tried to take the credit. They blew a guy out of prison in Panama. But they killed a bunch of their own people in Desert Storm. Somalia was a total debacle. And Bin Laden and his entourage made their way out of Afghanistan in a parade so big they probably had the Al Qaeda pipe and drum band leading the way. Talk to Delta, and it's always someone else's fault. No, they never interested me. If you've read my resume, you know my record as far as mission accomplishment."

"Point taken," said Payne-Best. "The younger cousins have had their problems."

Typical British condescending attitude, Avakian thought. Though he was more angry with the vanity of his own last sentence than with Payne-Best. "Not that the SAS has done that much better. But at least the British manage to keep their failures highly classified."

De Wet laughed loudly. "I'm starting to remember I liked you," he told Avakian. Then to Payne-Best, "Why don't you fucking get on with it?"

"Very well," said Payne-Best. "We are going to require your discretion in this."

It came out like steel, and Avakian didn't need it to remind him to look beyond the well-cut clothes and silky public school manners and realize that he was dealing with the kind of ruthless cannibal the British upper classes had been successfully producing since the Middle Ages. Well, he'd been insulting and they were still pitching him. It meant they wanted him badly. "If you know about me, you know I'm no gossip."

"Quite right," said Payne-Best. "Unlike so many in our business, unfortunately. Well then, let's put our cards on the table. Our intention is to effect a regime change here in Africa, and we would like to enlist your services."

Avakian knew he ought to get right up and walk out the door. But some irresistible impulse kept him in his seat. After a substantial pause, he said, "Why?"

"Why what?" De Wet demanded.

"Why me?" said Avakian. "You've been doing your thing for years now. You have your own people. Why do you need me all of a sudden?"

Payne-Best glanced over at De Wet.

"He's not a fucking idiot," De Wet said. "I'd think I was being set up, too."

"It seems we're victims of our own success," said Payne-Best. "Neither of us can travel anywhere in Africa without alarms ringing and red flags springing up. We have no freedom of action. So we require someone with no record of affiliation to us, who will not cause undue alarm to the governments and intelligence agencies on the continent. And who is also a resourceful military professional. We will handle the actual execution, but we need a man who can take care of all the advance work and logistics. Rather than contract this out, we want someone working directly for us. As far as past records of success, I think ours speaks for itself. What do you say?"

Avakian's sensitive ear detected some possible trust issues among the partnership. Now it was definitely time to walk out the door. But he didn't. He said, "What's the deal?"

"A million dollars flat fee upon completion," said Payne-Best. "Afterward, if you would prefer to stay on as an advisor to the new government, then a base salary to be negotiated plus a firm offer of 5% of the monthly net take. Insurance, of course, plus all your expenses. What do you say?"

"I say everyone gets promised the moon once

everything wraps up," said Avakian. "But delivery at the end of a deal is always a problem. People tend to get frugal after they get what they want, and contract enforcement is always an issue. At the risk of seeming unpatriotic, it would have to be a million euros. And of that a quarter of a million cash, upfront. Plus fifty thousand upfront for expenses."

"I said we would cover your expenses," Payne-Best replied.

"Sure you will," said Avakian. "But again, who knows how well everything will work out. There may not be anyone around when the time comes to hand in my receipts."

Payne-Best turned to De Wet. De Wet nodded dourly. "Tells me what I already know—he's not a fucking idiot."

"Fine," said Payne-Best. "But I must insist on U.S. dollars."

"Too much deficit financing," said Avakian. "Euros or gold. Your choice."

Payne-Best paused to think that over. "Very well, then. Euros. Done?"

Avakian had hoped that his conditions would scare them off and give him an easy way out the door. No hope for that now. Agreeing to that much upfront money meant they were real. And well financed. "I've got a couple of questions first. I know you want to maintain your operational security, but I'm going to need answers because they relate to my personal survival. First, who are we working for? I need to know if it's a government."

"No worries there," said Payne-Best. "We're working for ourselves, of course."

"You're financing this out of pocket?" Avakian said skeptically.

"No, of course not," said Payne-Best. "There are a group of private investors providing seed money for the enterprise. In the business and natural resources extraction fields. And if you expect me to provide their names then my friend Pieter is wrong, and you are a fucking idiot."

Avakian now saw where Sternkamp and all his issues fit into the picture. Signing an energy deal was a lot easier when you owned the government. "Fair enough, just as long as there are no governments involved."

"We've learned our lesson in the past," said De Wet. "When governments get what they want, they always welsh on a deal."

"I wish you wouldn't say that," Payne-Best mentioned. "I'm Welsh on my mother's side."

De Wet merely rolled his eyes.

"Next question," said Avakian. "What country is it?"

"You don't hear that until you tell us you're in," said De Wet.

"I'm not in until I know the country," Avakian retorted. "I need to know how big a nut you want to crack. Don't take this the wrong way, but it's either doable or you're stringing your backers along."

De Wet laughed coldly. "Take it the wrong way? What way do you want me to take it, mate?"

"Take it any way you want," Avakian said, just as cold and not backing down. He briefly examined the utensils on the table for a choice of weapons.

And, as he'd anticipated, Payne-Best had seen him do it. Along with De Wet preparing to knock the neck off his bottle of beer. "No need for all that." He got up and went over to confer privately with De Wet. There was a muttered argument, and finally he turned and told Avakian, "The country is Benin."

"Benin?" said Avakian. Central Africa, west coast. Just above the equator. Army probably no more than a few battalions. "Do they have oil? Because I'm pretty sure they don't have anything else."

"Offshore," said Payne-Best. "Potentially a bonanza."

"Potentially," said Avakian.

"In the slim chance it doesn't pan out," said Payne-Best, "there are other business opportunities."

Avakian wondered what they might be, though he was sure he wouldn't get an answer. "That's a former French colony."

"And what of it?" said Payne-Best.

"You know as well as I do," said Avakian. "It's no trick doing a coup in a former French colony. The trick is that if Paris doesn't like your new government a couple of battalions of French paratroopers show up on your doorstep a few days later. No one else in Europe has the balls, but the French still do that sort of thing."

"They won't in this case," said Payne-Best.

"They won't, or you hope?" said Avakian.

"We know," said De Wet. "Any more questions?"

"None that you're going to answer," said Avakian.

"Any and all questions will be answered once you sign on," said Payne-Best.

"So what do you say?" De Wet demanded.

Avakian had been watching them both closely for body language cues, and it seemed they were both telling the truth—as far as that went. "I say I don't believe in diving in until I check the bottom either," he replied.

Payne-Best examined *him* minutely for a few moments, then took out a business card. "Come to my house Monday evening after supper. If you can't make up your mind in a day, you can't make up your mind."

"If your answer is no don't show up," said De Wet. "And make sure you stay out of our fucking business."

Avakian took the card.

De Wet took a few steps forward until he was inside Avakian's personal space. "You go asking around about us, you be damn careful, mate. Any word of this gets out, we're going to be fucking angry."

"This isn't my first rodeo," said Avakian.

Payne-Best smiled wanly and turned to go. As they went out through the door Avakian heard De Wet say, "What the *fuck* did he mean by that?"

Chapter Three

HAVING LOST his taste for rugby, Avakian left the stadium and walked west on Stephan Way past the Green Point Common, nothing more than a wide expanse of dry grass where local farmers had once pastured their stock. He turned right on Kiewiet Lane and soon found himself on the Beach Road in front of the 1824 Green Point Lighthouse, white and red striped like a diagonal rugby jersey.

There was no beach, just a stone and concrete breakwater above a rocky shore. A low concrete post and steel pipe fence protected the top, and the wide paving stone promenade seemed to follow the shoreline for miles. Avakian eyed it longingly—it would be great to take a run on. The wind was brisk off the water, and the waves were building larger and thumping against the breakwater.

He turned around. Beyond the ugly modern concrete apartment buildings on Beach Road the older part of Cape Town swept up before him, 19th century houses and steep old streets rising toward Table Mountain in the distance, capped on this side by the prominent rock outcropping called the Lion's Head. That starkly beautiful broken granite backdrop, that the entire city wound around, was a reminder that you were in Africa. Otherwise Cape Town might just be another European city that blended a few older period touches with the skyscrapers and shopping malls.

Avakian sat down on the stairs that led down from the lighthouse to the water over an expanse of close-cropped grass burned by the salt air. The wind seemed to have driven everyone off the waterfront, but it was just what he needed to calm him down to the point where he could think.

You had to be curious, didn't you? You knew what was going to happen the minute those two walked in the door. Should have just tipped your hat and walked out. But no, you had to hear the offer.

He wondered whether that was the reason he'd been offered the Safoil job in the first place. After all, South Africa was overrun with security pros. They certainly didn't need to import one from the U.S..

Forget about that, he told himself. Focus on the fact that you're well and truly screwed. Just sitting there and listening had put him in an untenable position. The question was, who else knew what those two were plotting? If the word got around, with his name attached, then he was through. Even if he called them right now and said no he might wind up on any number of government and intelligence agency black-lists. Just landing in a country to do some security work could get him deported at the airport. Or, in those less civilized nations, immediately thrown into prison.

Not to mention that Payne-Best and De Wet were entirely capable of leaking his name around to force him to join them, knowing he'd have to leave the business and would need a financial score to set up retirement.

He had only two choices, and he hated both. Even though it was the age-old path to fortune, he was not going to participate in stealing a country and looting its resources. That left only the alternative. And it wasn't a decision to take lightly. Mainly due to everything he knew about the government agency involved. He was going to have to give the information to the CIA. Otherwise he might wake up one morning in the future to find that Benin or South Africa was demanding his extradition. And once a U.S. Attorney started gnawing on your hindquarters they could indict you in order to freeze all your assets and then sit back and let the case run on for years without even bringing you to trial.

"Shit," Avakian said out loud. Signing on with the intelligence services of other countries was like borrowing money from the mafia. Once you got started you were never going to repay the principle, and if you didn't make the vigorish every week that pleasant veneer would come off and you'd see what real ruthlessness was. The CIA was different. You had to worry about being sucked into a vast bureaucratic web of questionable competence and notorious unreliability.

Avakian sat there watching the pounding waves for another fifteen minutes, but couldn't come up with anything better. Surrendering to the inevitable, he unholstered his BlackBerry and tapped out an e-mail to a friend of his in Washington.

Phil, I'm in Cape Town.

Did the Packers cover the point spread on Monday night?
Oh, almost forgot:
Can I ask if Nancy could oblige, not some uptight lady?
Thanks, Pete.

The U.S. National Security Agency was incredibly efficient at intercepting international e-mails, so asking a friend to identify the local CIA assets could get both parties into a hell of a lot of trouble. Once snagged out of the ether the e-mails were scanned by supercomputers that looked for trigger words like CIA, agent, bomb, or Bin Laden, though the actual algorithms were much more sophisticated. If the computers found anything interesting they spit the message out for a human to read. Encrypting a message only told them you had something to hide and egged them on to break it. Avakian doubted that any of the e-mail encryption programs available on the open market were proof against the NSA.

So he and his friends relied on simple covered ciphers. Which they always signaled by asking if a sports team had covered the spread. The next paragraph was the cipher. In this case, the first letter of each word comprised the message. Avakian had spelled out: *CIA in consul?*

Of course, if anyone was specifically looking at your stuff it wouldn't take long to break the covered cipher, but then high technology was usually defeated by the simplest things.

With Washington six hours behind Cape Town, he ought to get an answer relatively soon.

There was also an e-mail from his girlfriend Judy. She was expecting him back in Denver in a day or two. This was going to require a little tap dancing. He carefully composed a reply and sent it off. She was used to frequent changes in his schedule, but Avakian was all too aware that, with women, there wasn't an infinite reservoir of that kind of good will.

Putting the BlackBerry away and finally looking up, he realized that he'd been preoccupied with his own troubles to his detriment. He was being watched by a couple of black teenagers.

Avakian's first thought was that Payne-Best and De Wet were having him followed until he made up his mind. It was something he'd think about doing in their place. But no, these kids were getting ready to rip him off.

He kicked himself for hanging around so long near a prominent tourist attraction like the lighthouse, especially on a blustery day when there weren't any people around. He'd parked his middle aged butt right in the middle of some gang's hunting ground. So much for the security professional.

Whenever the coercive power of a state fell away, be it Eastern Europe after the fall of communism, Hurricane Katrina in the U.S., or the transition to black majority rule in South Africa in 1994, the only people organized, equipped, and temperamentally prepared to fill the vacuum were criminals. South Africa was the only country in the world with a first world infrastructure and a third world population existing literally side by side. This combined a highly politicized black struggle against white racism with black kids who'd grown up in shacks without running water, education, or jobs, and watched white people driving by every day in Range Rovers. So of course all crime was seen through the prism of race. Whereas Avakian would ask whether white people were getting jacked because they were white, as *they* seemed to think, or because it was a good bet they had more money in their pockets and drove better cars.

Just as it was better to rip off a tourist in places tourists frequented, because they didn't know the local scene and wouldn't show up in court even if their assailants did get caught.

Well, you got yourself into this, he told himself. Now get yourself out. He put his sunglasses on to mask the direction of his gaze. The two teenagers had positioned themselves to cut him off on the shore walkway heading north, and also if he went back to the street.

Avakian stood up and took a couple of steps, and was surprised that they didn't make their move. One of them was on his phone. Okay, he got it. Two on one wasn't good enough odds. They were going to drive him into someone else waiting up ahead. A classic example of million year old hunting behavior, though he doubted that these particular predators would be aware of that.

The first piece of security advice Avakian always gave executive travelers was to carry a dummy wallet in their pocket. Salt it with fifty dollars in cash and a couple of expired credit cards from closed accounts. And have an old expired passport handy. If you got into a jam just hand them over without any argument and then you didn't have to spend the next week cancelling cards and replacing documents. He practiced what he preached, and his real wallet and passport were tucked away in a specially tailored pocket inside the front waistband of his trousers.

The only problem with that in South African was the signature violence of its street crime. Way too many people got casually shot during run of the mill muggings for him to contemplate blithely walking into one. Even if they didn't have guns, stab wounds took an annoyingly long time to heal. Since he wasn't armed Avakian intended to practice another thing that he always preached, which was to never bring your fists to a gunfight.

The ironic thing about mugging was that most people saw it coming. But either paralyzed by fear or hoping against hope, they just let their potential attackers walk right up to them and ask for a light, or the time, or for change to buy a soda. And when they helpfully stuck their hands into their pockets the weapons came out, or they got punched in the face.

The one thing they really needed to do, they didn't, because they were too embarrassed. Yet Avakian's worldview also didn't preclude running away whenever necessary. As soon as he got the lighthouse between him and the first pair he sprinted for the road. He only slowed slightly upon reaching it, then sped up through the traffic amid blowing horns. Pausing to glance behind would be a mistake. They'd either given it up or were running after him, and if it was the latter then he needed a barricade. You had to go with what you had, and what he had right in front of him was an ice cream shop on the ground floor of an apartment building.

In the reflection of the front window he could see the teenagers trying to cross the street against traffic. He was just in time.

The shop was deserted—it wasn't an ice cream day. Behind the counter was a tall, turbaned, and bearded young Sikh. Avakian snapped the door lock as he entered. The smile came off the Sikh's face and he reached under the counter.

Avakian held both hands up in front of him. "Do you see those young men out there?" he said quickly, pointing through the window. "They're planning on robbing your store. I overheard them talking and I thought I ought to come in and warn you."

"Ah, an American," the Sikh exclaimed. His hand came out from under the counter with a 9mm Beretta in it.

Now that's what I'm talking about, Avakian thought. And he'd been worried about ice cream shops. Well, the British empire had relied on the Sikhs for 125 years, why shouldn't he?

"Please do not be alarmed, sir," the Sikh said. "If you would, step around the end of the counter and join me."

Avakian did, just as one of the teenagers, hand inside his coat, rattled the locked door and stuck his face up to the door glass, trying to get a better view inside. Pretty damn bold—they didn't even care about the cops.

Behind the counter, the Sikh pointed to a closed circuit TV monitor. "Are those two the only miscreants, sir?"

Miscreants. Avakian liked that word. There were not only security cameras in the store, but the service alley behind and a full view of the sidewalk outside in both directions. A nice setup. "Those two," said Avakian, pointing. "And there. The other two coming up from the south."

"Very good, sir." The Sikh was immediately on the phone and, Avakian had to give due credit, provided beautiful descriptions. He kept an eye on his watch. It was always good to know the local response times.

Three minutes later two cars came bombing down

opposite sides of the road, lights flashing. The teenagers scattered and ran. Two made it before the shotguns came out. The other pair didn't.

C'mon, c'mon, Avakian thought, as the teenagers, laying on the ground, were searched. Then one of the uniforms triumphantly held up a pistol. That was it. Game over.

What really interested Avakian was that the Sikh had not called the police, and the police had not shown up. The patrol cars, which looked like police cars down to the flashing lights, had Armed Response written on the side. And bore the logo of an international security firm.

One of the ironic things about police states was that the police in them were always much better at crushing dissent than solving crime. Such was the case in South Africa's past. They hadn't served the public, they ordered them around. And, when necessary, beat a confession out of them. So when the ANC took over in 1994 their main priority was pulling the police's teeth. Most of the white senior officers were retired, and large-scale affirmative action took place. This resulted in a force that was undermanned, under-trained, underpaid, and prone to corruption in the face of the staggering crime wave that blew up once all those screws that had held society down were loosened.

In keeping with classical economic theory, this resulted in an explosion in the use of private security firms. They currently outnumbered the police by four to one. One of Avakian's tests for the relative stability of a country was the degree to which personal security had become privatized. Just as crime flowed into any vacuum in state power, protection went to those who could afford it. The poor, who supplied the foot soldiers of the criminal underclass and suffered from it in equal measure, lost out as always.

The Sikh secured the Beretta back under the counter. "Now the police will come," he said. "How can I thank you, sir? Only an American would come in to warn me. No one else. Please, anything you like. Free of charge."

"Well, it's really not necessary," said Avakian, until he saw the Sikh's face and remembered Sikh hospitality. "Maybe just a coffee to go. And if you have a back door, I'd just as soon not get involved with the police."

"Of course, of course," said the Sikh, snapping open a paper bag and stuffing it with takeout coffee and everything else he could lay his hands on. "You will be standing about all afternoon while they fill out forms, and your holiday will be ruined." He led Avakian through a door and the back room with the larger ice cream freezers. And carefully checked the view on another small TV monitor before popping the locks on a very thick reinforced steel door. "Thank you again sir." He stuffed a card into the paper sack and handed it over. "If I can ever be of service in the future."

Avakian accepted the bag and pressed his hands together. "*Sat Sri Akal.*" It was the Sikh greeting. God is true and timeless.

The Sikh beamed. He also pressed his hands together. "*Sat Sri Akal.* God bless you sir!"

"I'll say amen to that," Avakian muttered under his breath while raising a saluting hand over his shoulder.

On Bay Road behind the apartment building he consulted his BlackBerry for a Cape Town street map and a listing of hotels. He found a nice little inn that was just to the south in the Seapoint neighborhood.

Avakian didn't believe in big tourist hotels unless they were a job perk he had no say over. They were soft targets for anyone who wanted to kill a bunch of westerners with car bombs or commando teams armed with AK-47's. And he'd noticed a rental car office just down the street. He called both and made reservations.

With that done he walked back to the stadium. The game was over and the crowds filing out. No rioting between the opposing teams' supporters. Just went to show that there was a catharsis in rugby not present in soccer.

The limo was still in the parking lot. "Where to, sir?" the driver asked.

"Don't need you anymore, thanks," said Avakian, collecting the single small carry-on that was all he ever traveled with.

"You sure, sir?" said the driver, looking worried.

"Positive," Avakian replied, handing over a nice tip. He disappeared into the crowd of fans.

Chapter Four

AVAKIAN'S HOTEL was much too small to offer anything more than a bare bones continental breakfast, and that Sunday morning he felt the need for something more substantial. The nice thing about being near the sea was that there were always a lot of eateries that catered to both early and late morning risers.

Crossing the hotel lobby he noticed a young black woman waiting just outside the glass front door with her eyes on him. She was in her late twenties, early thirties. It was way too early in the morning for the professionals to be out, and if she was bait for a mugging the muscle wasn't in the vicinity. So who else would be hanging around a hotel?

As he stepped out onto the sidewalk she stepped into his path and said, "Mr. Avakian?"

"That's right," he said, smiling pleasantly and giving no outward indication of the alarm he felt at her knowing his name.

"My name is Patience Mbatha," she said, extending her hand.

In general, women who initiated a handshake were open minded, confident, and concerned about a good first impression. "How do you do," Avakian said, returning it. Nice and firm—I won't be dominated.

"I'm a writer for *South Africa* magazine. May I have a few minutes of your time?"

Great. That was all he needed. But Avakian kept it cordial. "To talk about what?"

"A foreign professional's impressions of the security situation in South Africa."

Yeah, right. On his second day in town. That definitely had to be a new world record, especially since he hadn't issued a press release to announce his arrival. He was reasonably sure he hadn't been tailed. But that didn't matter. The limo driver had his name, as did the stadium personnel. Not to mention the Safoil plane crew. Any one of them would cough that up for a few pieces of silver across their palm, and it had been more than enough time to call the hotels and see if there was an Avakian registered.

In his experience the surest way to incite the press was to tell them to get lost. Besides, he wanted to find out a few things himself. First of all, if she actually was with the press. How she'd run him down so quickly. And what she really wanted to talk to him about. "I'm about to have breakfast. Would you care to join me?"

She favored him with a really big, really warm smile. "That would be lovely."

They walked down the street and he stopped at the first place with a good crowd and a good smell. Avakian wasn't necessarily a booty man, but as he held the door open he paused to admire hers in her designer jeans.

They took an open booth. Patience Mbatha removed the leather jacket that matched her boots, and Avakian stood until she sat down.

She had high cheekbones and striking, almond-shaped eyes. She wore her hair very, very short, close to what would be a buzz cut on a man, and it accentuated an elegant forehead. Her complexion would be unremarkable to an American, since slavery had ensured that there were no African Americans with exclusively African heritage. The races had mixed the same way in South Africa, both during and after slavery, though the white supremacists there had the same professed horror of it. Under the apartheid system of rigid racial classification and separation the offspring of such unions had a category all to themselves. Set apart from white, black, and Asian, they were officially called colored. And ironically had a higher social status than blacks.

She unpacked half her voluminous bag before finding a notebook and a digital recorder. Then packed it all back up as Avakian watched, amused. "Do you mind if I record our interview?"

"This is going to have to be off the record," said Avakian.

"That's no problem," she said, putting the recorder back in her bag and opening the notebook.

"First of all," he said, "are you sure you have the right Avakian?"

Her eyes fluttered up from the notebook, and although she tried hard not to, she couldn't help laughing. "Excuse me?"

"I just like to get that out of the way," he said.

"These misunderstandings happen all the time." She was bright and bubbly and flirtatious enough for him to consciously remind himself to be on his guard.

"How many Avakians are there?"

"Oh, quite possibly tens of thousands. If not more."

"And retired American Army colonels?"

"Fewer," Avakian conceded.

"And security consultants?"

"Fewer still." Damn. But more information than you'd really like anyone to have on you was only a brief internet search away.

"Then I probably have the right one," she said, smiling.

Her diction was crisp and precise. Avakian had an idea where that had come from. After taking a lot of crap at West Point he'd worked hard to get working class Bethlehem Pennsylvania out of his speech. He guessed that for her education had been just as hard to come by, and "sounding black" something she'd had to deal with.

A waitress finally arrived.

"Just tea for me," Patience Mbatha said.

Avakian ordered poached eggs on toast and a side of oatmeal, or porridge when in the British Commonwealth.

After the waitress left he asked, "Is your name Xhosa?" One of the largest tribal groups in South Africa.

She gave him a dramatic pause, then finished it off with a little giggle. "Patience?"

Avakian grinned. "Very good."

She smiled back at him. "I'm sorry, Mr. Avakian. Yes, Mbatha is Xhosa."

"Please call me Pete. Shall I call you Mbatha?"

"If you like. But Patience will do."

"How long have you been a writer, Patience?"

"Seven years total. Three in my current job. But you know, Pete, if you keep asking questions I shall never get a chance to. Or is that your intention?"

"Perish the thought, Patience." Every interview, like every interrogation, was a battle of both wits and wills.

His coffee and her tea arrived. Avakian could see her working out the right angle to use on him. A little flirtation to loosen up the older white guy, followed by a few innocent softball questions. Then she'd surprise him with something. Because wanting story background was nothing but bullshit in its most basic form.

"Tell me, Pete, what brought you to South Africa?"

"I was consulting with a local company on the best ways to ensure the safety of their employees during foreign travel."

"And which company was that?"

"I'm positive they'd prefer to remain anonymous," said Avakian. "Even if I hadn't signed a non-disclosure agreement."

"And what are you up to now?"

Up to, Avakian thought. "A short holiday before I go back to the States. I've never visited Cape Town before."

"What is your impression of the current security situation in South Africa?"

She asked her questions from a head-down, looking up, false submissive posture, trying to appeal to him. The tone of her voice was all "help me." All in all very effective, Avakian thought. "I think I'd resent it if a South African who'd only been in

America for a few weeks commented on the security situation there."

"But we have one of the highest rates of violent crime in the world."

"Every South African I've spoken to seems to think so."

"Why do you think that is?"

"I really couldn't care less," Avakian said. Never go into any detail with a reporter.

Her eyebrows went up again. "What do you mean?"

"In my experience there are thousands of motives for a very short list of actions. I don't care *why* people steal. I don't care why they kill, or why they blow things up. I'm concerned with how to stop them from doing those things, or at least teaching others how not to be victimized by them. I have very little patience for whys."

"I would have thought that was the most important thing in preventing them doing it."

Avakian shook his head. "Even if they were inclined to be truthful and capable of being reflective, which they aren't, they hardly know themselves. Everyone always forgets the simple fact that most people with hard lives don't become criminals, and most people with serious grievances don't become terrorists. The why is usually because they want to, and they think they can get away with it."

"And you do this for companies."

"They're the ones who pay for it."

"I Googled you."

"Really? Am I interesting?"

"You don't have a website."

"I'm not on Facebook or MySpace either. Though

I actually know what those are, in case you were wondering."

"Now why would I wonder about that?" she said, smiling again.

"Oh, your generation is always skeptical about mine's relationship with technology. But I get all the work I need from word of mouth."

"I read of two cases where you helped American women whose foreign ex-husbands kidnapped their children and took them to Arab countries. You kidnapped them back."

"I recovered the children," Avakian corrected. "After American courts, which had jurisdiction in the marriages, granted legal custody to the mothers."

"And you took no money."

"The companies I work for pay enough that I can afford to do a limited amount of pro bono," Avakian said.

"Though I imagine the publicity was good for your business," she said.

"Actually, no," Avakian replied. "The first case was the friend of a friend, and the second came on the heels of that. I asked the mothers to keep it quiet, but it's a modern pathology that nothing of any note can happen without someone holding a press conference— not to mention that divorce is all about revenge. All the publicity got me was being declared persona non grata by Jordan and Saudi Arabia, and deluged by hundreds of other people I couldn't help because of that."

She was examining him again. "You'd prefer people think you're a harder man than you are?"

That was unexpected, and Avakian had to take a pause over it. "Who wouldn't?" he said finally.

"Yet you are a retired U.S. Army colonel who was awarded the Bronze Star twice."

That's right, flatter the old guy. "Always be skeptical about medals."

"You're advising me to be skeptical about your own heroism?"

"I'm advising you to be skeptical about *everyone's* heroism."

"Do you advise governments?"

"No. They have their own advisors." Nice little transition to throw him off balance. Now they were finally getting close to it.

"Do you give military advice?"

"No. I leave that line of work to others."

"But you know people who do."

"I had a long career as a soldier and a shorter one as a security consultant. I know a lot of people in both worlds."

"Have you ever done any mercenary work?"

"We're all mercenaries," said Avakian. "But if you mean the standard definition of a hired soldier in foreign service, no."

"Yet you know mercenaries."

"I've bumped into a few in my travels."

"Including Herbert Payne-Best."

Ah, the kicker arrives. "I know him."

"You met with him at the rugby match yesterday. Are you working with him?"

Well, that answered one question. So much for discretion and keeping your mouth shut or we'll kill you, and all that. But it was always the ones who yapped on about discretion who had their $40,000 a year secretary get them the mercenaries on line two. "I was a guest at the match. It turned out that he was a guest also."

"But you mentioned that you know him."

"I was in Sierra Leone in 1995, observing the situation there for the U.S. military. I met most of the people working for Corporate Solutions, including Payne-Best. Hadn't seen him since, until the game yesterday."

"You say you're not working with him."

"That's right."

"It seems you don't care whether I believe you or not."

"You're going to believe whatever you want, no matter what I say, so why should I get all bent out of shape about it?"

She put down her pen and raised her head to meet him eye to eye. "Pete, I must say your answers leave me torn. You've been very forthcoming, but I can't decide whether it's in order to tell me nothing."

She was no fool. "Patience, there's nothing I can do about that, either."

"Are you married, Pete?"

"Divorced."

"As am I. Occupational hazard for journalists."

"Soldiers, too."

Patience Mbatha seemed about to say something else, but didn't. She pushed her chair away from the table. "Well, Pete, I think I've taken up enough of your time. Thanks so much for tea."

"My pleasure," said Avakian, standing up.

"Do you have a card, should I need to contact you again?"

Avakian smiled. "You didn't have any trouble finding me. I'm sure you can do it again if need be."

Undaunted, she reached in her purse. "Here is mine, then."

Avakian dropped the card into his jacket pocket, making a mental note to toss it into the first trash can he saw. Neither he nor she needed anyone else to find that in his possession.

"Goodbye, then," she said, offering her hand again.

"Goodbye," said Avakian. He liked her, but she was definitely going to be a lot of trouble.

Chapter Five

AVAKIAN CERTAINLY WOULDN'T BOTHER VISITING the U.S. consulate on a Sunday. Not that he would bother visiting the U.S. consulate anyway. It was located far out in the Cape Town suburbs, the State Department's answer to security in the age of terrorism. Built like a bunker, fenced in like a prison camp. Everything except a moat and a drawbridge. He wondered why they even bothered. If you weren't going to interact with the people of the country you might as well pack up and go home and save the taxpayers a lot of money.

The e-mail had arrived Saturday evening. His friend Phil's reply used the second letter in each word to encrypt the message. Deciphered, it read:

Constance Springfield. 28. White. Blond.

Kind of young to be the person to talk to, but the whole CIA was young these days. Lots of turnover. Anyway, it was enough information to get him on track. But the weekend duty officer at the consulate wasn't likely to give him her address and phone number. And an internet search was inconclusive. There were a lot of Constance Springfields in Cape Town. She was bound to be unlisted, and he didn't have a whole lot of time to run her down.

Any competent South African private investigator would have been able to get her address for him in a few minutes. But then the fact that you'd wanted a U.S. diplomat's home address would cause the private detective to sell you to the local intelligence service.

He didn't even want to call one of the fixers he knew in Johannesburg, a retired police detective who could provide official information access numbers and authentication codes. That would still leave too many fingerprints behind to suit him. No, this particular job was too serious. There couldn't be any mistakes.

It was going to call for a little social engineering. And the weekends were a particularly good time for that. Doing it over the phone would require too much research and preparation. In person was best, but he would just as soon not leave behind any security camera images of himself. It would have to be a neutral location.

The magic of the internet gave Avakian quite a bit of information on the South African public utility Eskom. People might have different phone carriers, but everyone had electricity. He was particularly interested in the location of their dispatch stations.

On Sunday the repair crews would be on call, and Avakian understood what a holy thing the lunch hour was to a working man. After a short random drive in his rental car to make sure he didn't have a tail, he began cruising in ever increasing circles until he came across a diner with a repair van parked outside.

He went inside and luck was with him. Two guys in dark blue utility uniforms were sitting at the counter.

Avakian took a stool next to them and groaned loudly as he sat down. "The largest coffee you have, please," he told the waitress. "And if there are a couple of aspirins around, I'd be eternally grateful."

One utility worker was white, and the other black. The white guy chuckled and said to Avakian, "Rough night?"

"Fantastic night," said Avakian, hand clamped across his forehead. "I'm just paying the price."

"Bad head, you should eat something," the white guy said. The friendly type, a fountain of advice.

"I want to," said Avakian. "Last coffee I had didn't sit too well. I'll just see how this one goes down before I make too many demands on my stomach."

They both laughed. "American?" the white guy asked.

"That's right," said Avakian. He stuck his hand down the counter. "Name's Pete."

"Naas," said the white one, shaking it.

"Phinneas," said his black partner.

The waitress set his coffee down. "Here you are, love," she said, passing him four aspirins. "Couldn't make it through my day without these."

"Bless your heart," Avakian said gratefully, downing the tablets with the coffee.

"At least you're having a good holiday," said Naas.

"I was," said Avakian. "But I'm kicking myself this morning. I'm such an idiot." Always withhold the juicy details and let them drag the story out of you.

Naas, as expected, took the bait. "What happened?"

"Met this girl last night," said Avakian. "Blond. Great girl. Way out of my league." He nudged Naas with his elbow. "We've got this expression in the States. I looked good because she had her beer goggles on."

They both laughed at that. "Beer goggles," said Naas. "Good one."

"She came back to my hotel," said Avakian. "We got up this morning, and I haven't turned into a frog. I'm still a prince."

They laughed again.

"She wants to take me sightseeing today," said Avakian. "But I'm hung over so she's going to do some errands and give me a chance to recover. She writes down her address and phone number. And she's cute. She crumples it up into a ball and throws it at me in bed. She leaves, and I crawl down to the lobby to get some coffee. And when I come back to the room the bed is made and the maid threw away the balled-up paper with her address and phone number on it."

"No," Naas exclaimed.

"It's gone," Avakian said mournfully. "I did everything except dive in the hotel dumpster looking for it. So now she's at home waiting for me, thinking I'm the biggest jerk in the world. And I am *kicking* myself for being such an idiot."

"Wasn't your fault, man," said Phinneas.

"It was the bloody maid," said Naas.

"Makes no difference," said Avakian. "I went online and there are too many girls named Constance Springfield in Cape Town. No way am I going to find her." He sighed. "Who knows what might have been? I'm not getting any younger."

"What did you say her name was?" said Naas.

"Constance Springfield," Avakian said slowly.

"Know anything else about her?" Naas asked. Phinneas laid a warning hand on his forearm, but he shrugged it off.

"She's 28 and blond," said Avakian. "I couldn't remember where she said she lived if you put a gun to my head. Been trying all morning."

"Be right back," said Naas, getting up quickly.

"Where's he going?" Avakian asked Phinneas.

Phinneas just shook his head.

Through the window Avakian could see Naas on his cell phone, climbing in the repair van. He sipped his coffee and fought the smile off his face.

Naas returned and sat back down. He slapped a piece of paper down on the counter. "Here you go, mate."

"What's this?" Avakian said, picking it up. It was an address and phone number. The address was in the Rosebank section of the city, near the university. The number looked like an apartment. "I don't believe it! *That's* the address! I don't believe it! You guys can do that?" He leaned over and hugged Naas around the shoulders, and the feeling was genuine.

"Easy there, mate," said Naas, turning red.

Avakian gave the waitress two hundred rand. "Thank you, darlin'." And he put five hundred more on the counter. "Guys, lunch is on me. I can't thank you enough."

"Go get her," said Naas.

Avakian clapped them both on the back and dashed out of the coffee shop.

Naas thumbed through the bills. "Look," he said to

Phinneas. "We'll be eating on this for a while. American, eh? Good bloke."

"You get in trouble," said Phinneas.

"Ah," Naas said dismissively.

As part of his consulting work Avakian was used to demonstrating to businesses how he could walk into their buildings as a total stranger and walk away with their proprietary crown jewels. The human being was always the weakest link in any security system, in particular the innate tendencies to trust, accept someone at their word, be helpful, and absolutely love breaking the rules. It was how con artists made their money.

———

THE WAITER POURED him a glass of sauvignon blanc. He gave it a taste. "Mmmm, nice."

"Would you like to order an appetizer?" the waiter asked.

"Give me just a bit more time to think about it," Avakian said.

The restaurant was right on the waterfront, loud but not earsplitting. Casual, mellow crowd. Not too full on a Sunday night. It was off season so there weren't any American tourists with screaming kids who wouldn't eat anything but chicken fingers.

Avakian hadn't been in a hurry to get there because he knew she'd be late. When meeting an asset a case officer always wanted them to get there first so you could check them and the place out before making the commitment to walk in and sit down. The last thing you wanted, as a professional intelligence officer, was to be sitting down at a table while some source you'd supposedly been cultivating walked up, pulled out a gun, and blew your brains out. It had happened.

Avakian had already made the guy who'd come through to scope him out. He hoped this wouldn't take much longer. He was hungry.

He saw the blond coming in. Age was right. Man, she was really buttoned down and corporate. The tailored suit was almost severe.

She walked right up to the table. "Colonel Avakian?"

Avakian rose. "That's right."

She offered her hand. "Constance Springfield."

Her palm was down, signaling the intention to dominate. As Avakian grasped her hand and shook it lightly he turned it upright, reestablishing equality. "Call me Pete. Please join me."

"Thank you." As she sat down, she slid Avakian's military ID card under the lip of his plate. Red for retired.

"I'm glad you found me," Avakian said, pocketing the card. "It's not a great picture."

"Please call me Constance."

Great, Avakian thought. Wouldn't want to be letting our hair down all of a sudden. But then in his case there was no hair to let down. Hers, however, was straw-blonde, thin and straight. The eyes were blue. "Would you care for some wine? This Neil Ellis sauvignon isn't bad at all."

"Please."

At least she wasn't that much of a tight-ass. But Avakian reminded himself that his first impressions weren't always as accurate as he liked to think. Once before he'd met a woman he'd thought was a major league tight-ass, and he'd been totally wrong. He pulled the bottle out of the cooler and poured.

She raised her glass. "Cheers."

"Cheers," said Avakian, clinking it. Her free arm was on the table poised across her front like a barrier. The knees were pointed toward the door. She didn't want to be there.

"I don't often receive dinner invitations by messenger," she said.

She even had that east coast Martha Stewart clenched jaw way of speaking. Avakian was guessing Ivy League. The CIA didn't get as many of them as in years back, but it still got them. "Forgive my indirect approach, but I wasn't sure who else might be watching your apartment or listening to your phone." The 24 hour messenger service delivered the sealed envelope containing his ID card, the name of the restaurant, and the time right to her door. And she had to sign for it—no entrusting to the care of the doorman.

"And how did you happen to find me?"

Avakian just looked around. "This place came highly recommended. I've always found that the chalkboard, live lobster tank, wood beam, flags on the ceiling kind of seafood restaurant is either very good or very bad. No in-between. Have you eaten here?"

"No, but I hear it's quite good."

She was nervous, and Avakian understood why. People imagined CIA officers out ruthlessly beating the bushes for agents to recruit. There were a few superstars like that, but for most of them it really didn't work that way. Screwing up your approach might get you ejected from the country you were working in, never to be sent overseas again. So if you wanted to cover your ass, you asked headquarters for permission before you made a run at a prospect. They didn't want to risk being held responsible for your screw-up, so they said no. And then you were covered. You could go back to working in the embassy, responding to routine queries, and having coffee with the local intelligence types.

He'd gone and short-circuited this whole process, and now she was feeling out on a limb. Join the club, Avakian thought. "You should tell your friend with the salon tan to buy some South African suits," he suggested. "American cut clothes always make you stand out in a foreign country."

As he'd intended, she was giving him much deeper appraisal, signaled by the closed hand on the chin, finger pointing up along the side of the face.

The waiter reappeared and asked, "Are you ready to order?"

"Not trying to sway you in any way," Avakian said across the table. "But what do you think about the seafood platter for two?"

"That would be fine," she said, closing the menu.

Well, she either wasn't a vegetarian or she wasn't going to eat it. "Local fish, if you please," Avakian said to the waiter. "Whatever is freshest."

"Dorado is best today," the waiter said.

"Freshest or what you were told to move?" Avakian countered. "Before you answer, keep in mind that we're outstanding tippers."

The waiter broke into a smile. "Absolutely the freshest."

Avakian knew restaurants, and he wasn't all that confident about fresh fish on a Sunday. He'd been weighing commissioning the death of a couple of the lobsters swimming around in the tank, but he only really liked the northern variety. "All right."

"Something to start?" said the waiter.

Avakian glanced over the table again.

Constance Springfield reopened her menu. "Tomato, Avocado, and Mozzarella salad," she said with a touch of impatience.

"How am I going to feel about grilled sardines?" Avakian asked the waiter.

"If you're a sardine man, you'll love them," he said definitively.

"I'm a sardine man," said Avakian.

The waiter left. Avakian said, "I had an incredibly hard time finding a restaurant open on Sunday in this town. Is that some residual Dutch Calvinism, or do South African chefs like their Sundays off?"

"I'm afraid I wouldn't know," she said.

So she wasn't all that great at waiting patiently and gently humoring people until they opened up. Which made Avakian wonder what other essential trade skills she was lacking. When reporters were more engaging than intelligence officers, then the intelligence agency had a problem. The sad part of it was, once he told her the purpose of the meeting she was going to be all over him. "Okay, Constance, put your cell phone in the table." Meaning, start recording. "I've got a story to tell you."

He paused once when the appetizers arrived. His hotel desk had been right—this restaurant was the real deal. Everyone's opinion was colored by the badly canned variety, but sardines came much larger and a few whole grilled ones with just some olive oil and rock salt were a thing of beauty. These didn't even need the peppers and onion they came with.

Avakian's impressions of Willem Sternkamp took them through the arrival of the main course.

The dorado fillets were arranged on the tray along with prawns, more sardines, black mussels, lemons, and the lemon butter sauce they'd ordered. Everything was simply but expertly grilled, and everything was fresh. And to Avakian's mind that was all seafood really needed. The blood orange and saffron reductions beloved by the high end restaurant world were only there to jack up the price and cover up fish that had spent too much time in the coolers.

The detailed account of Payne-Best and De Wet took him all the way through dinner. Springfield only picked at her food and, as predicted, had a hard time containing her rising excitement. The arm barrier was gone, her knees were pointed straight at him, and she was mirroring all his body language. Avakian knew the deal. This was a career-maker, dropped right into her lap. A CIA case officer might spend years fruitlessly trying to scratch up an intelligence source on the inside of an conspiracy like this. He'd started off as some pain in the ass old fart retired colonel who'd ruined a decent Sunday night, and now he was a ticket to upper management.

"And you're going to Payne-Best's house tomorrow," she said.

"It might have been better to ask me my plans," said Avakian, as if he were back instructing one of his junior officers. "And if the answer was no, then you could begin gently moving me in that direction."

The look that flashed over her face then was priceless. Oh, she did not care for that at all. Avakian briefly let himself extrapolate, based on her age and position. First in her class, aced all the tests. But not really in order to learn anything—to be first in her class. He made a mental note to keep his eyes open and make sure all that ambition didn't bulldoze him right into the middle of a whole lot of trouble.

"Yes," he said. "I am going to Payne-Best's house tomorrow. I'll get as many details as I can. But I make no promises after that. Most likely I'll be on a plane back to the States just as fast as I can reserve a seat. Then you and your people can decide whether to blow their op or let it run and keep watching. Makes no difference to me."

"You came to us because you realized the importance of the information," she said. "We appreciate the time you're taking out of your busy professional schedule. And we'd like to make sure that…"

"I'm not angling for a payday," Avakian interjected. "I don't want any money, not even expenses. Oh, Uncle Sam can pick up the dinner check, but that's it. I'll keep going until I think it's time to bail out. And then we'll part, on whatever terms, hopefully as grownups."

"You've spent your life serving your country," she said. "And…"

"And that's why I tend to be skeptical about appeals to my patriotism," he said. "But one of these days, if you play your cards right, I just might show you my American flag tattoo." He suddenly knew how a woman felt when a guy kept hitting on her with a string of pickup lines he'd memorized from the pages of Maxim. A seventy-five billion dollar intelligence budget, and this was the best they could do? It was professionally depressing. Instead of going down the agent recruitment checklist she should have been working on developing a relationship and some empathy, finding out what drove him, and using that to keep him on the team.

"I'm sorry," she said. "You've gone out of your way, and you've put yourself at risk to bring us this. I really can't ask for anything else."

"Sure you can," said Avakian. "And you probably will. But that was much better. I'm just saying, try not to be offended if, when you do, I'm not receptive."

"We should probably discuss some procedures for staying in contact," she said.

"Face to face only," Avakian stated. "I'm not writing any reports. Not on paper, computer, PDA, or flash drive. No e-mails, no dead drops, no wireless transmissions. Everyone brings their A game to a personal meeting. When I have something to talk about, I'll send you a dinner invitation in one way or another. That's it."

"We have a technique for meetings…," she said.

"Yeah, I know," said Avakian. Unlike most men he didn't like to interrupt a woman when she was talking, but he also had no intention of listening to something he had no intention of doing. "If I say it's Wednesday at nine, we subtract 25 hours and it's actually Tuesday at eight, or some nonsense like that. Except if either of us happen to forget the comm plan and show up on the wrong day, and we have to do it all over again. So let's just say that if I invite you to dinner Tuesday at eight, it's actually Tuesday at eight."

"We don't necessarily have to meet at a restaurant," she said.

"They're loud. They're anonymous, people are always coming and going, and the staff see so many customers a night it's hard to place a face. A man and a woman get caught in a hotel room with their clothes on and they're an intelligence officer and a source. If we're seen in a Cape Town restaurant, then I was eating here alone, you came in to try and recruit me, I let you pay for dinner and told you to get lost. I can talk my way out of a jam with a cover story like that. If we show up with the same tee time and play a round of golf together, I can't."

"At least there should be some means of emergency contact," she said insistently. "What if we learned something that could affect your safety? We wouldn't even have your cell number."

One drunken night in a Panama City bar a CIA paramilitary officer had told Avakian an interesting story of the time the CIA sent out an informational mailing to all its officers on a new diversity policy. In official envelopes that had "Central Intelligence Agency" written on the return address. Only one problem. Someone screwed up and it got mailed it out to *all* their officers, including the ones working under deep cover in foreign countries. Funny story, but only if you weren't the poor schmuck in Lebanon who found that potential death sentence burning a hole in your mailbox. He could just imagine being someplace where the local spooks paid particular attention to international cell calls and having one from a U.S. embassy, or worse, Langley Virginia area code come banging in. "I'll take care of my own security," he said. "If you want to, give me your number."

She wrote it down on a card and slid it across the table.

Avakian memorized the number. "Okay, got it."

Constance Springfield dropped the card in her purse and gave a frustrated sigh. "I think you're making a mistake. But you did work on a few special projects, didn't you?"

She was referring to the dark, or covert side of special forces. Where you operated in very small teams, or individually, in non-military long hair and civilian clothes. "You've seen my record, I'm sure," said Avakian.

"I have," she replied.

Avakian thought it was good to never forget who you were dealing with. "What do you say to some dessert?"

"None for me, thanks."

"I'm kind of full myself. Thanks for letting me eat all the sardines. It was very important to our relationship."

"What?"

"Never mind."

The waiter brought the check and put it beside Avakian. He slid it across the table to Constance Springfield.

One of the waiter's eyebrows went up ever so slightly.

"My niece got me out of the nursing home for my birthday," Avakian told him.

A nervous little laugh spilled out of the waiter. "Happy birthday."

"Big tip," Avakian ordered Springfield.

Chapter Six

BISHOPSCOURT WAS one of the more exclusive Cape Town suburbs. The traditional seat of the Archbishop of Cape Town, an old neighborhood of new mansions and new money. Small but by no means cramped. Only 350 homes, most every one on at least an acre of land. And of course well walled and gated. In a way it reminded Avakian of Beverly Hills. Except in Beverly Hills even the walls didn't keep the riches from being on display. Here you could sense the insecurity. The streets were very heavily wooded, and there was nothing to see but trees and walls, as if the haves felt a shared need to keep what was behind them out of sight of the have nots.

He had the cab let him off at least a block away, just in case anyone later questioned the driver about his destination.

Just like Beverly Hills, it seemed that no one in the neighborhood did any walking. There wasn't another soul on either side of the street.

Avakian believed in keeping the senses extended to

their working limits. If you paid attention they'd let you know if there was anything to worry about. A contradiction in terms to the Bluetooth earpiece and iPod wearing population, sealed off within a wall of sound, but he didn't begrudge them. Lions and tigers and bears were becoming scarce in the world, and the herd needed to be thinned somehow.

So as he heard the car behind him slow down he checked it out in his peripheral vision. Another private security patrol vehicle. It crossed out of its lane, pulling over to the curb and slowing down to match his pace.

Avakian bent over until he was eye to eye with the driver. South Africa drove on the left, and the driver was on the right side of the car. "Evening, gents. What's going on?"

"American," the driver said to his fellow security guard, as if that explained such eccentric behavior. Then, to Avakian, "Lose your way, sir?"

"No," said Avakian. "My cab let me off at the wrong house. I'm just going down to the end of the street."

"Expected, are you?" the driver asked.

"That's right," said Avakian. "Friends of friends, you know?"

"Would you like a ride?"

"No thanks," said Avakian. "It's a beautiful evening for a walk, isn't it?"

"It is, sir, but you should be careful walking the streets after dark."

"I will," Avakian assured him. "Thanks for stopping, guys."

The driver cut back over to his lane with a squeal of tires, and sped off down the road.

Avakian grinned. Let the crazy Yank get his head broken. He wasn't on the list of paying customers.

A short ways down Avakian took a fork onto a road that was even darker and greener. The right number was discreetly mounted on a stone wall next to a wrought iron vehicle gate. Avakian pressed the intercom button and looked into the security camera.

"Ja?" a voice came through the speaker.

"Peter Avakian."

"Where is your vehicle?"

Avakian believed that everyone had a finite supply of patience, and he liked to save his for when it was really needed. He made a point of looking over his shoulder, then back to the camera. "I knew I forgot something."

There was a long pause after that, then the gate opened with a whirring of electric motor.

Avakian walked up the drive. Palms lining the way, of course. Grounds landscaped to within an inch of their life. Two peacocks were pecking away on the lawn, and since it was Africa he had to wonder whether they were wild or just part of the landscape design. There had to be at least a pool and tennis court out back. Avakian had to remind himself not to act like the disgruntled proletarian.

The house brought him up short. Not because it was a mansion, he'd been expecting that. It was the brown sandstone, columns, and tiled roof. The arabesques carved into the stone. Northern Africa come to Southern Africa.

Barring his way to the front door was the classic British Commonwealth retired Regimental Sergeant Major type. Beer gut hanging like a cannonball over the belt, hair cut too short for civilian clothes plus the obligatory greased-down comb-over, and a walrus moustache with the tips carefully waxed. Wearing what had become an international cliché, or what Avakian liked to call the I'm-the-bodyguard-shoot- me-first outfit: khaki vest and khaki tactical trousers, both with multiple Velcro pockets for all your spare magazines and grenades and knives and multi-tools and flashlights and first aid kits and what have you. A retired military man's idea of going totally incognito: civilian clothing worn like a uniform.

"Colonel Avakian?"

He'd said that as if he expected Avakian to come to attention, in lieu of salute. So of course Avakian made his reply even more laconic than usual. "That's right."

"You're expected."

"Yeah, I know," said Avakian. "That's why I'm here."

Glaring, the RSM stood aside to let him proceed down the walk. As he passed, Avakian said, as an aside, "You forgot your shooting glasses."

He rang the bell. The door was opened by a very attractive brunette in her early thirties, heavily made up, with expensive highlights in her hair and a dress that had to have come from Paris. Avakian had heard that Payne-Best had acquired a young wife, and she had to be it. She was wearing a set of diamond studs in her ears that wouldn't have shamed a hip-hop star. They were dwarfed only by the size of the rock on her left hand.

"Hello," she said brightly, in a plummy London accent. "I'm Emma Payne-Best."

"Peter Avakian."

"Why Mr. Avakian," she exclaimed. "You are not at all as my husband described you to me."

"And yet you're as lovely as I had been told," said Avakian.

She laughed and took his arm. "You must continue to flatter me as I lead you to Herbert."

Very expensive perfume. Mrs. Payne-Best had a very sexual way about her, the kind of woman who could unzip your fly just by looking at you. "I must say, I'm enormously impressed by your home," Avakian lied. The inside was Moroccan to a degree that even a Moroccan might have found embarrassing. Domed ceilings with Islamic star grids and colored tile inserts, textile hangings on the walls, carved wood *mashrabiyyas* fitted to the windows.

"I was definitely influenced by the Alhambra, of course," she said. "Then when we visited Morocco I found my inspiration. We imported some genuine Moroccan craftsmen to do the work. Lovely men. Brought their prayer rugs and stayed for months."

Avakian imagined the fun the Moroccans must have had going over the top with the décor. He tried to tally up a dollar value on the work but quit before it depressed him. He could probably live for five years on the proceeds from just the furnishings of the room they were walking through. "You must have done the decorating yourself."

"What makes you say that?"

Avakian turned to fix her in his gaze. "I look at you, and I look at your elegant home, and they just seem to match."

She gave him a quick look of frank reappraisal, and he thought he felt his zipper move. Then, unaccountably, she began to blush. "Well, I had help of course."

As they neared the back of the house the sounds of

talking and laughing grew louder. There were quite a few people there. Payne-Best was standing in a small group, glass in hand, looking politely bored as only an Englishman can when someone else is talking.

"Herbert," his wife demanded. "Wherever did you find this charming man?"

"Out in the jungle, my dear," Payne-Best replied.

"I certainly doubt it," she said. "I must say, he's a breath of fresh air."

"You mean, compared to my other guests?" Payne-Best said.

"I did not say that, Herbert."

"You didn't have to, my dear."

A little flash of temperament rose up in her eyes, though she visibly tamped it back down. "In any event…Mr. Avakian?"

"Please call me Peter," Avakian said.

"And you must call me Emma. I hope we will be seeing more of you, Peter."

Avakian took her offered hand, lifted it up to his mouth, and kissed it lightly. "I hope so too, Emma."

She favored him with a dazzling smile before moving over to smooth out the group of guests Payne-Best had not bothered to introduce Avakian to.

"Lovely girl," Avakian said to Payne-Best.

"She is that," said Payne-Best, giving no indication that he'd picked up the emphasis on girl. "Can't quite decide whether she keeps me young or will be the death of me. What are you drinking?"

"Scotch," said Avakian.

Payne-Best led him over to an antique table against the wall, on which sat an army of bottles. "Blend or malt?"

Avakian pointed to the bottle of Glenlivet.

"A Speyside man, eh?" said Payne-Best. "I prefer the Laphroaig myself."

"Too peaty for me," said Avakian.

Payne-Best picked up the bottle. "Water? Ice?"

"I'll forgive the anti-American stereotyping," said Avakian. "You can just pour it into a glass, thanks."

"I shall do just that," said Payne-Best, handing Avakian the glass in question. He started to raise his own, then paused. "Assuming that your being here indicates a yes. Though from what I've heard, you might show up personally to tell me to get fucked."

"It's a yes," said Avakian.

"Then good luck to us," said Payne-Best.

They touched glasses.

"Good luck," Avakian said. He'd always liked to say he didn't believe in luck, but lately he'd begun to change his mind. "It was a fine idea, having a group of people over as cover for our meeting."

Payne-Best only smiled.

"So when do we meet the African and the Eastern European?" said Avakian.

Payne-Best's eyes narrowed. "What do you know about them?"

"I see two sets of bodyguards," said Avakian, using his scotch glass as a pointer to cast about the room. "The salt and pepper teams aren't mixing. As a matter of fact, they don't seem to like each other very much."

"Quite the Sherlock Holmes," said Payne-Best. "Follow me."

They went down a long hallway into what had to be Payne-Best's private study, because this particular room blasted free from the Moorish theme of the rest of the house. It was all dark paneling and leather club chairs. A massive mahogany desk. Even a 19th century hunting print on the wall. Exile in guy-ville, Avakian thought. All the testosterone made him feel like shooting a spot of game, or riding to the hounds.

"You know De Wet, of course," said Payne-Best. "And allow me to introduce Henry Okong and Dmitri Volkov."

Avakian had to hold back a double-take at the mention of those last two names. De Wet was leaning against the fireplace mantle, beer bottle still in hand, still trying to stare him down. The first one to get up and move in to shake his hand was a black man with a head shaved as bald as Avakian's, except he was about six feet tall and weighed close to three hundred pounds. His onyx skin was set against a resplendent white shirt.

Avakian's hand was enveloped in a much larger one, but the handshake was surprisingly gentle, as if the owner had learned to check himself. "*The* Henry Okong?" Avakian inquired. "Who uses the nom de guerre Jomo?"

"The very same," came the smiling, soft-spoken reply, the British accent indicating another Nigerian private school product like Avakian's friend General Medani.

Up until this moment Avakian hadn't been entirely sure that Henry Okong, or Jomo, actually existed in the flesh. Of course, every Nigerian criminal had a hundred different ID's. Yet here he was, standing before him. According to the legend Okong had started off as an engineer in the Nigerian merchant marine. And, like any good entrepreneur, identified and took advantage of a business opportunity in the coastal delta where virtually all Nigeria's oil production took place. In particular the fact that the locals there had some definite grievances against the Nigerian government and international oil companies. They didn't enjoy being shoved off their land by the oil drillers. Then there was the massive pollution. Oil companies only cleaned up after themselves in countries where the cost of cleanup was less than that of bribing politicians, regulators, and judges. The natives particularly resented the fact that the oil money went away and none of it came back to the delta. The local politicians and foreign oil company employees lived like kings while they had precious little access to electricity or clean water or education.

Another thing Okong noticed was that the criminal gangs, or cults as Avakian's friend the general had called them, were already in place. He hired this pool of mercenary talent to steal crude oil from the companies' pipelines. They siphoned it off into small barges, and ran the barges out to Okong's leased freighters waiting offshore. The freighters returned with cash, high-end military weaponry that made the cults even more formidable, and premium western consumer products. As far as the locals were concerned Okong delivered the spoils, while the government didn't. Since the cults were hired on a job by job basis there was no organization for the Nigerian government to target.

After millions of dollars went back and forth Okong raised his sights a little higher and decided to take on the Nigerian government directly. To make it look like he actually had an organization he created MLND, or Movement for the Liberation of the Niger Delta, and gave it a leader, the otherwise anonymous Jomo. All that took was a computer and a fax machine. E-mails and communiqués to global news organizations announced MLND's claims against the corrupt government and the evil oil companies.

Then instead of just stealing oil he had his people destroy pipelines and drilling rigs and kidnap the foreign workers. Announcements of attacks minutes after they'd happened established MLND's credibility with the media. When people started writing about you, then you were a movement. Pretty soon Okong had cut off nearly 25% of Nigerian daily production, and the resulting higher oil prices put even more money in his pocket. Causing chaos was easy, and enough of the right kind would drive the Nigerian state out of the delta. Which was his ultimate goal. Then the oil companies would have to deal with him exclusively.

None of this was new. Guerrilla movements had always dabbled in crime: the Irish Republican Army ran drugs and protection rackets to finance itself. And criminal gangs frequently picked up the banner of liberation movements to give themselves an aura of legitimacy. But Avakian considered MLND the inevitable next step, and you could take your pick as far as definitions: a business in the guise of a guerrilla movement, or a guerrilla movement run as a business. What made it perfect was that Henry Okong didn't have to concern himself with the day to day heartburn of actually running either a criminal gang or guerrilla movement. He just subcontracted it all out on a cash or barter basis.

Avakian had also heard rumors of Colombian cocaine crossing over to Africa and up into Europe on those very same freighters.

All in all, a security professional's nightmare. Or limitless opportunity for future contracts, whichever way you looked at it. Avakian found it odd to be staring face to face at the future of his business. "I've followed your career very closely," was all he said.

Okong smiled. "From what I have heard of you, I have no doubt."

The next man to take up Avakian's hand was Okong's physical opposite. Slim and white, and not just white but eastern European pale. Curly light brown hair and a bushy moustache. A canary yellow silk shirt open to display the chest hair. And a solid gold neck chain of huge links that looked like it easily weighed five pounds. Tacky and nouveau riche to the well-bred civilian eye, but Avakian recognized its purpose. It was the kind of portable universal currency that a traveler might wear to exchange for his life in the dark places of the world. In excellent though Russian-accented English the man said, "Dmitri Volkov."

"Greetings, pilot," Avakian said in Russian.

"Very good," Volkov replied in Russian. "You have heard of me, too. How far does your Russian go?"

"Not much farther," said Avakian. There was certainly no question about Volkov's existence. He was perhaps the world's biggest independent arms dealer. A man with a fleet of surplus Russian military cargo planes who for the right price could obtain and deliver anything from a T-72 tank all gassed up and ready to go to a thousand AK-47's, no questions asked. The most successful survivor of a business that had boomed up after the fall of the Berlin Wall. In those good old days a Russian with the right contacts needed only to fly onto a military base in the former Soviet Union, hand the commanding officer a suitcase full of dollars, pick whatever weapons he wanted right out of those overstocked armories, load up the plane, and fly off.

Volkov had come to the fore by establishing a reputation for reliability, and his pilots would go anywhere. Prior to 9/11 he ran guns to the Afghan Northern Alliance, and when one of his crews was forced down in Taliban territory he got them out by agreeing to deliver for the Taliban, too. The UN would sanction one of his air cargo companies, and the next day the planes would have new tail numbers and be working for a new front company in a new country. Then the UN would contract him to fly aid to some remote part of Africa, because no one else would do it. And after dropping off the corn meal and powdered milk, the next day he'd fly in again with a few loads of arms for the local rebel group that created the refugees. The U.S. State department would work with Interpol to try to get him arrested while the U.S. military, desperate for airlift to move supplies to Iraq, would hire one of his United Arab Emirates fronts.

Another model entrepreneur of the 21st century international underground economy, Avakian thought. Now he knew where Okong got his guns. And where Payne-Best had obtained his front money. Talk about business opportunities. If these two buccaneers ever managed to steal themselves a country, where they could operate freely, the sky would be the limit.

"Your English is excellent," said Avakian. "Where did you pick it up?"

"The Military Institute of Foreign Languages, in Moscow," said Volkov.

"Then I assume you were a military officer," said Avakian. "Air Force?"

"Yes," said Volkov.

Back in Special Forces Avakian always like to tell his intelligence sergeants how a couple of innocent questions could fill in a lot of blanks. A junior Air Force officer, which Volkov must have been at the time, would not have attended the Russian military's most prestigious language school unless he was also an officer of the GRU, Russian military intelligence. It explained where he had gotten the seed money to start his business. After the fall of the Soviet Union the GRU would have been happy to give one of their alumni a couple of old transport planes that otherwise would have sat rusting on a runway, in exchange for a piece of the action and future considerations. It also explained why whenever Volkov got himself into trouble he ran home to Moscow and, in response to western queries, the authorities could never seem to find him.

"And your Russian?" Volkov went on. "The American Defense Language Institute?"

"I learned my Spanish there," said Avakian. "My Russian shows the effects of learning it on my own."

"I congratulate you for making the effort," said Volkov. Meaning, of course, how unlike an American to learn foreign languages.

An impatient Payne-Best put an end to the pleasantries. "First things first," he said, handing Avakian a sheaf of papers and gesturing toward the desk. "Give these a look over and a signature, if you would."

With an amused smile on his face, Avakian took a seat behind the desk and began thumbing through the documents. Everyone else had settled into the club chairs on the other side of the room, talking softly enough that he couldn't hear them.

It seemed that he was to be working for a company called Chromium Futures. Of course, it didn't take much to register an offshore company. As Avakian went over them in detail, it wasn't the documents themselves that he found genuinely puzzling, but the very idea of them. He spent much more time trying to discern the motive than actually reading them. Because he couldn't accept them on face value, he kept looking for the trap.

Finally he dropped the papers on the desk and stood up.

"Everything all right?" Payne-Best asked.

"Straightforward employment contract," said Avakian. "Hope no one gets bent out of shape when I don't sign it."

"Why not?" Payne-Best demanded. "It is straightforward, as you said."

"I appreciate your commitment to good corporate governance," said Avakian. "But I'm not leaving any paper trail of my involvement in this little venture."

De Wet was slouched in his chair, smirking. Okong and Volkov were clearly indifferent.

"But my dear fellow," said Payne-Best. "The documents don't mention your involvement with this venture. They simply record your employment with a neutral corporation."

"Whatever," said Avakian. "If you need tax advantages, have your gardener sign them. My signature's not going on anything."

"Perhaps I should explain," said Payne-Best. The typical Englishman, tamping down his frustration and attempting to reason with the heathen. "You need to understand politicians, old boy. Treacherous bastards, won't keep agreements. Our company will have binding contracts with the new President of Benin."

Avakian could hardly credit such childish naiveté. Could it be as simple as that? "If this venture goes sour

I don't think a Benin court is going to rule in our favor. And I don't think a judgment rendered by a court in…" he glanced at the contract again…"the Isle of Man is going to be upheld in Benin. But you go ahead and make all the contracts and letters of agreement you want. Just don't expect me to sign them. If that's an issue then I'll wish you all luck and say farewell right now."

Avakian waited near the door while they had a whispered discussion that ended with De Wet's rising voice telling Payne-Best, "…now stop fucking about."

"Very well," said Payne-Best, turning back to Avakian and noble in defeat. "No signatures required."

Avakian returned to the desk and wrote on a single sheet of paper over the hard wood surface, to leave no impression. "Here's my bank account and routing number," he said, passing it to Payne-Best. "I'll expect 300,000 euros to be deposited within 24 hours." He kept an account with a bank in Lichtenstein to hold the receipts for all his jobs that paid in euros.

De Wet just looked bored. Payne-Best glanced over at Okong, who nodded. Which told Avakian who the power behind the throne was. And where the majority financing was coming from.

Volkov was grinning broadly. "I like this man," he announced to the room. And then to Avakian, "No bullshit. You stay all business, soldier. We have some success."

"Very well," said Payne-Best, trying to return himself to the center of the room. "Let's get down to it, eh?"

He walked over to the hunting print and pulled it away from the wall, revealing a safe with a digital keypad lock.

Low chuckles from the assembly. "A safe behind a portrait?" said Okong. "Is this not a cliché, my friend?"

"Quite," said Payne-Best, punching in the combination. He was careful to keep his body between them and the lock, though Avakian made a point of looking.

Payne-Best brought a stack of file folders over to a long table and began laying everything out. Topographic and street maps of the adjoining coastal cities of Porto Novo and Cotonou, Benin's administrative capital and de facto one. A stack of commercial satellite photographs.

"Here you are, gentlemen," said Payne-Best. "Benin. West Africa, between Nigeria and Togo."

All the better for Okong to have a safe haven right next to Nigeria, Avakian thought. A port, an airport—what more could a smuggler want?

"Population approximately seven million," Payne-Best went on. "Depending upon how many have died of AIDS this week."

Cold chuckles around the table.

"Official language, French," said Payne-Best, in crisp military briefer fashion. "Fon and Yoruba in the south, at least six major tribal languages in the north. Government: former Marxist people's republic, now an actual republic. Which means they have elections, but the government still never changes."

"Nothing changes a government like a few bullets," said De Wet.

Avakian never would have guessed that De Wet was such a humorist. "What about the new government?" he said, asking another of his intelligence-gathering questions. "I'm assuming you've Googled Benin political opposition and visited their Paris apartment?"

"As far as that goes, it's not your concern," De Wet said bluntly.

Which meant that the representatives of the new government were on retainer, Avakian thought, so there would be some black faces on display to the world as soon as the smell of gunpowder had left the air. Well, that was the CIA's problem.

"Moving on," said Payne-Best. "Armed forces. Total army personnel 7,300 depending upon who shows up for work on any given morning. Three infantry battalions, one commando/airborne battalion, one armored squadron, one artillery battery, and one engineer battalion."

"A joke," said De Wet.

"I'm assuming that the airborne and the armor are positioned near the capital," said Avakian. Governments made sure their most elite troops were also the most politically reliable. And tanks on the streets both stopped coups and started them, so they were always kept under thumb also.

"Correct," said Payne-Best. "Order of battle is 20 Russian PT-76 light tanks. Armored cars are a mixed lot. About twenty French VBL, 14 Russian BRDM-2, and 7 old American second world war era M-8 Greyhounds. Personnel carriers, 16 ex-Belgian M-113's. And knowing what I do about African vehicle maintenance, I would estimate that, at best, 10% of that force is capable of engine starts and driving a hundred meters without breakdown."

"Even if they can get out of the garage, there's nothing there that can take an RPG hit," said De Wet. The Russian RPG-7 rocket-propelled grenade launcher, merely an updated bazooka, was the world standard for man-portable antitank weapons.

"And the artillery?" said Avakian.

"Twelve L-118 British 105mm Light Guns," said Payne-Best. "And 4 old American M-101 howitzers. No one I've spoken to can recall the last time they fired a round."

"What about Air Force?" said Avakian.

"Fourteen aircraft total," said Payne-Best. "Seven helicopters and the rest transports. In various states of repair. Only two Augusta's of the Presidential flight can be relied upon to take off and land without incident."

"A cakewalk," said De Wet.

Avakian would be inclined to agree.

"Primary objectives," said Payne-Best, tapping the map of Cotonou. "Presidential palace. Airport. Military and Gendarmerie barracks. Television station. Three radio stations. As for the force, our current thinking is that a battalion minus ought to do the job. Probably no more than two reinforced companies with medium mortars, sustained-fire machineguns, and plenty of RPG-7's."

"One night and done," said De Wet.

Nods around the table.

That sounded so better than people running screaming for their lives as machinegun fire skipped down city streets, rockets slammed into buildings, and mortar rounds set everything on fire with elegant cascading sprays of inextinguishable white phosphorus particles. But that was military planning for you. The process, and it wasn't an accident, made it so very easy to divorce action from consequences. Avakian waited, but no one said anything else. "And you're planning to insert, how?"

"Airport," said Payne-Best.

"Using your notorious 727 that I assume you have stashed away somewhere in the region?" said Avakian. "Or maybe a couple of colleague Volkov's Illushins?"

"That's right," said De Wet.

"You don't like it," Volkov said, watching Avakian's face.

Avakian doubted whether either Payne-Best or De Wet had done even a training air assault with anything larger than a 64-man SAS squadron. In their mercenary work they were used to loading their force into airliners, flying to friendly airstrips, getting organized, and then going into battle. "It's hard to go from sitting in a plane right into the assault. If they're waiting for you on the ground it's even harder."

"Why would they be waiting?" Okong broke in.

"You don't plan for everything to go right," Avakian explained. "You plan for what you'll do if it goes wrong."

"We'll do the planning," said De Wet.

"Fine," Avakian replied. "You do the planning. But you wanted me to handle moving supplies, right? I assume colleague Volkov will be supplying the arms. You want me to fly them into South Africa or some other country in the vicinity on the assumption that the authorities have been take care of? I don't think so. You want me to babysit some airport warehouse filled with tons of ordnance while I wait for you to jet in with a few hundred guys who are supposed to be, what? Soccer fans heading to a tournament? The world's most physically fit all-male tour group on their way to celebrate gay pride week somewhere? You can forget it."

That had them all looking at each other. Avakian knew the type from special forces. The hard cases only wanted to plan the attack, leaving all the boring details of supplies and how to get there to the limp-wristed logisticians.

It was De Wet who unexpectedly said, "What's your better idea, mate?"

"Any place you're getting the weapons from is a place where you can arrange for customs to look the other way while you put them on a ship," Avakian said. "I assume colleague Okong can arrange a ship or two. I can bring those ships anywhere and park them in a harbor. As long as I'm not unloading cargo there's no customs inspection. Bring your troops aboard whenever you like. Sail to the coast of Benin and put your whole force right on the beach via rubber boat. If you like, uncrate one of your Hind gunships and fly it right off the deck."

They were looking at each other again.

"I'll tell you what," said Avakian. "You can do what you like. You want me to recon Benin, I'll do it for the 300 grand and then we'll all part friends."

"You've got a lot of bloody conditions, mate," said De Wet.

"I've got a pretty robust survival instinct," Avakian replied. "Three hundred grand isn't worth 20 years in an African prison for smuggling guns."

Volkov was amused. "We have a saying in Russia. An enemy will agree, but a friend will argue."

"We will have to talk this over," said Payne-Best.

"Suit yourselves," said Avakian. "I'll be checking out your bookshelves."

He took his glass of scotch and did just that. With any luck they'd throw him out the door. Gazing at Payne-Best's books it occurred to him that all military men had the same libraries.

When they were done talking De Wet came over. "You're a right pain in the arse, mate," he informed Avakian. "But you make sense, I'll give you that. I wasn't too thrilled with the aviation option myself. But everyone was looking at the bottom line: they already had the planes. You woke them up. So you're on."

"Since we're all buddy-buddy now," said Avakian. "What the hell was the deal with those employment contracts?"

"Payne-Best," said De Wet. "Silly bugger wants to pretend he's a fucking businessman running a company instead of a bloody mercenary."

So it was as simple as that, Avakian thought. There wasn't a lot of difference between illusions and delusions. Something he ought to keep in mind himself.

Having met with nothing but failure in every attempt to get himself fired, he rejoined the group at the planning table. Peering at the maps, it suddenly dawned on him that they were waiting for him to say something. Well, lead, follow, or get out of the way. "I'm assuming that you want the on-site reconnaissance done first, before you determine the final composition of the assault force and the weapons load you're going to need?"

"Correct," said Payne-Best. "What we need is…"

He was interrupted by a loud crash and woman's piercing scream. In an instant later that blended into a cacophony of yelling and the thumping of bodies hitting more solid objects.

Volkov, Okong, Payne-Best, and De Wet all drew pistols from beneath their clothing. Okong was halfway to the door leading to the patio outside when De Wet bellowed, "It's not the fucking police! It's your fucking bodyguards!"

At that everyone dashed out into the main house. Except Avakian. He walked over to the wall safe and twisted the handle. No, Payne-Best had locked it.

No time to boot up the computer and take a look. There was a Sig-Sauer 9mm pistol in the top desk drawer, but nothing else interesting. Avakian gave it some thought, but photographing Payne-Best's rolodex was not something he wanted to be doing when everyone came back. The crashing had stopped, and there was just yelling now, so he ambled down the hall to see what all the fuss was about.

De Wet was standing in the center of the room, face flushed with anger, pistol thoughtfully pointed down towards the floor. Volkov was on one side shouting at his bodyguards, and Okong doing the same in the other neutral corner. Based on one bloody nose and a few ripped shirts, the mutual dislike he'd sensed in both camps had degenerated into open conflict.

Of them all Payne-Best had the worst of it. Everyone else just had to break up a little fight between armed men, while he was trying to calm his wife. Who was not crying. Not hysterical. But rather shouting at him at the top of her lungs. "Never! Never have I been so mortified. Those thugs you brought into my home brawling in front of my friends. By tomorrow the news will be all over."

"My dear...," said Payne-Best.

"And the furniture! The side table and both lamps. Ruined! Do you have any idea how long it took me to find those lamps, Herbert? Do you?"

"Yes, my dear," said Payne-Best. And he turned to the guests, who seemed fewer in number than when Avakian had come in. Doubtless some had bolted for the exits when hostilities ensued. "A thousand apologies, everyone. Just a bit of a misunderstanding. All over now. Please, have a drink." He opened the double doors that led out to the pool and motioned violently to Volkov and Okong, mouthing the words: get them out.

Volkov and Okong herded their troops out the door, banishing them to opposite ends of the yard.

While this was going on, De Wet noticed Avakian on the periphery. "Thanks for all the help, mate."

"Not in my employment contract," said Avakian. The bar table was unbroken, so he paused to recharge his glass with another two fingers of scotch. "Besides, it seems I'm the only one around here who's not packing heat."

"Excuse me," said a mature female voice behind them.

Avakian turned, and there was an elegantly dressed, silver-haired matron, face flushed and moist from all the excitement. "Yes?"

"Could you possibly pour me a large vodka?" she said.

"Certainly," Avakian replied. Evaluating his customer with the eye of the barkeep he'd been in his younger years, he loaded a glass with ice and filled it to the brim with Stolichnaya. "Lemon? Lime?"

"Thank you, no." She took the glass and drained it in three swallows, throat muscles pumping up and down. "How very exciting."

"Quite," said Avakian. He was waiting for her to wipe her mouth on her sleeve, but De Wet's hand on his arm was beckoning him back to the study. "Please excuse me."

"Of course," she said, turning to the man next to

her, who was queuing up for a drink himself. "Could you pour me a large vodka, please?"

On the way back to the study Avakian said to De Wet, "A little racial tension between the camps?"

"Who fucking knows? Bloody Russians can't stay away from the booze even when they're on the job. And the bloody Nigerians. Stiff-necked blacks always looking for an insult."

It was always the human resources issues, Avakian thought.

In the study Okong was shouting at Volkov. "Keep your Russian animals under control!"

"Control?" Volkov shouted back. "If my men did not follow orders all yours would be dead. You know nothing of discipline!"

Avakian began scouting out available cover, in case this little alpha male struggle for dominance culminated in pistols being drawn again.

But Payne-Best solved that, though totally unintentionally. "Do you have any idea what that ruined furniture cost?"

Next to him De Wet sighed loudly. Avakian didn't get far along in his countdown before the other two halted their squabble and rounded on Payne-Best.

"Furniture?" Volkov bellowed. "You are talking to us of furniture? You want perhaps me to write you a check?"

And then Okong followed it up with, "Just because your wife has squandered your money, do not think you can present us with any bills."

"I don't know about you," Avakian said under his breath, "but I'm feeling so much better about our little conspiracy."

"Don't be a drama queen," De Wet ordered. "You

never worked with generals? This is par for the course."

"That true about Payne-Best?" Avakian muttered.

"Don't pretend you can't use the cash," De Wet retorted.

"There's a difference between wanting it and needing to have it," said Avakian.

"I was never at the top," said De Wet. "I was paid, but never a piece of the action. This is my time. Payne-Best has a style he needs to maintain, that's his business. You mind yours."

At least Avakian now knew why the men he thought wouldn't need this gig actually needed it badly. Neither of them had been among the top people in Corporate Solutions. And now it was time to finish defusing the situation. "Gentlemen," he said in a tone firm enough to cut through the noise.

It gave him the silence he wanted. "Gentlemen," he repeated, in a lower register now that he had their attention. "It's getting late. What do you say we finish up our business?"

They stared at him for a moment, then Volkov began to laugh. "What do you say?" he demanded. "The voice of reason." Then to Avakian alone. "This ability, it is worth money, my friend. And I know what I speak of. Negotiation is my business." He thrust a hand toward Avakian, as if presenting a beauty queen. "The quiet man who keeps his head."

"Right," said Payne-Best, who always seemed just a bit tardy in salvaging a situation.

"You want me to do a close-target recce of all the objectives in Benin," Avakian said, leaning over the table and picking up the conversational threat as if nothing had happened. He also intentionally used the

British military term. "You want a surf zone and beach reconnaissance. You want a detailed look at the airport in case a beach landing isn't tenable. You want a sense of the security situation in Cotonou; equipment, morale, and training of the police and military, and their routines. You want the schedule for the changing of the guard at Buckingham Palace. In short, you want the view from the ground."

"Exactly," said Payne-Best. He tapped the maps on the table. "Which of these do you need to take with you?"

"None," said Avakian. "I'm not walking around either South Africa or Benin with military topographic maps or sat photos in my pocket."

"When will you leave?" said Volkov.

"I'll start making arrangements as soon as the money is deposited into my account," said Avakian. "As far as details, I'll be keeping my itinerary to myself. I won't be checking in on the phone while I'm there, or sending any e-mail updates. I'll give you a call when I get back."

"Is all that paranoia really necessary?" Payne-Best asked. "We want you to complete the mission, after all."

"I'm sure you do," said Avakian. "My concern is anyone who doesn't."

"No one outside this room knows anything about the operation," Payne-Best said coldly.

No one except all the other guests who saw that little bodyguard rumpus and then watched the five of them return to the study together. But Avakian didn't mention that. What he said was, "All the better then. Let's hope it stays that way." He looked around the table. "This is usually the point where threats are communicated. Rather than bothering with all that, let's just say that I have no desire to spend the rest of my life on the run from any or all of you gentlemen. You checked me out. You know that when I'm hired the job gets done. Let's just say you're aware of my concerns, and I'm aware of yours."

"Couldn't have put it better myself," said De Wet.

Chapter Seven

AVAKIAN KNEW that the CIA would want to hear everything about his meeting with the conspirators as soon as possible. And that was exactly why he had no intention of telling them. At least not just yet. For the very same reason he refused to share his Benin itinerary with the coup plotters. This kind of business attracted some major control freaks, and if you gave them the opportunity and your cell number they'd be micromanaging your every move. More important, there was always the chance that at any point someone higher up in the CIA might decide that it was time to put an end to the plot, probably by notifying either the South African or Benin governments. Such a person would not consider Peter Avakian's welfare a high priority, and if the plug got pulled at the wrong time he might very well find himself in a Benin jail trying to explain to unsympathetic ears that he was actually one of the good guys, working for the CIA. Who of course would never admit it.

You needed a visa to visit Benin. Which ordinarily

wouldn't be a problem, except that the country was so poor it only had ten embassies around the world. And none of them was in South Africa. The best he could come up with was a two-day trip. South African Airways from Cape Town to Johannesburg, then on to Nairobi, Kenya. Then Kenya Airways from Nairobi to Lagos, Nigeria. A day layover to pick up a visa at the Benin Embassy in Lagos, then the next day's Kenya Airways flight to Cotonou, Benin. There were more direct routes, but only with African airlines that no sane person with any other alternative ought to contemplate flying on.

As he drove around Cape Town doing some last minute shopping Avakian had a sense of being followed. In a way it was reassuring that it had finally happened. Not that he planned to do anything about it. Always better to let them think you were oblivious. Might be mercenaries, or the CIA, or even South African security doing routine surveillance. The list was getting longer every day.

It happened when he stepped out of the Cape Town pharmacy with his prescription in hand. Atovaquone and proguanil, an anti-malaria combination that he'd have to take in Benin. At least they'd come up with something better than mefloquine. That stuff always gave him terrible nightmares.

The car door slamming attracted his attention. Avakian turned and put on his sunglasses while he waited for Patience Mbatha to make her away across the parking lot to him.

"This is what happens when I don't give you my phone number?" he said. "You stalk me?"

"I stalk you because you won't give me your phone number," she replied.

"Touché," said Avakian.

"I need to talk to you."

Avakian looked out over the parking lot. Amateurs. Always the biggest problem. "I didn't figure you were here to get a prescription filled. Are you aware that you're under surveillance at this very moment?"

She started to whirl about, but he clamped a hand on her shoulder. "Do *not* look around."

"Under surveillance by who?" she said.

"No idea. I didn't plan to walk up and ask them who they were representing." He thought it over. "Were you in the cab?"

"Yes."

"And how long have *you* been following me?"

"Since you left your hotel."

At least it would give him an alibi if someone saw her tailing him. "Anyone else with you? The truth, if you please. I know how many people have been following me, but now I need to separate the players."

"It was just me."

Good. That meant two cars switching off, and maybe one backup in parallel he hadn't seen yet. That was better than the team of four vehicles he thought he'd been looking at. "That just leaves open the question of whether they're following me, you, or both of us. Now don't move your head. Do you see the tallest office building, over my shoulder, two blocks down the street?"

"Yes."

"Walk directly there. Go inside, take the stairs to the first floor. Wait for me right beside the elevator. I may be fifteen minutes or more. If I don't show up after forty-five minutes, then walk back to your car and leave the area. Now read that back to me."

"Excuse me?"

"Repeat what I just said."

She did.

"Great," he said. "Now I'm going to give you some body language as if I'm telling you to get lost. Feel free to stomp off angrily."

"What?"

Avakian held a hand up to her face, as if telling her to shut up. Then he waved his finger back and forth under her nose, as if delivering a lecture. It was condescending enough that she didn't need to be Meryl Streep to act angry. Then, for the finale, a dismissive flip of the hand and he said, "Take off now."

She surprised him by getting up in his face and yelling, "Fuck you!"

Avakian had to work to keep from laughing. He hoped she found that cathartic.

He sat in his car and watched. She went down the street but the surveillance didn't. He kept watching in case they had someone farther down the street as a cutoff, but nothing picked her up when she crossed the intersection to the next block.

So it was all on him. That was good. It was always nice to know who was following you, but you could tell a lot from the numbers and the level of professionalism.

If you had multiple cars, eyeball vans with one-way glass and cameras, multiple walkers with everyone changing clothes and taking bicycles out of their trunks, then your ass was in trouble because you had the first team on you and they were official.

Or if you just kept bumping into a single, but everywhere you went, then they'd wired a GPS into your car. Probably with an ignition kill switch for whenever they decided to scoop you up.

This bunch was the same two cars. So it could be anyone. CIA. Mercenaries. Nigerians. Russians. Local cops investigating the Nigerians or Russians. Or anyone else, for that matter.

Avakian stayed on foot, and took a much more roundabout route to the office building. They stayed with him, but they stayed in their cars.

As he walked in he glanced at the building directory and went right for the elevators. Patience Mbatha was standing right there when the door opened onto the first floor, and Avakian stepped out. It was an older building and he didn't see any security cameras in the corridors, but they probably had them in the elevators.

"Where are we going?" she said.

"Eighth floor," Avakian replied.

No security cameras in the stairwells. And, thankfully, Patience wasn't even breathing hard. On the eighth Avakian followed the numbers until he found what he was looking for. "Here we go," he said, opening the door for her.

"Do you have a medical condition?" Patience asked.

"No."

"Then why are we in a doctor's office?"

Avakian motioned her toward a chair. "Because it's a doctor's office. They barely pay attention to you if you're signed in. Otherwise you're just waiting for someone."

She gave him one of those reappraising looks he was getting used to. "You're quite capable, aren't you Mr. Avakian."

"Pete," Avakian said. He wouldn't have been

surprised if she'd been scared out of her wits. Instead she was all geeked up over the cloak and dagger stuff. Which was not really a good thing. "Now, you said you wanted to talk to me?"

"Who would be following you?"

"I told you, I have no idea. Have you been doing things that would get people interested in following everyone you've been meeting?"

"I?" she said, all surprised. "Why would they be following me?"

Avakian wasn't about to tell her she wasn't being followed. "You're the one running around interviewing people about mercenaries."

"Don't talk about me," she retorted. "You were at Payne-Best's house two days ago."

Avakian kicked himself for not considering the obvious. Yeah, he'd taken a cab and then walked on foot. But as movie stars knew all too well, all it took was a photographer hiding in the bushes with a long lens shooting everyone who came in and out of a house. "You got me interested. So when he called and invited me over for drinks, I went."

"Are you working with him?"

Now he was going to find out how much gossiping Payne-Best's civilian friends had done. "No. But I wouldn't be surprised if they're in the process of doing some corporate headhunting."

Her expression was pure skepticism. "You expect me to believe you're not working with them."

"If I was, I'd hardly be sitting here talking to you."

That provoked a little reevaluation. He could see that she was at least thinking about buying it.

"I know they're planning a coup somewhere in Africa," Patience said. "And I know that Dmitri Volkov is part of it. Please don't tell me you didn't talk to him at Payne-Best's house."

This operation was as leaky as a sieve. It made Avakian wonder why he'd bothered to go to the CIA at all. Then again, if history proved anything it was that hustling journalists were a lot better at digging up information than the CIA. He decided to roll the dice. "Of course he was there. But I didn't speak to him."

"Please."

"He's not the kind of guy you walk up to and say hello. Have you seen his bodyguards?"

"So you were at a party with the world's foremost gunrunner yet you didn't speak to him."

"No. And if you're thinking of trying for an interview I don't recommend you springing out of the bushes at him all of a sudden."

"Then what do *you* think Payne-Best and Volkov were doing together?"

Avakian was reassured that she hadn't mentioned Okong. But then even he hadn't known what the man looked like until they were introduced. "Who's being disingenuous now? Mercenaries need guns, and gunrunners need customers." He paused. "Either that, or their kids are on the football team together at some private school, and their wives are best friends."

"I should think the second part was less likely."

"I probably wouldn't either if I was a reporter." Oh, no. He could tell by the look on her face. She'd made up her mind about him and was going to put in the shot. Always be closing.

Patience didn't disappoint. "Pete, you can help me with this story. Exposing these people would be very important."

Man, she was just *glistening* with ambition. "If I'm

sure of one thing," Avakian said, "it's that your magazine cannot afford my hourly rate."

"We should have dinner tonight and discuss it."

Okay, that was it. He wasn't joining any more
teams. "Patience, you've been flirting up a storm, and
I'm sure that has everything to do with my rugged
good looks and nothing to do with your story."

"That was unfair, Pete. To both of us."

It always was when you got your hand caught in
the cookie jar. "Maybe so. You're a very attractive
woman, but there's a lady back in America I'm in
love with. But that's not why I'm not going to meet
with you again. You're messing with dangerous
people, and you're putting me in danger. Which to
me means you either don't care that you're putting
me in danger or you're oblivious to the fact that
you're putting me in danger. Both are equally bad.
"

Now she was pouting. "You're being very unfair."

"Maybe. But let me tell you something. If I was
working for the mercenaries I wouldn't just not be
sitting here talking with you. I'd be giving them your
name. And you'd be dead."

"Isn't that rather dramatic?"

"No, it's good advice from the security professional,
if you'll take it. You need to ask yourself whether this
scoop is worth it, on a strict cost-benefit basis. I'm not
saying don't write about it, but maybe it would be
better to wait and file your story after whatever it is
happens. Because these are people who would think
nothing of having you shot down in the street and
making it look like an everyday robbery. And it
wouldn't cost them any more than the amount of
money they normally carry around in their pockets on

a given day. Happens to journalists in Russia every month."

"This is South Africa."

"Yes," said Avakian. "It is. I can give you the name of a reporter who was gunned down on the streets of Oakland, California."

"And they would do that?"

"You'd better believe it. Sooner or later the fact that you're interviewing people about them is going to make its way back. Not from me. But someone will talk. Guaranteed."

As he pretty much expected, knowing women of a certain type as he did, that didn't faze her. It excited her. What was the cliché line, that you couldn't watch a movie these days without hearing? This isn't a game. But it was. The most exciting game in the world. Just one you could get yourself killed playing. He looked at his watch. "We've been here too long. We need to leave."

He rose and led the way out the door. As he turned the corner on the way to the elevator Avakian nearly collided with a tall black man in a business suit. From the startled look on the guy's face it was clear that he was walking the halls looking for them.

Rather than jump back Avakian let momentum carry him into the man. By way of separating themselves he grabbed him by the arm and turned him around so he couldn't see Patience. "Oh, I'm really sorry."

The black guy opened his mouth to say something, but it got shut off by a loud clacking sound. His mouth opened even wider and he fell to his knees and then onto the carpet, shaking.

Patience Mbatha stood behind him holding a stun gun in her hand.

Great. That left Avakian only one move. He took a step forward and drove his heel into a spot right behind the guy's ear.

The black man's head bounced twice on the carpet, and he was unconscious.

Fortunately the corridor was empty. Avakian grabbed him under the arms and dragged him down the hall toward a men's room they'd passed. "You want to open the door for me?" he said to Patience. No one in the men's room either, which was another jackpot avoided.

Avakian dumped the still-unconscious man in a stall and frisked him.

Patience was standing in the middle of the men's room, looking around like it was her first time in one and she wanted to remember the view. "What are you looking for?"

"ID," said Avakian. "I'm really hoping he's not with the National Intelligence Agency." That was South African counterintelligence. But they spent most of their time spying on factions within the ANC on behalf of other factions within the ANC.

Patience's stun gun was back in her purse, and she had a hand up to her mouth. "What if he is?"

"I'm thinking a heartfelt apology won't be sufficient," Avakian replied.

No credential case, thankfully. He was packing a 9mm Beretta that Avakian didn't touch. No walkie-talkie, which was good. All cell phone calls would go to voice mail and they'd think he had no bars. Nothing but regular ID and credit cards in the wallet, not even a private detective license. Avakian wiped them all off and carefully replaced the wallet in the man's pocket.

"Now it's definitely time to go," he said, grabbing a sheet of towel paper to wipe Patience's fingerprints off the door handle on the way out.

"Is he alive?" she said.

"I don't know," Avakian said. "I didn't check."

"Shouldn't we…?"

"No, we shouldn't call an ambulance."

"Did I do the wrong thing?"

"What's done is done," said Avakian, pushing her out the door and wiping it down. "I'm taking the elevator to the street. I'll leave and draw them all off. You take the stairs up to the top floor and wait a good half hour. No less. Then walk down and go out the back door. Walk at least a quarter of a mile before you catch a cab. Don't take it right to your door—get out and walk home. Okay, repeat that back."

She did. "Thank you, Pete."

"Goodbye, Patience. And I really mean goodbye. Don't get in touch with me again. And remember what I said about dropping this."

"Goodbye, Pete." Patience seemed about to say something else, but instead turned and headed down the corridor toward the stairs.

There was another black guy in a suit covering the lobby, but Avakian didn't even look at him as he walked out. He went directly back to his car and they all fell in behind him. If they had left someone back at the office building to look for the missing man the odds were fair that they'd miss Patience.

Avakian was driving aimlessly through the Cape Town business district, thinking about his next moves, when his BlackBerry buzzed. He checked the screen and pulled over to take the call. Unbelievable. The psychic powers of women, even over incredible distances, never ceased to amaze him. It wasn't even eight in the morning in Denver. "Hi, Judy."

"It's nice to finally hear your voice."

"Well, the time difference isn't helping us out."

"Pete, you know as well as I do that the only time you send text messages is when there's something you think I don't want to hear."

Avakian thought that was a little unfair, though he did concede that technology made it much easier to be a weasel. "Now Judy, I told you personally that I was going to be delayed coming home."

"But you still haven't told me why, other than "business.""

"And I still can't, not over an international phone line."

"The thought of what you might be getting yourself into is giving me stomach pains."

"Judy, it's nothing like Beijing."

"Pete, you're gone for over a month, and then a few days before you're due to come home you get involved in something else? That you can't tell me about over the phone? Please don't insult my intelligence."

The China incident that Payne-Best alluded to during their first meeting, well, Judy had been a big part of that. Avakian had been contracting with the U.S. government on security for a conference of foreign ministers in Beijing and she was working as a doctor with the U.S. women's gymnastics team, in town for an exhibition. After the assassination of the President of Taiwan, a surprise guest for the conference, Taiwan had a coup d'état and China began firing missiles at them. During their first date. Total chaos in Beijing that night, and when a couple of soldiers who stopped them tried to molest Judy Avakian had killed them both. After that they'd run for the Mongolian border together. She was the most amazing woman he'd ever met. Not to mention no fool. She'd seen it all in his company, including patching him up after he got shot in the leg at a Chinese checkpoint, and was going to be hard to satisfy on this. Avakian dropped his voice. "Judy, I just said it's nothing like Beijing."

"I'm just not enjoying sweating it out back here and letting my imagination run wild."

"Honey, I understand. It's just that I made some commitments here. And I don't want to give you a date for coming home and have to break it again."

A pause over the line. *"I miss you."*

"I really miss you, too."

"Pete, I don't want to fight over the phone."

Why did people always tell you they didn't want to do what they were actually doing? "I don't, either."

"I know perfectly well that you're drawn to action even more than most small boys, and I spend a lot of my time putting small boys back together. And you need to know that I'm not made to be the sit-at-home Army wife."

She knew the wounds from his first and only failed marriage hadn't healed completely even after all these years. Nice of her to open them back up. "I know I screwed that up once. I don't want to screw it up with you."

"I'm sorry, Pete. Just having to do this over the phone's made me incredibly bitchy."

You didn't have to do anything, Avakian thought bitterly. "All I can say is, when I get home we'll take some time off and talk this through."

"Don't take too long. I've got to go, Pete."

"Bye," Avakian said helplessly.

She clicked off.

Avakian sighed as he pocketed the phone. You'll never learn, he told himself. All duty's ever given you is a good hard kick in the ass. Now there was one more thing hanging over his head. He was beginning to know how knife jugglers felt.

Chapter Eight

THE MINISTER of Trade and Industry examined Avakian's business card again. Unusually enough, it was his real business card. "And what is the company you are working for, Mr. Avakian?"

"That's the awkward part, sir," Avakian replied. "I've been engaged by a group of companies, all in the oil production equipment and services field. The deterioration in the security situation in Nigeria has led them explore the possibility of moving at least a portion of their port, cargo handling, and warehousing operations to other countries in the general vicinity. As I'm sure you understand, this is a delicate matter in view of longstanding contracts and relationships. So until the companies involved make a decision to pursue this course of action, they have required me to maintain their confidentiality."

He waited until the interpreter put that into French. Evidently his very basic command of that language was so jarring that the deputy minister he'd initially spoken to had immediately summoned a translator.

The Minister was both well dressed and extremely well fed, in marked contrast to everyone Avakian had come into contact with in Benin so far. "And yet you are here."

"My employers felt it would be extremely disrespectful to conduct their surveys in secret," said Avakian. "I am here at their request, as a courtesy, to begin what they hope will be a fruitful relationship."

"The government of Benin welcomes all responsible commerce, free trade, and investment," said the Minister.

"That's very gratifying," said Avakian. "As I'm sure you've realized, the infrastructure investments my employers are prepared to make would be considerable. They would both welcome and require the assistance of local contractors and suppliers."

Everyone in the room was able to visualize the big old carrot Avakian was dangling. He wasn't one of those who moaned about political corruption in developing countries. If he'd been proposing the same kind of project on the Gulf coast of the United States he'd have quickly found himself buried under a pile of politicians trying to stick their hands into his pockets. The only difference was that American politicians had made corruption legal in the form of campaign contributions. Avakian's theory of natural selection dictated that the higher you went in a country's political hierarchy, the bigger the crook you were dealing with. Honest politicians only a did a term on the local town council.

The Minister was obviously appreciating the possibilities, but still playing his cards tight. "You must understand, Monsieur Avakian, that we receive many individuals with many proposals. If they all came to pass, Benin would be as developed as France today."

Avakian knew that long before the Nigerian prince with the five million dollars there had been generations of white men showing up with a briefcase, a shoeshine, and a smile to scam the African. "I understand perfectly, sir. But I require nothing. My presence here is simply a courtesy to inform you of my presence and intentions before I begin work."

"You have not yet mentioned exactly what your work is."

"To complete a general survey of the security situation in Cotonou and Porto Novo," said Avakian. "Particularly the port operations."

"And by security you mean?"

"Crime. Law enforcement. Cargo handling in the port. Warehousing. Transport."

"Benin is a safe and peaceful nation, Monsieur Avakian. I am certain your report will be favorable."

"I have every expectation that it will be, sir. I understand that it is illegal to take photographs of official buildings in your country, and as that may be necessary in the course of my work I wanted to avoid any misunderstandings."

"I understand. I will order the appropriate permissions to be issued to you."

Avakian knew that people had died of old age waiting for African bureaucracies to generate official documents. "Thank you, your Excellency. Perhaps the Ministry could recommend someone…an official escort, a translator…who could personally forestall any difficulties as I travel about your country."

"I am sure it could be arranged."

Avakian was sure the Minister had some relative hanging around with the ability to drive a car and pad a bill. "I'm grateful to your Excellency for making time in what I'm sure is a very busy schedule." Actually, he hadn't heard a phone ring the entire time he was there.

"The pleasure was mine, Monsieur Avakian. I wish you success. If there is any further assistance we can provide, please feel free to contact my offices."

Avakian stood, and they shook hands.

"Good day," the Minister said, dismissing him.

"Good day, sir."

Avakian was enormously pleased with himself. Benin was one of those countries that still had a lot of the residual paranoia of a people's republic. Tourists had gotten roughed up taking pictures in front of banks. So why sneak around in your ninja outfit and risk getting thrown into the clink when a good cover story could get you official permission to nose around to your heart's content? Not to mention that the authorities' total focus would now be on finding out who he was working for, in order to gauge the potential for future bribes, rather than wondering if he was some kind of spy.

So he was practically clicking his heels as he was walked down the Ministry hallway, when a door opened and he found himself in the midst of half a dozen Chinese in business suits.

There were Chinese trade delegations signing deals all over Africa. They desperately needed energy, raw materials, and markets, and were very popular with the local governments because, unlike the West, they couldn't care less about annoying little details like human rights. Whether their efforts would come to naught like every other great power's venture into Africa, they were definitely serious about it.

Uncharacteristically rattled, Avakian put his head down and kept moving. Even when he bumped into one of them he didn't say a word, so as not to give away his nationality. But once he was clear of the group he couldn't resist looking back over his shoulder. And when he did one of the Chinese, probably the group intelligence officer, was ready with a cell phone and snapped his picture.

Dammit. Avakian began calculating how long it would take his photo to make its way to Beijing and back. He was going to have to move fast and wrap up his business in Benin before that happened. It was always something.

Chapter Nine

AVAKIAN'S EYES only flickered over the piles of garbage in the street but Laurent, draped over the front seat, didn't miss a thing. "Terrible, is it not, Monsieur Pierre? These *nègres*, they keep their bad habit. No one want to do anything."

Nègres was negroes, also a slur in Benin. Laurent was one of those Africans who liked to run down the brothers. Probably had a lot of success ingratiating himself with the white man doing it too, Avakian thought. As expected, Laurent was the cousin of the brother of the Minister of Trade and Industry, or something like that. Avakian had gotten a bit lost during the lengthy explanation. Definitely part of the local elite. There to be a minder, but also hard at work on making his own fortune.

In his early twenties, Laurent wasn't fat like his relative the Minister but definitely fed well. Avakian had started using body shape to determine everyone's social status in Benin.

A definite go-getter, Laurent considered Benin

much too small a canvas for a man of his ambitions. He'd actually shown up on time that morning at the Marina Hotel, a rare enough occurrence in Avakian's experience that he'd invited Laurent and the driver to join him for breakfast. They both acted as if no one they'd ever taken around had made that kind of offer before, which Avakian, remembering the people he'd bodyguarded for, didn't doubt for a second.

The driver, Fabrice, was a reed thin beaten-down man in his early thirties who looked twenty years older. Laurent addressed him imperiously in Fon, one of the local tribal language of southern Benin. French was the official language but only the city elite spoke it fluently. However most of the residents of Cotonou, like Fabrice, understood French phrases even if they didn't strictly speak the language. No matter the language, though, Fabrice said very little. He just contentedly ram-fed himself from the hotel buffet.

Laurent, on the other hand, hadn't wasted a second of potential conversational opportunity. Before he'd even finished his coffee Avakian had declined hash, cocaine, ecstasy, and a wide range of girls available for any imaginable perversion. Not for the first time he reflected that the one advantage Americans still had overseas was that everyone wanted to go to America. Even the most die-hard Yankee hater was still willing to suspend their principles for at least a week's vacation in New York or Miami. And in Africa they firmly believed that every American was allowed to bring a certain number of foreigners home with them, like duty-free perfume.

Since Laurent never took his eyes off him, all Avakian had to do was look at something and Laurent was offering to arrange it. Even sunglasses didn't help.

It seemed his fate on this trip to dislike the one he could communicate with, and like the one he couldn't communicate with.

They went to the port first, because everyone would be expecting it. It was one of the largest in Western Africa, eight berthing stations of which one was for container and one for roll on-roll off. It could use some work, though. The channel was silted up and needed to be dredged, the cranes were rusting and the warehouses peeling. Security wasn't bad, for Africa. Cement wall around the port, and reasonable control at the gates. Of course people were going to slip over the fences and lift something, but nothing big like a container was getting out without organized payoffs. There were a lot of workers who didn't seem to be doing anything in particular, but Avakian had no doubt things got done, the African way. He knew how hard it was to work in the steaming heat when you were hungry. With a painful twinge he remembered arrogant young Green Beret Captain Avakian in El Salvador wondering aloud what it was going to take to get these people *moving*. And then one of his staff sergeants gently telling him that there wasn't much staying power in a bowl of rice and beans.

"They have to change their mentality," Laurent was saying. "There is no passion. This country, it is a cemetery. Not like America."

Avakian tried not to say much, because it only sent Laurent off on another soliloquy on the Protestant work ethic. He was starting to wonder if the kid wasn't tweaked on some of his own chemicals.

After the port they took in the town, Avakian supposedly working off the map in his lap but actually the one in his head. Cotonou was spread out, so it was easy to just circle around. Heavy traffic moving sedately at about thirty miles per hour. Not a lot of cars sharing the road with their Nissan, but thousands of motorcycles. Little 50cc two strokes and scooters moving in swarms. At the traffic lights what little order there was fell apart, and as the bikes backed up they formed dense billowing masses that shifted shape like single cell organisms. They were the reason there was a permanent bluish haze to the air. And probably why even the palm trees looked sad and droopy. In Cotonou if you didn't own a bike you got around by the motorcycle taxis that were easily picked out of the swarms by the drivers' bright yellow shirts. A passenger just hopped on the back and offered up the necessary prayers to their deity.

When the driving got touchy Fabrice either hunched up his shoulders around his ears or lowered his head into his body, Avakian couldn't decide which. It usually happened trying to negotiate the swarms of bikes.

"These zemis, they are maddening," Laurent said. "No rules are followed, not like America."

"What does 'zemi' mean?" Avakian asked.

"'Get there fast', in Fon," Laurent replied.

"It would be better if they were called 'get there alive'," said Avakian.

Laurent started laughing. But it didn't tail off. It grew louder and more hysterical, until he was rolling around in the front seat and even Fabrice was looking over at him.

"It's okay, Laurent," Avakian said. "You can stop now."

Except for that gorgeous African landscape Cape Town might as well have been Europe. Even though the gap between rich and poor was as wide as the Grand Canyon, you didn't see how the poor lived unless you went looking for them. Or they went looking for you. But Cotonou was Africa. Multiple story bank buildings existed literally side by side with miniature neighborhoods of huts nailed together from scrap. There were no parks. Every open space belonged to the street vendors, the hut villages, or was used as the local landfill. One of those countries where government services were a dream, and everyone just made do. The power had gone out that morning, which it did all the time, and three people had gotten trapped in the elevator at Avakian's hotel. Another reason to take the stairs.

Cotonou was women walking down the streets with baskets on their heads, and seeing a truck pass by was a rarity but some guy pushing eight 55-gallon steel drums on a two-wheeled cart commonplace. There weren't many stores. The economy seemed to be based on markets, and like every ex-Marxist economy that had opened up there were people selling things every-where. Every street was jammed with the stalls of the more prosperous vendors. The less affluent worked under umbrellas so beaten up they'd even lost their original color. And the bottom of the heap had to be content with selling their stuff from a pile on the pave-ment, or a basket on their head.

Cotonou was also a coastal city that might be blown away at any moment by a tropical storm. Poured concrete was the preferred building material, and it was pretty dirty and pretty chipped. Otherwise there was a lot of masonry and not much steel, a jarring contrast of new and crumbling, paved main streets and naked dirt side roads. Fall didn't mean much on the equator. Bright sun and then an instant later dark rain clouds, a downpour so thick you couldn't see through it, and then another instantaneous transition back to sun and so hot that the pavement dried while you were looking at it.

Avakian's general principle when scouting out a place was to do all the general work first. Just in case.

All it took was a little practice. Sit up next to the side window of your car and it looked like you were talking on your cell phone instead of using it to take video of your surroundings.

The tail appeared in the late morning. A blue Toyota with tinted windows. They were probably government, having just tossed the contents of his hotel room looking for information on his supposed employers. As a matter of fact, Avakian was amazed that Laurent hadn't pumped him for that information already, since restraint wasn't exactly the kid's middle name.

The Presidential Palace was practically on the beach. Which made for a nice view and handy recreational opportunities, but wasn't too smart from a defensive standpoint. Of course there was a wall, and a checkpoint access road on the city side. Avakian imagined it might delay determined attackers with breaching explosives for at least a minute or two.

After a short time spent gazing at the palace and noting the security measures he said, "Okay, let's go." Pointing to the totally deserted road crossing the front of it.

Fabrice hesitated, and said something to Laurent. Avakian didn't have to speak Fon to know that Fabrice was warning that there would be trouble. Then

Laurent yelling back. Listen to the Monsieur. Do as you are told.

Without another word Fabrice shifted and pulled out. They hadn't gone far when a green French jeep full of soldiers shot up behind them. No lights or sirens. They accomplished their mission by shouting and brandishing weapons until Avakian said to pull over. Not that he even considered it, but they certainly wouldn't be able to outrun anything in the Nissan. Every time they went over a pothole the car rattled like a tin can full of pebbles.

Fabrice just sighed quietly, in the manner of a foot soldier whose accurate prediction of disaster had gone unheeded.

"I will handle this," Laurent announced, springing out of the car.

Couldn't wait to display his executive abilities, Avakian thought. This was going to be a show.

The soldiers wore the red berets of paratroopers. Their camouflage uniforms in the old French lizard pattern, polished jump boots with white laces, and relatively un-battered AK-47's all said elite Presidential guard unit.

Laurent characteristically began by shouting and waving his arms. Giving them the old "do you know who I am?" Which only worked, Avakian thought, if they were inclined to be impressed by who you were.

He began the usual countdown, and didn't get far before one of the soldiers angrily rammed his rifle barrel into Laurent's stomach. The kid folded in half like a lawn chair. Evidently the Minister of Trade and Industry didn't carry much water with the Presidential Guard.

Fabrice gave Avakian an imploring look over the front seat.

Avakian should have guessed that Laurent was the type who could walk into an Amish quilting circle and start a riot. He kept his sunglasses on and donned the straw dress hat that matched his suit. Had to protect the bald head from the equatorial sun. He reached into his pocket so he'd have what he needed already in his hand without any sudden moves.

It was one thing to know you needed to maintain an aura of confidence, quite another to go walking up on a bunch of excitable soldiers with marginal weapons handling skills and probably no idea whether their rifles were set on safe or full auto. But doing so with your knees knocking together was a recipe for disaster. Like any other animals, humans had no trouble sensing fear.

Avakian didn't believe there was such a thing as a fearless person. Too stupid, unbalanced, or chemically altered to be able to imagine or care about the probable result of a course of action, yes. Fearless, no. His solution was always to get seriously pissed off. You could be scared or angry, but not both. So he took a moment to work himself up into a decent froth.

It also helped if you'd done it before. Avakian had lost count of the number of checkpoints and road-blocks he'd negotiated in his time. If asked, he would have admitted that this was why he did what he did. A situation where, if you didn't read it perfectly and make every single right move at the exact right time, the absolute best that could happen was getting a rifle barrel rammed into your gut. The worst? Well…

As soon as he stepped from the car every weapon was immediately pointed in his direction. Avakian acted as if they didn't exist. The soldiers had no idea what they were dealing with, and he knew that window of psychological ascendancy was extremely narrow. He lifted up his sunglasses to briefly stare at Laurent sprawled on the pavement trying to get his wind back. Then the shades were down and he was looking at the soldiers, followed by a stern, official snap, "*Qu'est-ce que c'est?*"

Whether or not they spoke French was an issue, but the sergeant in charge of the group got ahold of himself and sputtered out in rapid and bad French, "This road is forbidden!"

Avakian looked at him, nodded his head slowly as if he were thinking it over, and said matter-of-factly in his just as terrible French, "A mistake." And at that he shook open the pack of Marlboros in his hand and offered each of the soldiers a cigarette.

Which threw everything off balance. Of course they weren't going to decline. Avakian didn't smoke, but he knew that even smuggled American cigarettes were not inexpensive items in central Africa. After everyone had one Avakian passed the pack to the sergeant and didn't expect to see it back. Then the butane lighter, though he didn't light up for them. He wasn't surprised to see that disappear, either.

Once they were all puffing away happily the mood had shifted. Laurent had struggled back to his feet and Avakian didn't want the vibe messed with. He aimed his thumb in the direction of the car and Laurent meekly obeyed, making a show of limping away and holding his stomach.

Avakian glanced briefly at him, then back at the soldiers, shaking his head in disapproval. "A mistake," he repeated. "No problem, eh? I have meetings."

"No problem," said the sergeant. He pointed a finger at the car and shook it sternly.

"*Merci, chef,*" said Avakian. "*Bon jour.*"

"*Bon jour, monsieur,*" the soldiers chorused, waving their burning cigarettes in salute.

Avakian took one last look at them before ambling back to the car. No heavy weapons in the jeep, and only one extra AK magazine pouch on their belts. They looked spiffy in their camouflage, but they weren't set up for any kind of real fight.

Laurent was slumped in the front seat, in a definite funk. Fabrice, clearly pleased to have been spared a beating, not to mention the confiscation of his vehicle, was giving him a toothy smile of approval.

"*Allez,*" said Avakian, gesturing with his hand before settling back in the seat with a couple of deep exhalations to bleed off the tension.

Fabrice turned front and started the engine. Avakian didn't look back. But if that blue Toyota kept following them the occupants were going to need to have some baksheesh handy.

He consulted his watch. If he didn't do something Laurent was going to be pissy the whole rest of the day. "Laurent, take us somewhere good for lunch." Then, seeing the reaction, quickly added some additional guidance. "Local Benin food, though. Nothing else."

Laurent's face dropped, and Avakian knew he'd nearly been on the hook for multiple courses of overpriced French food at some joint for skittish tourists. No way. The only other cuisine he'd be willing to consider was Lebanese. When in doubt, the Lebanese restaurant was always the best one in any city.

This set off a spirited argument in Fon between

Laurent and a newly assertive Fabrice. It went on until Avakian loudly cleared his throat. The victor wasn't in question, because Fabrice was driving with his first smile of the day while Laurent fell into another front seat sulk.

Avakian was curious, because the restaurants in the city were mainly for tourists. When the locals ate out, they did so from the street vendors.

They traveled along the Oueme river, which passed through town from a lagoon north of the city and emptied into the sea. The name Cotonou meant mouth of the river of death. The kings of Dahomey had exported slaves to the coast down that river. Africans hadn't been just the victims of the slave trade.

The journey took a while down dirt roads, dodging chickens and potholes the size of the car. It culminated at the bottom of a steep hill that had rocks banging the underside of the car like machinegun fire. Avakian hoped they were going to eat well, as there seemed to be no assurance they'd be able to make it back up that hill.

The road was fronted by about ten tiny shops, with the usual curious kids running around. The restaurant was screened in using a vast collection of different types of screen. It had an actual thatched roof. Well, you wanted authentic, Avakian thought. You got authentic. There was no sign.

"What's the name of the place?" he asked Laurent.

He only shrugged, which Avakian took to mean either it had no name, or Laurent was still in a snit. Probably both, since he'd gotten used to the fact that there were no signs on anything or for anything in Benin.

As they walked in they passed a 6X6 foot charcoal

grill upon which the better part of a pig was cooking. That definitely jacked up his sense of anticipation.

Fabrice spoke to the owner and they were led to a wood picnic table with bench seats.

Another conversation in Fon. "They have beer or Coca Cola, Monsieur Pierre," said Laurent.

"Coke for me," said Avakian. "You guys can have beer if you want. Just tell them to leave the cap on my bottle." A basic food safety tip for developing countries. Always beverages with bubbles in them, and always with the cap on to avoid recycling or adulteration. No fruit juice, no ice. Stay away from raw fruit, raw veggies, and all milk products and you'd probably be all right.

Their drinks were borne in by a pretty young girl who couldn't have been over twelve. She wore a white headscarf and a long lime green dress with a pattern of blue and white sea shells. Rich or poor, Africans dressed up. Bare feet. She probably didn't go to school because her father needed waitresses. She giggled adorably when Avakian thanked her in Fon, then cast her eyes down at the floor when Laurent spoke to her. Language barrier or no, Avakian knew aggressive flirting when he heard it. He just stared at Laurent until the kid happened to glance over with his usual "ain't I cool" expression. The look shut him up. Just as well, because Fabrice looked like he wanted to kill him.

Avakian's Coke was in the old fashioned glass bottle, a nice little trip down memory lane. He took out his key ring to uncap it.

"Monsieur Pierre, what is that?" Laurent asked, pointing to the substantial chunk of metal on the ring.

Trying to get back in the good graces. "Just a key ring ornament," said Avakian. Actually, it was an

Okinawan tekko. A two-fingered brass knuckles, but so stylized that they didn't look like brass knuckles. An object that had so far eluded the imaginative powers of every airport screener around the world. Just part of his traveler's emergency kit.

After the flirting incident the owner brought out the food himself. Avakian guessed that the cuts you were served depended on what you were willing to pony up. The plates of the rich white foreigner and his friends were loaded with sliced tenderloin, pieces of liver, belly crackling, and a meaty bone. There was a plate with strips of onion and two sauces, and another plate with another sauce in the center surrounded by large pats of a mashed starch.

"What is that, Laurent?" Avakian asked, pointing to the starch.

"Yam," Laurent replied, mouth already full of pork.

Avakian tried a sample. It wasn't sweet potato. More a tuber like Puerto Rican iname. He rolled some into a small ball and tried the sauces. One was bean, the other two were different varieties of hot pepper. Nice.

The pork was well done, a necessity in the tropics. The slow cooking for tenderness was also necessary, as this pig had never been fed grain and had spent its life running around loose. But great flavor, enough to make Avakian continue his long running feud with tasteless and rubbery factory-raised American pork. The taste was more like Cuban barbecue than anything else he'd run into. Not really surprising considering the number of central Africans who'd been dragged off as slaves to the new world.

They ate with their right hands, the left being

reserved for bathroom functions in most cultures. The mashed yam was particularly good dragged through the pork juices. Avakian always approved of hot pepper sauce. It gave you a nice cooling sweat in the heat, and in his opinion few pathogens could survive exposure to it.

Just like breakfast, Fabrice was eating like he'd never seen food before. Laurent was pouting again. Avakian concentrated on lunch and ignored him. He would have liked to talk to the owner about his recipes, particularly one of those pepper sauces, but after Laurent's disrespect to the daughter that was out of the question. Another missed opportunity.

Avakian passed up the fresh pineapple. His dessert was a capsule of ciprofloxacin with the last of his Coke. An old Green Beret trick, he resorted to the powerful antibiotic only when he couldn't afford to be laid up with Montezuma's Revenge. One cipro after a meal and it didn't matter what bugs were in the food or on the utensils.

The total bill came to less than twenty dollars, and that was probably with a hefty white man's surcharge. Avakian's tip doubled that, leaving behind a colorful pile of the CFA francs that were the exchange of the former French colonies of Western Africa.

Emerging from the shade of the restaurant the midday heat nearly knocked them over. The neighborhood kids had been watching the white man eat through the screening and were waiting for them outside. Avakian passed out a handful of coins, and they all ran off to one of the nearby shops screaming with excitement as Laurent shook his head.

Fabrice backed down the road so they could make a good run at the hill. From the back seat Avakian could see that his neck was now hunched down into his body like a turtle, no doubt cringing inwardly at every rock that dinged his meal ticket. Halfway up the hill the tires spun on the dirt and they were enveloped in a cloud of dust. Avakian thought they'd be heading back down, if not rolling back down, but Fabrice gave it more gas and they made it to the top, engine screaming.

After that bit of excitement Laurent fell asleep in the front seat. Fabrice didn't look that much more alert, so Avakian said, "*L'hotel.*"

Instead of indulging in siesta he changed into his swim trunks and headed for the nearby beach. To his surprise both Laurent and Fabrice insisted on coming along. Avakian didn't credit the bond they'd developed —the guys were making sure nothing happened to the money man. Fabrice took his nap in the car, refusing to leave his baby to the mercy of the environment. While Avakian swam Laurent went to sleep in one of the thatched-roofed open wall cabanas on the beach.

Anyone watching would have thought that Avakian was slowly swimming laps. A few hundred yards out into the water, then slowly returning to the water's edge, and back out to sea. A little farther down the beach each time. Good exercise.

He was actually doing a beach survey. He had twenty five feet of line in his pocket, that he'd marked at one foot intervals, and a weight on one end. As he swam he took depth soundings. Back in South Africa he'd use the data to make a complete hydrographic sketch of the beach, including the condition of the bottom, the slope, the types of sand, and any under-water obstacles like sand bars, debris, or wrecked boats. When he was finished he sat on the sand and for exactly ten minutes by his watch recorded the height, period, and drift of every surf breaker. There was a strong inshore current, and change of tide around here had to produce some nasty rips.

Refreshed by the exercise and cooled by the Atlantic, Avakian was ready to get back to work. He momentarily thought about leaving Laurent asleep in the cabana, but he needed a translator. Besides, there were five or six young men hanging around the beach looking for an easy mark. They'd already strolled by once while he was swimming to see if there were any valuables on his towel. If he left Laurent out there the kid would be walking back home naked, if he was lucky. And he didn't open his mouth.

With his towel under his arm, Avakian leaned into the cabana. "Laurent." No response. "Laurent!" Maybe he was dead. He snapped his towel at a leg. Not a twitch. Avakian grabbed a bare foot and shook it. Nothing. But there was a pulse, at least.

Avakian had seen this in the Army. Sleeping so soundly they literally needed to be hit with a baseball bat in order to wake up. Not the best quality in a soldier. Still holding onto the foot, he backed up fast. As Laurent landed on the sand, his head hit the edge of the cabana platform. He moaned and slowly opened his eyes.

"Back to work," Avakian said. Every time you thought you were done dealing with privates, you were proved wrong.

In the late afternoon Fabrice refused to park any closer to the paracommando barracks than a quarter of a mile. Avakian didn't blame him for not wanting to risk a Laurent-provoked beat-down, but the decision was problematic because the blue Toyota had shown back up. He hoped they hadn't any trouble with the soldiers earlier in the day.

The sun was going down, and it wasn't the safest looking street in the world. Every military base every-where was the same—they attracted vice like a magnet. Fabrice wasn't about to leave his car, but after seeing them both sleep Avakian decided it would pay to be careful. When he and Laurent reached the end of the block he called over one of the little kids that were running around in packs. He was a street kid, so he didn't get too close. Avakian held up a 5 euro note cupped in his palm, and the kid's eyes went wide at the sight of that vast and incredible fortune.

"Watch that car," Avakian said. He was pointing and Laurent was translating. "And when I come back you get the other half." He ripped the note in two and handed over one piece to the kid.

"He says he will guard it with his life," said Laurent.

"I just want him to keep his eyes on it," Avakian said. "Tell him not to get involved with anything, just let me know everything that happens anywhere near it."

Twenty yards farther down the street and Avakian gave another kid half of another 5 euro note. To watch the first kid.

A couple of soldiers with slung rifles were lounging in front of the barracks gate. Avakian considered that at least an approximation of guard duty. He asked to see the commanding officer. Not around. Probably a late tee time. The second in command? No. Was there at least a duty officer?

One of the soldiers trudged off on a search, and returned fifteen minutes later with a young lieutenant.

Looking bewildered, as young lieutenants had a tendency to do.

Avakian nearly smiled like the Cheshire Cat. Had not the Ministry of Trade and Industry informed them of his visit? No. Well, he was a retired colonel of the United States Army. Would it be possible to get a tour of the barracks?

The lieutenant thought that over. "My colonel, I have no orders."

"What do you think *your* colonel would say?" Avakian countered. "Would he turn me away, or greet me as a fellow paratrooper and give me a tour?"

The lieutenant's brow wrinkled up. "It would be my honor to give the colonel a tour."

"Spoken like a future colonel," Avakian said. Now, a future *general* wouldn't have done anything that had even the remotest chance of getting him into trouble, but that was something else entirely.

Live in one military barracks and you'd be at home anywhere in the world. They all looked that much the same. There wasn't much to see, but every detail was telling if you knew what you were looking at. The general layout of the buildings went into Avakian's head. If it took fifteen minutes to dig up an officer on a week night then the level of alert wasn't high, to say the least. The level of training was checked off when the lieutenant answered Avakian's casually posed question that they hadn't been to the field on exercises in more than four months. All the weapons and ammo were carefully locked away, so it would take them some time to get into action. And a quick head count in each platoon living space told Avakian that the number of troops available for duty on a given day was a far cry from the battalion's organizational strength on paper.

If Payne-Best and De Wet managed to get ashore with any kind of force these soldiers were history. Even if they didn't take off running at the sound of the first gunshot.

The sun had set by the time they were finished. Avakian thanked the lieutenant profusely and promised a letter of appreciation to his colonel. The kid had never heard of anything like that, and he sent Avakian off with his snappiest salute.

"Monsieur Pierre, we are finished for the day?" Laurent asked plaintively on the way back to the car.

"What was all that talk before about passion?" Avakian demanded.

Laurent only managed an embarrassed grin.

"Yeah, we're done for the day," Avakian said.

A hot night had everyone in the street. The whole neighborhood was hanging out. A different kind of music was playing every fifteen feet—the machine-made disco beat that mostly disappeared from American music in the early 1980's but had been a staple of European pop ever since. The omelet men were cooking eggs on their portable stoves, and everyone was drinking beer. No street lights, just the dim illumination spilling from everyone's windows. The vendors worked from kerosene lanterns over their tables or a few bare bulbs on jury-rigged wiring from the nearest power line.

The second kid was gazing down the street with the concentration of a bird dog. He reported that the first kid had been on the job the whole time, and hadn't spoken to anyone. Avakian palmed him the other half of the 5 euro bill in a handshake, so none of those sharp eyes would see the money transfer and take it off him. The kid wasn't stupid—he wasn't going to give anyone the chance. He couldn't have disappeared into the darkness any faster if he'd dematerialized.

The first kid sprinted down the street to meet them. The words came out in a furious rush, then a short pause to draw in a ragged breath, and another headlong rush of words. It reminded Avakian so much of his son at that age he had to grin. But that smile gave way to alarm watching Laurent's face as he listened to the kid. "A man walked by the car, left, and then came back. The driver did not see him. The man crawled under the car very quickly. He got up and left. The driver did not see him do it."

"Was anyone with the man who went under the car?" Avakian demanded.

"No."

"Is the man or anyone else with him waiting in the area?" said Avakian.

"No. He left and did not return."

"Not within sight?" said Avakian.

"The boy did not see him," said Laurent.

"What did the man look like?" said Avakian.

The boy pressed an index finger in the corner of each eye and pulled the skin back. Laurent said something to him, and they went back and forth for a while.

"What?" Avakian said impatiently.

"It cannot be right," said Laurent.

"Just tell me exactly what he said," Avakian replied, his tone of voice a warning in itself.

Laurent blocked on the English word, so he said it in French. "*Chinois*."

Chinese. "Call Fabrice on his cell phone," Avakian ordered. "Tell him to leave the car and come meet us here."

"I will tell him myself," Laurent said excitedly, and took off running down the street.

"No!" Avakian shouted after him. But Laurent was gone.

Avakian gave the little boy the other half of the banknote, and he was gone in a flash.

Laurent had reached the car and was leaning in the window, gesticulating wildly as always. The driver's door opened up, and Avakian was willing them to do what they'd been told. But Fabrice jumped out and immediately crawled under the car with a flashlight. Avakian's stomach twisted. Maybe it was just a GPS tracker.

The bang and the simultaneous flash triggered a lifetime's training, and Avakian instantly threw himself onto the ground. The blast wave skipped by like a hot breeze, and when he lifted up his head an instant later there was a pall of smoke. That drifted away quickly into the night sky to reveal the silhouette of the car in the faint street light, except the car was opened up like the blooming of a jagged metal flower. There were no flames, just the smoldering remnants of a high order explosion.

Chapter Ten

AVAKIAN PUSHED himself up off the pavement as some people ran by him screaming and others ran toward the car to look. As for himself, he joined everyone leaving the area. Any pro would have eyes on that car. And having seen that their target hadn't been blown up, there probably was someone with a weapon waiting for him to come running up and check for survivors. If Laurent and Fabrice were alive, which he sincerely doubted, then they were going to have to rely on their own countrymen.

Returning to the paracommando barracks would raise questions that he didn't feel like answering. Avakian tried to walk down the street as if he belonged there, which of course he didn't. Based upon all the eyes he was feeling on him, this neighborhood saw a white man in a suit out walking alone at night about as often as it snowed.

He wasn't worried about that as much as he was about what it would take to get out of there. He was going to have to hail one of those motorcycle taxis. And there was nothing, absolutely nothing Peter Avakian hated more than motorcycles. He was simultaneously walking around trying to find one and using the time to figure a way out of it. He had nothing—it was going to have to be the motorcycle.

A bunch of kids were following him, just for something to do. It was the last thing he needed, but trying to shoo them away would be fruitless and only attract more attention.

Avakian turned the corner, and there was a guy on a motorcycle. No yellow shirt, but he probably wouldn't be averse to making some money. He looked like a safe driver. No, that was a rationalization.

"*Bon soir*," Avakian said.

The biker turned around in his seat to face him, and did a double take at the sight of a white man. "*Bon soir.*"

Avakian had been working the pitch over in his head to make sure he had the French both right and simple. As he opened his mouth the driver kicked his bike into life and drove off in one smooth motion.

Avakian just stood and stared. It couldn't have been anything he said. Maybe the guy was just prejudiced.

There was too much music on the street to hear well, but the security expert thought it would be a good idea to look behind him. Four young studs in their 20's, showing off the muscles in wife-beaters and silver jewelry. And there was no place to run.

They spread out around him, casually but practiced. The leader of the pack was just over six feet tall and spent a lot of time on his biceps and pecs. He smiled, as if to make the point that he was harmless. "*Hey, yovo.*"

Avakian had listened to Laurent and Fabrice enough to know that yovo was white man in Fon.

"*Cadeau, eh?*" said the leader. "*Cadeau pour nous.*"

Cadeau was gift. Everyone in Cotonou wanted to be gifted.

Avakian put on submissive body language, and a squeaked out a frightened little, "*Oh, oui.*" He reached into his pocket as if to grab some money and slipped his first two fingers into the holes of the tekko brass knuckles, gathering the rest of the key ring into his palm to stop any jingling. Shoulders hunched down and looking at the hand in his pocket, he took a step forward as if to hand it over, carefully closing the distance with the leader. He kept his eyes down, but in his peripheral vision he could see they were all passing each other gloating looks over an easy mark.

Avakian's hand shot out of his pocket, coming up from his hips, his whole body uncoiling behind it. He caught the leader flush on the hinge of the jaw and the brass knuckles contacting bone sounded like a pistol shot. The leader was unconscious before he hit the ground, the side of his face ripped open by the metal.

The momentum of the punch carried Avakian forward, and he had to dance over the leader's legs to keep from falling. He charged through the hole in the circle he'd just created and whirled about before he could get stabbed in the back.

But the other three were frozen in both shock and indecision. Avakian sprang at them, bellowing, "C'mon!"

They turned and ran down the street.

Not wanting to wait around until they regrouped or rounded up help, Avakian ran in the opposite direction.

Unless you were Bruce Lee, four on one was a guaranteed beating. But one ought never underestimate the powerful impression made when the leader of the pack was laid out with a single punch.

As he ran down the street Avakian could make out a motorcycle silhouetted in the light of a street vendor's table. As he got closer he could see that the bike was fueling up at a gasoline vendor's table. The gas was smuggled in from Nigeria and offered in any quantity a customer might desire, from a soda bottle to a five gallon jug. It was sold for half the price of the government-run gas stations. Typical of Africa, a burning gasoline lantern hung perched over the table of gasoline bottles.

Avakian slowed down to a walk. All running up on someone in the dark would get him was another drive off.

The vendor and the biker were both staring at him like they'd just seen Godzilla show up on their street.

"*Bon soir, monsieurs,*" said Avakian.

"*Bon soir,*" they both replied cautiously.

"*Aller à motorcyclette?*" said Avakian, pointing to himself. "*À l'Hotel de Marina?*" He showed the driver the color of his money.

The sight of the cash transformed the biker from skeptical to eager, as money had a way of doing. "*Oui, oui.*" He seemed to be composing a response, then gave up and pantomimed that he had to gas up first.

Avakian stepped in to grab the bottle and give him a hand. As he leaned over the front of the man, the biker fell forward across his ride, his whole body spasming as if he'd had a seizure.

Avakian instinctively dodged to his right, and the globe of the vendor's lantern shattered right next to his head. It didn't go out. The mantle flared and everything got twice as bright.

Avakian threw some of the francs in his hand down onto the table, grabbed a whiskey bottle full of gasoline, and ran.

A very good marksman had shot the biker in the head and put another bullet into the lantern. Both meant for him. Only the simple fact that he hadn't been standing still saved his life. That spasming was characteristic of a head shot, when the dying brain fired incoherent electrical impulses through the body in its final moments.

And it had been a silenced weapon. He hadn't even heard the crack of a bullet, which meant both a sound suppressor on the weapon and the bullet slowed to subsonic velocity. So it was probably a pistol. He factored that into his tactical planning, because it determined how close his adversary would have to be in order to take a shot. He hadn't seen a thing, which meant they were good.

Avakian followed the recon man's rule to never run in a straight line. He turned at the next intersection, and again as soon as he could.

When he felt like he'd opened the distance he paused in the entrance of a narrow alley between two buildings. It was risky, because if he had multiple adversaries it would give them a chance to fix him in position and work their way around. But he really needed to know what he was up against.

Avakian crouched down as he peeked around the

corner of the building, so his head would not be at eye level. There was a group of locals congregating around a building stoop on the other end of the street. Loud and laughing, a portable radio playing. A few more people walking by. All Africans.

The concrete exploded next to his eye.

Chapter Eleven

AVAKIAN FELL BACK into the alley. He couldn't see out of his right eye. He touched his face and felt blood. It was like a handful of grit in the eye. Either it was really a handful of grit, or he no longer had an eye. No time to worry about that right now, and no place to run except into the alley. Dumb, Avakian. Dumb move.

About twenty feet in the alley was blocked by a small mountain of garbage. It wasn't like western trash. In Africa anything like cardboard or glass or metal was recycled like gold. This was just an enormous stinking pile of the daily refuse of life.

Avakian began climbing the lower slope of the hill, near one of the building walls. He immediately sunk down below his knees, giving thought to being sucked down into it like quicksand. The smell was horrendous, and he felt like he might puke at any moment. If he got cut on anything the infection would probably kill him before he had a chance to get shot.

To make a step he had to pull each foot up and clear of the pile and swing it forward. And each one he took caused the rats swarming over the pile to scurry away from him in panic. The only thing keeping him upright was that one supporting hand against the wall of the building. Expecting a shot in the back at any second, he struggled to force his way forward.

Finally his feet touched solid ground again. As he walked forward he shook each leg like a cat that had accidentally stepped into water. The alley was pitch dark and there was only a quarter moon, so he felt his way forward carefully.

Great. A concrete wall. Not high, but still over Avakian height. And like every wall in the third world it was bound to be topped with broken glass. Nothing to stand on, and nothing in the garbage pile like a piece of cardboard or old carpet to throw over the top to protect him. But there was a drainpipe coming down the side of the building. Avakian gave it a shake. It was attached none too securely. He grabbed it anyway and pulled himself up, walking up the wall with his feet. The drainpipe gave a metal groan as it gradually pulled away from the building. Avakian just climbed faster. He felt himself coming away from the building along with the drainpipe. He reached out for the top of the wall with his foot. As expected, the wall was topped with broken glass bottles cemented into place, but there was a short lip on both sides where the concrete had been troweled down. The only problem was, even with his leg fully extended his foot was still a good six inches from the wall. And that drainpipe was going to come down any second.

Avakian jumped. One foot landed on the lip at the

top of the wall. He windmilled his arms like a tightrope walker who was about to lose it. He tried to get his other foot on the lip at the other side of the wall, but there was no hope. Having only one working eye didn't make it any easier. It was either fall groin-first onto the glass, or jump again very quickly. He grabbed ahold of the bottle of gasoline in his suit jacket pocket and jumped.

The ground on the other side of the wall was in black darkness. In the air he put both feet together, and when they hit ground he rolled onto his hip in perfect parachute landing fall. He landed on nothing but dirt. Avakian was grateful for that, but he hated having to rely on nothing but luck.

He came off the ground gingerly. The older he got, the harder those falls were to make. Continuing down the alley was the damndest thing. He wasn't surprised that there were no fire escapes, but there were also no doors on either side. No windows at ground level, and the ones higher up were both out of reach and barred to boot. Nothing to do but keep moving forward.

The alley took a dogleg turn at the jutting corner of a third building, and became only half as wide. At least there wasn't any crap to wade through. It was precisely while Avakian was thinking this single positive thought that the alley stopped at the back wall of yet another building. Totally boxed in. No windows. There was a ground floor door in the building right in front of him, but it had been completely bricked over.

A dead end. And totally screwed. No way out but back the way he'd come.

Avakian took a couple of deep breaths to forestall panic and made a complete circuit of his surroundings to see if there was anything he'd missed. Another drainpipe, a ground floor trap door or sewer grate, anything he might use for a tool or weapon. Nothing. Good work, Avakian. Fine job of trapping yourself. The Chinese were going to laugh themselves sick as they nailed his scalp to the wall back in Beijing.

Maybe there was something. He ran back to the wall and leaped up to try and get one hand on the clean edge. Too short, dammit. He took a longer start and nearly wrenched his back on the leap, but he got a hand on the top. He reached up with his free hand and felt around for loose glass. Couldn't hold on much longer. He got ahold of the bottom part of a bottle and yanked it out, dropping back to the ground.

Useless. His brass knuckles were a more effective weapon. But maybe…

He wrapped the chunk of bottle in his suit jacket and stamped on it. That produced a couple of nice handfuls of small glass pieces.

Avakian thought he heard something and backed away to that last corner, where he could see the top of the wall.

Barely see, that is. Only one eye, and the other was really hurting. He didn't want to poke at it and risk permanent damage it if the eye wasn't already beyond repair. All he could smell was the garbage he'd crawled through. But at least his ears still worked.

The Chinese ought to be hard on his heels by now. Once there wasn't an ambush at the mouth of that alley they'd be pretty sure he was unarmed. They wouldn't risk losing him in the darkness.

The trouble was picking anything out over the sounds of a city at night, even though muffled between two buildings. Pots banging, kids yelling, people arguing, music playing.

He focused all his concentration on it. Minutes passed with no result, but this was not the time to be impatient. Then, finally, on the other side of the wall. The faintest creak of metal.

Someone was checking out the drainpipe. Well, they were there. And they were coming. Nothing to do but prepare the last stand of Peter Avakian.

He made one more check of his surroundings to measure distances and angles. If you had time you always wanted to turn around and prepare the killing zone of an ambush from the perspective of anyone venturing into it. Just before that corner he shook out his jacket, scattering the glass pieces across the width of the alley.

At least he had the whiskey bottle full of gasoline. Another of Avakian's rules. If you're in a jam and see a weapon, grab it. You could always toss it away later if you didn't need it. He pulled out the cork that sealed the bottle and stuffed in his pocket handkerchief as a wick. A Molotov cocktail wasn't much against a pistol, but it was better than brass knuckles. He felt around in his pocket before realizing with alarm that those soldiers had walked off with his lighter earlier in the day. No lighter, no matches, no flint. Not even two sticks to rub together. Without a spark, all that bottle was good for was a club.

Okay, think. He took a few more breaths to steady himself and tried to concentrate. He had nothing. Making a kite to attract lightning and tying on a key wasn't exactly feasible. Lightning? No, no electric lines, outlets, or meters anywhere within reach. Okay, Avakian, be systematic. Inventory everything on you, and see if there's anything you can use.

He did just that, knowing there wasn't much time

before his adversary or adversaries came over that wall. Take it easy. One by one. Nothing. Wait. Cell phones. Cell phones? He'd never seen it actually done, he just remembered reading about the theory. Well, it was better than nothing, which was all he had otherwise.

Every time Avakian visited a new city he bought a prepaid cell phone so he wouldn't have to give any of the locals he was working with his regular numbers. He opened that one up and removed the battery.

He didn't hear the approach as much as he felt it. Timing was going to be crucial, and the other guy had all the advantages. He was completely fatalistic about his prospects, hoping only to put up a good show, as the British would say, before they gunned him down.

The alley corner was crucial. No one was going to come around it until they were absolutely ready, and that would be too late for him.

Avakian waited on one knee, the Molotov cocktail on the ground before him and the cell phone battery next to it. He cleared his mind and concentrated on breathing quietly but regularly. Waiting for the sound.

Whoever it was moved like a cat. Avakian didn't even hear him come over the wall. While he'd probably sounded like a water buffalo.

Just one soft crunch of glass as a foot stepped on it and immediately backed away.

Avakian smashed his brass knuckles down onto the cell phone battery. The positive and negative poles of a rechargeable lithium ion battery were separated by a piece of plastic as thin as cellophane. And, as everyone knew, a fully charged cell phone battery was very hot. The brass knuckles pierced the battery case and Avakian pulled his hand back quickly. Nothing.

Avakian reared back and hit it again. This time the battery seemed to spit up flame in front of him and a hot piece of metal hit his hand. Avakian touched the gas bottle handkerchief wick to the sputtering battery, and the wick flared up. He sprang to his feet and charged around the corner.

By the light of the burning wick Avakian saw his adversary creeping along the wall. The pistol came up the same time Avakian threw the Molotov cocktail. Not at the man, at the wall beside him. As he let it go he felt a bullet fly by his cheek.

The Chinese was already diving out of the way as the cocktail hit the wall and exploded.

But that was what Avakian intended. No one who wasn't in a wheelchair was going to get hit with a flaming bottle they saw coming. But the Chinese was diving out of the way of the burning gas, not shooting at him. He'd followed up his throw with a desperate headlong charge. He slammed into the Chinese, leading with his shoulder. The impact knocked the man clean off his feet and sent the pistol flying.

Avakian aimed a kick that would have smashed a skull, but it hit nothing but ground as the Chinese had already recovered and rolled clear. Shit, he was fast.

Avakian swung his right hand to finish the fight with the brass knuckles, but a block to his right forearm sent an electric shock all the way up his shoulder and turned his hand numb.

The Chinese's right hand was coming up toward his head, and Avakian just managed to get his left forearm in the way. Another burning blow as the knife blade that would have gone into his neck instead went through his forearm.

Instead of responding to instinct and pulling back

Avakian drove forward, bellowing like a bull and using that forearm and the knife to pin the Chinese's knife hand against the wall. A kick thudded off his shins that he barely paid attention to.

They were belly to belly up against the wall. No room to throw a punch, and his right hand couldn't make a fist anyway. Avakian spat into the Chinese's eyes and sent a knee at his groin to gain just a little separation. With his own right arm pinned the Chinese was on the defensive and trying to hold back Avakian's with his left. Avakian used all his strength to punch that arm up between their bodies and grab with his thumb and forefinger at the Chinese's eye sockets.

A shrill yell. Avakian took a step back, pulling back with his thumb and forefinger. With the extra room he swung his left arm around the Chinese's neck and could feel the knife blade grinding away in his forearm as he did it.

Once his arm closed around the neck Avakian left his feet and dropped deadweight to the ground, twisting his body so the Chinese was falling onto his back while he was falling onto his stomach, the two of them locked together.

Avakian's body weight was greater than any punch. The Chinese's chin was being forced onto his chest, with Avakian's arm as a fulcrum. Too many forces were involved—something had to give. The Chinese's neck broke as they hit the ground.

Avakian felt the sickening lack of resistance in the neck tucked into his arm. He was face to face with the Chinese, who had long black bangs covering his forehead. The man's eyes were opened and blinking, though Avakian knew that wouldn't be for long. No central nervous system meant no breathing. He lay there on the ground and watched, and after a minute or so the eyes stopped blinking and went fixed.

Avakian just lay there on the ground. It took every last bit of his willpower to get himself moving. Focus, Pete. Set priorities. Okay, first aid.

The handle of a folding knife was sticking straight out of his forearm. The only good thing was that blade hadn't come out the other side. Too much adrenaline was still racing through his system for it to hurt, but it surely would soon. From a first aid standpoint, the one thing you did not want to do was remove any object that had pierced your body. Major vessels could have been cut, and the projectile might be the only thing holding them closed and keeping you from bleeding out. Better to let them do it in the emergency room.

Having said all that, Avakian wasn't about to go walking around Cotonou with a knife sticking out of his arm. And he had no intention of visiting any hospitals in Benin.

Fortunately, a bad injury in the recent past had spurred him into carrying a wound dressing around in the back pocket of his pants. A plastic wrapped rectangle about the same size as a candy bar.

He ripped the plastic open with his teeth and spread the compress out. Taking a deep breath, he grabbed the knife handle and pulled it out. Shit. His forearm muscles were locked up so tight the blade wasn't moving.

Avakian pulled up his shirt tail and wrapped it around his hand for a better grip, since he was slick with sweat and blood. Another deep breath, and he yanked at the knife with all his might. The blade came out of his arm with a sound like a champagne cork popping. Now he was really sick to his stomach.

He gave it a second to see if there was any arterial pump that might require a tourniquet, then slapped the compress over the wound and tied the gauze down tight. He had to take a short breather after that.

Avakian popped another ciprofloxacin, dry, thinking about garbage piles and flesh-eating bacteria.

Move. Get moving. He searched the Chinese, retrieving two spare pistol magazines and all his cash. By all rights he should have been the one laying there. He'd never seen anyone faster, or better at moving in the dark. More raw strength, and the luck of being in such tight quarters where he could use it to his advantage was all that had saved him.

Avakian had a button-sized Photon Micro Light LED flashlight on his key ring. He squeezed it on and searched the alley. The knife was wiped clean and went into his pocket. Then he found what he'd really been looking for, and it was definitely a surprise. He'd never actually seen a Chinese Type 67 pistol outside a Special Forces small arms recognition manual. Small and chunky, with a short barrel that looked like a round piece of pipe that was actually a built-in sound suppressor. Avakian could hardly believe the shooting the Chinese had done with that. The pistol with its little .32 caliber bullet was designed for killing people quietly at point blank range. A shot of over 15 yards was scarcely credible, and he'd easily made them at over three times that distance.

Avakian inserted a fresh magazine into the pistol, clicked the safety on, and stuck it into his belt. He felt like curling up and going to sleep, and that feeling was going to be even more pronounced after the inevitable adrenaline crash, but he knew he had to get out of there. No way had that Chinese been driving around all day by himself.

Ready to move, Avakian put his jacket back on to cover his blood-soaked shirtsleeve. He hobbled down the alley and stopped at the wall. Now how the hell was he going to get over that with two bum arms?

He looked back at the Chinese. Sorry buddy, but if it's any consolation I wouldn't mind if you did the same with me.

Avakian dragged the Chinese over to the base of the wall, pulled off his shirt and trousers, and bent him at the waist. He balled the clothes up in his hands, took another running charge at the wall, and used the Chinese's body as a step.

The clothes padded his hands from the glass, and the angle of the broken bottles actually made it easier to pull himself up. God, everything hurt, especially his arm. He left the clothes on top of the wall to protect his body as he rolled over the glass, and dropped to the other side.

Avakian felt like crying. His left arm was on fire. The right had a rising knot the size of a ping pong ball on the bone. And the shins that had been kicked didn't feel much better. He looked back on that wall as if it had been the Matterhorn. Pushing on, he waded back through the garbage heap.

The entrance to the street was the place for more decisions. Avakian had trouble believing there wasn't another Chinese intelligence officer in the vicinity who'd stayed behind to cover his partner's entrance into the alley. But maybe they'd gone in different direc- tions to try and head him off? Couldn't count on it. He knew the final answer would only come when he exited the alley and someone took a shot at him. Since he was in no hurry to add a gunshot wound to his list of injuries, he decided to sit tight for a while.

The same group of locals was still at the far corner, listening to a portable radio. Avakian carefully watched for any signs of impatient movement in likely hiding places, but the street was quiet.

Lethargically watching motorcycles buzz past, Avakian suddenly shook his head as if to wake himself up. He'd either been beaten worse than he thought, or he was really getting old. That was it. Screw nego-tiation.

He heard more bikes going along the perpendic-ular blocks on either side, but nothing else on this one. More minutes passed. Then that familiar puttering noise that changed pitch on a downshift, the sound rising back up as it came closer.

Avakian ran into the street with the pistol drawn. He knew he must look like the Creature From the Black Lagoon, one eye crusted over with dried blood, clothes ripped, blood spattered, lurching stiff-legged.

He could see the wide-eyed driver think about speeding around him, but the pistol aimed between his eyes put a stop to that idea. Avakian grabbed the handle bar with his left hand and motioned with the pistol for the driver to get off the bike. He shook his head wildly, and Avakian gestured more emphatically. Incredibly, the driver tried to gun the throttle and take off. As the bike lurched forward Avakian cracked him across the bridge of the nose with the butt of the pistol. The driver fell off the seat. The bike kept going until the hand came off the throttle, and it fell over.

Everyone who had been hanging out at the end of the street shouted and started running toward him. Avakian picked up the bike, a Yamaha 50, as if it were a live cobra. He straddled it and got his foot on the start pedal. Okay, fast downward motions. He did just that, and the biked coughed impolitely. It knew, the frigging machines knew all about him. Easy Avakian. A little choke and try again. If any Chinese were firing at him, they were much worse shots than the first guy.

The engine caught. Avakian sat back with a feeling of superiority and engaged the clutch. The bike shot forward fifteen feet and stalled. Goddamned fucking piece of shit! Another kick, and another cough. Easy, baby, I didn't mean it. That was my bad. Is there a compression release on this thing? Screw it.

All the yelling was helping him to gauge the distance, and the crowd was almost on him. Avakian sincerely did not want to shoot anyone who didn't absolutely need to be shot tonight. Another kick, and the engine caught in a burst of choking exhaust. That smuggled Nigerian gas wasn't premium quality. Avakian released the clutch with the greatest of care, just ahead of all those pounding feet.

At first the bike wasn't much faster than a sprinting man, and a couple of dedicated souls were still trying for him. Avakian could almost feel the hands grabbing for his clothing. He shifted gears with the same delicacy he would have used to arm a nuclear weapon, and finally separated from the mob.

Besides a previous unpleasant incident as a passenger, he'd only driven a motorcycle once before. A dirt bike in the hills around Aspen, chasing after his lunatic girlfriend on another bike. A little aversion therapy, was what his doctor called it. Noisy, stinking things; one false move and they'd kill you. Just too dangerous. After checking that block in order to satisfy a certain someone he'd happily gone back to his mountain bicycle.

He was feeling slightly more comfortable now, and at the next intersection ran through the gears smoothly. As he slowed down for a traffic light the light went from red to black. As did everything else. The power was out again. Maybe his luck was taking a turn for the better.

Illumination gradually flickered up in the surrounding buildings and huts as the resilient residents of Cotonou lit lamps and candles. On the street there were only the solitary floating blobs of motorcycle and scooter headlights.

Avakian heard a high-revving un-muffled engine coming up behind him. He knew he wasn't going very fast, so he pulled over to let them pass. The bike he was riding did not have any rearview mirrors, of course, and something made him take a cautious look behind—though that was not at all safe. He almost dumped the bike at the sight of another driver bent down over his handlebars and a passenger swinging a long metal bar at him.

Avakian swerved and braked, and the metal bar hummed by out of range. It was the former owner of the bike he was now riding. Avakian couldn't believe it. No one wanted their shit ripped off, but coming after the thief on another bike like some kind of modern day joust? Well, the heat of passion was usually when good sense went away.

Now they were dropping back to take another swing at him. This was getting ridiculous. Avakian gave the bike some gas and swerved farther out of reach, pulling the pistol from his waistband. As soon as he went one-handed the bike wobbled alarmingly and the fear clenched up his stomach. This provoked a definite murderous impulse, and as they also sped up and swerved back into him he raised the pistol. Heat of passion, Avakian. Heat of passion. He lowered the pistol and shot out their front tire. The bike went down and dropped the two Africans face-first into the street.

Avakian returned the pistol to his trousers, feeling worse about this than anything else that had happened. Sorry, man. I know a stolen bike is a lot of money to a poor guy, but if you make it a choice between you and me, it's going to have to be me.

After that little fright he made a few turns to be sure there was no one else following him.

Once clear of the old neighborhood he stopped in front the street stall of a clothing peddler. Who, to give him credit, recovered quickly from the shock of a bloody and battered bald white man, stinking of garbage, roaring up on a motorcycle. Business, after all, was business.

It was always helpful to know your sizes in both inches and centimeters. Without even getting off the bike Avakian picked out a shirt, a belt, and some socks, but the proprietor didn't have a pair of trousers in his unique combination of waist and inseam. He pantomimed "just a minute" and sent a little kid dashing off into the darkness. Avakian patiently took a seat on the motorcycle. He'd seen this before.

Every other vendor on the street, recognizing a sport, came running up with samples of their wares. While he was waiting Avakian picked up a bar of soap and a towel. The man who sold him the soap was very insistent about a bottle of shampoo also. Avakian said, "You're joking," in French, and the whole crowd had a laugh.

Five minutes later, as he was tiring of examining local handicrafts, the kid returned with the right size trousers. No showroom. No warehouse. It just happened. Africans were so unbelievably resilient and resourceful. They didn't need billion dollar aid packages and European rock star philanthropists. All they really needed was halfway decent government, and not to be ripped off. Unfortunately those were the two things they were least likely to get.

Avakian paid up, gifted the kid, and positioned the bag of clothes so he could sit on it. Took another five kicks to get the bike started again, with everyone offering him helpful advice. Goddamned things.

He drove straight to the beach, taking the bike across the sand all the way down to the water's edge. The Chinese were sure to be waiting back at his hotel. Transferring the contents of his pockets to the clothing bag, he walked into the water and stripped down. Not too far, though—a bull shark hunting at night didn't draw much water. He let the current take his suit to parts unknown and scrubbed himself down with the soap. As the crust of dried blood came off his eye he discovered that he could still see. First good news of the evening.

Three figures were coming down the beach toward him as he stepped from the ocean. A stark naked Avakian held up the pistol in profile so they could see it clearly. They stopped in their tracks, held a quick caucus, and headed in the other direction.

Avakian donned his new wardrobe and his old shoes, which he'd scrubbed off in the water. Took four kicks to get the bike started this time. Goddamned thing.

———

IF THE CHINESE were waiting at his hotel, they were definitely staking out the airport. Which meant that alternative transportation out of the country would need to be arranged. Avakian walked soundlessly down the quay until he had a good feeling about one of the fishing boats.

There was a young boy sleeping on deck. A fine idea in principle, but young boys tended to sleep soundly. Then again, you weren't going to get many volunteers to sleep out on deck and guard a boat. Matching his movements with the faint rocking of the boat with the tide, he slipped over the railing and slowly and quietly crossed the deck. There was a fishing knife in the kid's right hand.

Leaning down, Avakian clamped his palm firmly over the kid's mouth while simultaneously pinning the knife arm with his foot.

The boy's eye's popped open in panic, then grew even wider when he saw that his attacker was a white man.

Avakian retrieved the knife and held a finger up to his mouth for silence. "*Apportez-moi le capitaine*," he said in a mild tone. Then he released the boy, giving him a gentle pat on the chest.

To his credit, the kid didn't scream. He stood up and remained there, frozen in place.

Avakian motioned him toward the boat's cabin. "*Apportez-moi le capitaine*," he repeated.

The boy backed toward it, keeping his eyes on Avakian at all time.

Avakian took a seat on the stern rail, within

jumping distance of the quay in case everyone over-reacted.

Less than a minute later a black man in his late thirties charged out on deck, wearing only his shorts and brandishing a machete.

Avakian just sat there on the rail with his arms crossed. He smelled alcohol, so the skipper must have had a few pops before bed. Retaining his relaxed posture, he just looked at the machete and smiled.

The captain halted, at a loss as to what to do. Avakian could hardly blame him. Probably didn't have many bald, big-nosed white men coming aboard without permission in the wee hours of the morning. Or any, for that matter. Time to fill the void of indecision before the skipper fell back into his default setting, which was probably to turn nasty. "Do you speak English?" he asked, hoping that a Benin fisherman who sailed nearby Nigerian waters would speak some in order to deal with the Nigerian navy.

This cowed the captain, who let the machete drop to his side and stood up a bit straighter. "Yes, sir."

"What is your name?" said Avakian, intentionally keeping his English simple and the atmosphere cordial.

"Prosper," the captain replied. "Prosper Kassa."

"*Bon*," said Avakian. "I am Jean Smith."

"American?" said Prosper.

Avakian ignored the question. "I want you to take me to Lagos. Can you do that?" Nigeria was right next door, and Lagos was the closest port to Cotonou with an international airport.

"Hire my boat?" said Prosper. "To Lagos?"

Avakian nodded patiently. After all, the poor guy had just gotten up, and needed a little time to shake off the cobwebs.

"When?" said Prosper.

"Now," said Avakian.

Prosper shook his head. "Fish in morning."

Avakian gestured to the boy, who came right over. He was loving the expression on the captain's face. Just walk right up to the white man, you idiot kid. Avakian handed him some currency, and pointed to the skipper.

The boy dutifully walked the cash over. Forgetting about everything else, Prosper Kassa tucked the machete under his armpit and started counting.

Avakian enjoyed watching his expression change as he flipped through the five 100 euro notes. The captain's legs began shaking. He could double the value of this fortune in francs on the black market exchange, or hold onto it for even more value in the future. He looked up from the cash to Mr. John Smith. "Lagos," said Avakian. "Now."

Prosper was unconsciously petting the money like a new puppy. "You kill me. Take my boat."

"I don't know the waters and I don't want a boat," Avakian said reasonably. "I want to go to Lagos. Now."

Prosper fought to concentrate, searching for the word. "Seven hundred euro."

Avakian lost his avuncular expression and gave Prosper his coldest stare, to end the negotiations. "Five hundred. Lagos. Now."

Avakian could see Prosper doing the math. Of course the American was in some kind of trouble. Maybe a spy. Perhaps when he returned from Lagos the police would be waiting for him. That against five hundred euros for one night's work. He looked down again at the money in his hand, and snapped at the boy to hurry up and cast off.

Avakian settled back at the stern and pulled out his

Thuraya satellite phone. Fifty miles by sea to Lagos. He'd have to wake another Nigerian fixer and find a good private clinic to get his arm cleaned out and stitched up. It was hurting like a bastard. And he'd better book a morning flight back to South Africa right now.

Chapter Twelve

THE CLERK WAS WEARING a white plastic pocket protector. He said it would take a minute or two to get everything together.

"No problem," Avakian replied. "I'll just look around some more."

He walked back through the aisles, stopping at the one where the man who had followed him into the store was loitering.

At least the CIA officer who'd covered Springfield in the seafood restaurant had taken his advice and bought a South African suit. Avakian dug out the bottle of eye drops that had been prescribed for his scratched cornea and applied a dose.

"What do you need industrial testing equipment for?" the voice next to him said.

Blinking hard, Avakian screwed the dropper back into the bottle.

The CIA man said, "She wants to talk to you."

Avakian turned and looked at him for the first

time. "Look, kid, if I ever see your face again, I'll burn you so bad you'll be on the next plane home."

The CIA man puffed himself up and said, "I'm not a kid."

"Then don't act like one," Avakian replied. He turned on his heels and returned to the counter to sign his credit card slip. Patience and professionalism seemed to be bygone virtues these days. He'd have to make an issue of that. Now, what else was on his shopping list? Handcuffs. Sex shop or police supply? Sex shop. Make it more interesting for anyone following him.

The clerk in the shop on Long Street was wearing a black latex bustier, sleeve tattoos on both arms, ten rings in each ear, and a metal rod through her eyebrow.

"Tell me," Avakian asked, eyeing the bustier. "Doesn't that get kind of hot and uncomfortable over the course of the working day?"

"I love latex," she said, drawing out the love until it was a sentence all its own.

"But hard to get into?" Avakian inquired.

"Baby powder," she replied.

Of course. You used the same thing for wetsuits.

"Now what do you think of these, darling?" she said, holding up a pair of handcuffs with fluffy pink marabou padding on the wrists. "We also have them in white and black."

"I'm more old school," said Avakian. "What about just plain cuffs?"

She reached under the counter and retrieved the genuine article. "Oh, you're bad."

"You don't know the half of it," he said.

"How would you like me to use them on you?" she asked. "I know what to do with bad boys."

"Sorry, I have a bad heart," Avakian said.

"Pussy," she said.

Avakian was driving to his next destination when his BlackBerry buzzed. Shit. It was very early in the morning in Denver. Didn't sleep well and decided to pick up the phone. Either that or somehow she'd sensed where he'd been shopping. He pulled over and parked to take this one.

Now, what was the right voice? If you tried to be upbeat and pleasant it sounded like you were happy to be away from home. Neutral, maybe a little tired. "Hi, Judy, what's up?"

"Where are you?"

Look out for squalls. That flat monotone was as clear a warning as you were likely to get. "Cape Town."

"And when do you think you'll be done?"

"Soon, very soon. I'm really close to wrapping everything up."

"Really close, Pete?"

"Believe me, I'd love to give you a firm date."

"But you won't."

"I can't, honey." Dammit, how could you explain to people? The odds were that his calls were being monitored. And even the most inconsequential detail he gave up was something that someone might be able to use against him. Even yes, you're right, I'm doing something dangerous but I've got it under control. Normal people just couldn't work themselves into the mindset of being under surveillance.

"Pete, I'm just not cut out for this. I've tried, I really have. I know I was the one who suggested that you go back to work, and

I take full responsibility for that. Maybe it was for the best, because it showed me that I love you but I can't take the stress of worrying and wondering what might be happening to you when you're gone."

She paused for breath. Jesus, thought Avakian. She'd written it down so she'd get it right. She'd written it down and she was holding the paper as she read it into the phone. "Judy," he interrupted. "If I ever asked you for anything I'm asking it now. Don't say what you're about to say. Not right now, not over the phone. Say it to me later. Say it to me in person. But don't say it on the phone right now."

Another pause, and he was silently chanting invocations on his end.

"I'm sorry, Pete. I just can't do it. If I didn't care about you so much I wouldn't go through the day worrying myself sick. It's affecting my life. It's affecting my work. And I'm not going to make you promise you'll never do it again, because I know how much you love it. I've tried to think of another way out of this, but I just can't." She was crying. *"So I have to say goodbye."*

Avakian almost blurted out that she couldn't do that because he loved her, but that would just be too pathetic. Not to mention useless. "I just want you to know," he said. "If you broke up with me face to face in Denver or anywhere else, I'd accept it. But not like this. You're going to have to tell me one more time, in person. But not over the phone, not now. I don't accept it."

"You're going to have to," she said, still crying. And hung up.

Avakian held the BlackBerry at arm's length, shaking it back and forth, pumping out deep breaths in an effort to keep from throwing it into the windshield. Finally he tossed it into the back seat. What a wonderful thing, language. I love you so I have to break up with you.

He grasped the steering wheel, closed his eyes, and tried to do a little biofeedback to calm down. No, you are going to finish your errands. You are going to go back to the hotel, put your PT gear on, and go work out. You are not going to the nearest bar and start drinking. Because if you do, someone is going to get hurt.

Chapter Thirteen

AVAKIAN TRUDGED up the stairs of his hotel. Sweat plastered the running jacket to his torso, and grass was stuck to his ankles from when he'd gone off-road. He glanced at his watch. Two hours and seventeen minutes. Probably something like seventeen miles. Well, he'd had a few things to work out.

He didn't feel like eating, though he knew he'd be hungry as soon as he rehydrated. A restaurant was not something he thought he could face. Maybe order a pizza and see if he was tired enough to sleep. He'd have to sit down with the CIA soon, and he'd need to be sharp.

He spent a lot of time in the shower and felt halfway human afterward. Walking around in the white terry hotel robe he noticed that the room had acquired that stale familiarity that came from living in one too long.

A knock at the door. Avakian sighed out loud. Great. He took a few breaths and tried to put himself in the right frame of mind. It was going to require a conscious effort to keep from ripping everyone in his path a new one this evening.

He checked the peephole. Oh, no. The absolute last thing he needed today, so of course he got it. Patience Mbatha was standing outside his door. Another insistent knock. Avakian gave some serious consideration to playing dead. He would if he thought it would work, but she'd only stake him out. No sense postponing the inevitable. Change? No, maybe with a little luck it would get her on her way faster. Okay, Pete, put on a smile for company. He looked at himself in the mirror. Sorry, a smile was out of reach today.

He opened the door. She must have been working off the look on his face, because the first thing she said was, "I'm so sorry to disturb you."

Avakian just stood at the door. He wasn't really in the mood to say: no, that's quite all right.

"Please," she said. "May I come in?"

"It's not really a good time," said Avakian.

She burst into tears.

Christ. So much for the universe not giving you more than you could handle. Avakian would have thought he was pretty much maxed out. He stepped away from the door. "Come on in."

At least there was nothing to be embarrassed about. The habits of an Army lifetime meant the room was squared away, and the habits of the security professional meant he was always ready to pack and leave on five minutes' notice. "Have a seat." He didn't apologize for the robe. Nobody invited her to drop by unannounced.

Patience sat down and pulled a tissue from her purse to wipe her eyes. "I'm being followed. There are two men watching my apartment."

Avakian's first reaction was: no shit. It wasn't like he hadn't warned her. Now just shut up, he told himself. She got herself into it. No need for you to get involved.

She started crying again.

"How do you know you're being followed?" he said. You asshole, he told himself immediately afterward.

"Two white men in the same car," she said between eye dabs. "They are everywhere I go. I look out my window, and they are parked in the street."

And of course you brought them right here, was Avakian's next thought. Save him from amateurs. Another heaping slice of complication piled atop an already precarious existence. "Stop interviewing people for your story. Take a vacation somewhere. They'll figure it out and eventually go away."

"You said they would shoot me down in the street."

"Get on a plane," said Avakian. "Right now. Go somewhere."

She shook her head fiercely. "They'll follow me everywhere I go."

"This isn't the movies," Avakian explained patiently. "You're not being tailed by SPECTRE. They don't have the resources to follow you everywhere. You go to the airport and the guys following you will have to call someone for permission to buy a ticket. And they probably won't get it. A couple of weeks in the sun and you're home free."

"I'm not going anywhere," she said. "I'm too afraid to even go back to my apartment."

"You shouldn't. If you won't leave town then you should stay with friends."

"But what if something happened to them while

I'm staying there?" she demanded, almost hysterically. "I could never forgive myself."

"Then get a hotel room," said Avakian, tiring of trying to reason with her. "Leave your car, walk a few blocks, go into a store, leave the back way, hail a cab, and check into a hotel. Don't register under your own name. Same advice. In a week everything will have blown over."

"Could I stay here?"

Avakian picked up the phone and called the front desk. Anything to bring this to a conclusion. But the hotel was fully booked.

"I meant, could I stay here with you," said Patience Mbatha. "Please, just for one night. I'm so afraid."

"That is definitely *not* a good idea," Avakian said with finality.

She held her stomach. "I'm sorry, I'm not well. May I use your bathroom?"

Avakian pointed to it.

The second the door closed he shot up out of his chair, slowing drastically halfway up. Man, he was stiff. That's what came from being over fifty and running nearly three times your normal distance. He briefly stretched his back and commenced pacing. Okay, as soon as she gets out of the bathroom she's out of here. No matter if she starts bawling again. Just be ready, activate the frigging shields. No matter what little tricks she comes up with that she inherited along with those two X chromosomes. And if she turns up dead, you okay with that? I'm not the protector of the whole goddamned world. I warned her. I told her the score right off the bat and she didn't want to hear it. And now she's in the shit it's poor me and someone's got to help me. Why did he have to be the only adult in the whole goddamned world? Nobody wanted to listen, and nobody wanted to accept the consequences of their actions after they didn't listen. That was the trouble with the whole goddamned world. Okay, he'd take her through everything she needed to do. But then she'd have to do it herself. He was sick of being everyone's white knight. Every time he did it, he got jammed right up the ass for his trouble.

He was pumped up with fresh determination, ready to take care of business. The only trouble was that she was still in the bathroom. He looked at the clock on the night stand. Jeez, she'd been in there more than fifteen minutes. No sounds of throwing up. Okay, time to take the bull by the horns. He knocked on the door. "Patience. Patience?"

The bathroom door swung open, and Patience Mbatha was completely naked. She threw her arms tightly around his neck and kissed him, hard.

Avakian fell back under the assault. He made a noise like, "Mrrp," because her tongue was in his mouth. He put his hands on her hips and tried to give her a little push to separate them, but she was still wrapped around his neck and pushed him back even harder. Staggering backward, his legs hit the edge of the bed and he fell onto it with her on top of him. Jeez her hair smelled good. And she was quite a talented kisser. Her nipples were as hard against his chest, and she was sliding her pelvis up and down against his groin. His hands fell down her back and around that magnificent rear end. Jesus Christ, Avakian, what the hell are you doing? This was Africa, where AIDS was epidemic and the wages of sin really were death.

He tried to pull back from the kiss, but she wasn't having any of that. He finally got his arms under her and pushed her up, but he ended up with two handfuls of breast. Patience moaned loudly, and the sound went right through his central nervous system. Oh, no. "Listen, Patience…"

She held a hand up to his face, and in it was a foil-wrapped condom. "Don't worry," she told him.

Crap, Avakian thought.

Chapter Fourteen

"DON'T YOU TRUST ME?" said Patience.

Avakian was in front of the sink with a towel around his waist. A snowy cap of shaving cream sat atop his head with a narrow shaven track of exposed skin right down the middle. The razor was in his hand. She was standing behind him, but they were face to face in the mirror. "You ought to know better than to ask questions whose answers you don't want to hear."

"You don't trust me."

Avakian carefully ran the razor over the top of his head, carving another path in the shaving cream. "Since you brought it up, no. I like you, but I don't trust you."

"How can you say that after last night?" she demanded.

Avakian rinsed the razor off and tapped it in the sink. "Look, Patience, you and I both know that you slept with me because you want something. Now, that doesn't make you bad. Whether it was for refuge, or protection, or something you haven't mentioned yet, it's okay. You let me know when the time is right."

"I can't believe you said that," she said, whipping back into the room and out of his view in the mirror.

"You wouldn't be getting upset if I wasn't right," Avakian called out. "Why don't we have some breakfast and discuss it? But whatever it is, I won't go for it just because we slept together."

Some stomping around in the room. And then, fully dressed, she charged across his field of view again. "What of the woman you said you were in love with? Can she trust *you*? Then she was gone and slammed the door behind her.

Avakian looked up into the mirror at his tired, middle-aged face. Great question. Just the latest in a whole series of mistakes he seemed to be making lately. As he always said, you should never expect people to act in any way other than their own self interest. And now that seemed to apply to himself, too. Well, the spirit was willing. But the flesh? Definitely weak.

Chapter Fifteen

THE STEAK HOUSE was in a hotel on Greenmarket square, in the city center. Yet another modern city that had lost most of its historic buildings, the square was a remnant of old Cape Town, the former vegetable market of the name now a flea market. But the stalls Avakian had passed by on his way through were nothing like Cotonou. The average citizen of Benin wouldn't have been able to afford a handkerchief there. At the other end of the square was the Burgher Watch House, home of the first town council and much later the first city hall. He'd wandered inside to check it out. Sometime around the First World War they had done the interior in English Arts and Crafts, which was about the farthest thing from the old Dutch you could imagine.

The restaurant was a contrast of light walls and dark wood ceiling beams and tables. The clientele was much more upscale and quiet than the patrons of the seafood place.

Avakian actually had trouble picking out the CIA

advance guard this time, though he guessed it was one of the guys at the bar. That had been a condition of his dinner invitation: leave the idiot at home.

Constance Springfield hurried in and sat down. No handshake, just a smile as if they were old friends. "We've been worried about you."

"You should," said Avakian. "One of your guys comes up to me in public, in the middle of a Cape Town store. If anyone else has me under surveillance, you should worry about me a lot. What kind of amateur hour bullshit is that?"

"He said he made sure the store was clear before he made his approach."

Avakian could hardly believe his ears. "Let's forget about the security cameras in the store. I'm sure no one else would notice an American diplomat entering right after me and then leaving right after me."

"No one knows he's with us."

"Only took *me* five seconds to make him the first time," said Avakian.

She leaned over the table to say it. "You didn't give us any way to get in touch with you."

"Yeah, there was a reason for that," said Avakian. "To keep someone from doing something dumb and compromising me. Imagine me being worried about something like that?"

"I apologize," she said.

Fortunately the sommelier appeared with the decanted bottle of wine he'd ordered. He poured a sample for Avakian, who held it up and gave it a swirl to check the ropes, then leaned his own substantial nose over the glass to see about the wine's. Finally a slurp. "Oh, that's really outstanding," he told the sommelier.

"Thank you, sir," the man replied.

"Better open up another bottle," said Avakian. He'd ordered the most expensive Bordeaux on the list. He took another sip. "Don't worry," he told Springfield. "I'll get over it somehow."

The waiter arrived on the heels of the sommelier. Avakian had heard people say that South African restaurant service was terrible, but he had no gripes about it so far. He gestured for Springfield to go ahead.

"Just the barbecue chicken salad," she said.

Maybe she was on a diet. Or maybe she'd gotten a look at the label on the wine bottle. "Roquefort and biltong salad, please," said Avakian. "And the 450 gram fillet, medium rare, with roasted cherry tomatoes and feta. Sauce on the side, not on the steak." Biltong was African wind dried meat, and he was really interested to see how it went with the blue cheese.

He only provided an edited version of his adventures so far. Everything on the mercenaries. Springfield had a lot of questions about Volkov, and even more on Henry Okong. Avakian wasn't surprised that the CIA knew as little about him as everyone else.

He was much more selective about Benin. Bringing the Chinese into the story might have all kinds of unforeseen repercussions. The CIA would definitely freak, and since he wasn't sure in what direction he kept it all to himself. Besides, you didn't want to casually mention over dinner that you'd been running around an African city killing Chinese diplomats.

"You really have an excellent memory," said Springfield. "And quite an eye for detail."

"As you well know," said Avakian. "You can't always write things down."

"What are you going to do next?"

Avakian had to give her credit. She was learning. The bulldozer hadn't been brought to dinner this time. "Set up a meeting and give them my report on Benin. If that's what you want."

"What do you mean?"

"Do you want me to give them the real recon information and say a coup is completely feasible, or do you want me to tell them something else?"

He had to admit he enjoyed watching the thinly suppressed panic that provoked. Clearly she'd failed to anticipate the question and neglected to ask for orders. Now would she make an independent decision and accept the blame if it was wrong?

"Excuse me for a moment," she said.

Avakian suppressed a smile as she left for the powder room. Or the parking lot. Or wherever she could get enough bars on her secure phone.

The waiter arrived with his steak while she was gone. Avakian was always skeptical about tenderloin. Tender, yes, but sometimes not a lot of flavor. But this was grass-fed beef, properly aged, and there was no mushiness at all. And tenderloin really took well to charcoal grilling. Great crust on the outside. If the meat was good it didn't need sauce, and this meat was good. And he loved roasted cherry tomatoes, the way they popped in your mouth. Feta was just the right cheese with them. He savored those blissful bites in silence before Springfield returned.

"Go ahead and give them the real report," she said.

"Okay. I don't know what you're going to do about those people, and I certainly don't expect you to tell me. But the next step is lining up the weapons for the operation. I don't think I want to do that."

"Why not?"

"Because if they have any suspicions about me, that's when I'll probably trip on a big old banana skin and hurt myself." He was thinking about Patience as much as the CIA on that. In truth, he didn't even want to have another meeting with the mercenaries.

"We're very interested in the origin of the arms, the players involved, and the smuggling routes," said Springfield. "This is an opportunity to get a look inside Volkov's operation that may not come around again. And we'd like to know a good deal more about the other financial backers, particularly the South African oil interests."

"I'm sure you would," said Avakian. "I'll try to get you as much of that info as I can. But I don't think I'll be going out to get those guns."

"We wish you would."

"Remember when I said there'd be a time when I tipped my hat?" he said. "This would be that time."

Springfield passed a folded piece of paper over the table. Avakian didn't open it up, instead spearing a cherry tomato with his fork. "And what might this be?"

"A section of the no-fly list."

Avakian finished chewing and shook the paper open. It was the end of the A's, and there was Peter G. Avakian. Which meant that, assuming he was able to make his way home, his future travels would be confined to driving around America in a Winnebago. "I'm assuming this is a future list, not the current one."

"Yes, but it could become current at any time."

That the CIA might resort to blackmail wasn't exactly unexpected, and Avakian imagined it must be a pretty sweet moment for Springfield after all the smack he'd talked earlier. Whether it was girlfriends or the

CIA, pleading accomplished exactly nothing. And even if he wanted to give that impression, it was still contrary to his nature. "Seems that the music has stopped, and I'm without a chair. Okay, Constance, it looks like I'm going into the arms business."

"It's really for the best," she said.

"Oh, I'm sure," Avakian replied.

Chapter Sixteen

MINDFUL THAT SOMEONE from Patience Mbatha's magazine team, or anyone else for that matter, might still be camped out within sight of Payne-Best's front gate, Avakian took a Bishopscourt side street and followed the path of the property wall. Sure enough, there was an access door set into the wall. Most countries with fire codes required them.

The door was solid steel with just a lock on the outside, no knob. The lock was one of the best, which was good. High-end locks had more precise tolerances which caused the pins to move freely. And hardened steel locks were less prone to damage when they were bumped.

Avakian sorted through his key ring for the right size bump key. Which was a normal key blank that had been cut down much lower than a standard key, just below the first groove. And instead of the irregular teeth of a standard key it had one triangular tooth at the end followed by four smaller ones at regular intervals, like the blades of a saw.

Avakian slipped the bump key into the lock, one notch out along the keyway. Then he struck the end of the key with a rock, driving it into the lock. The force separated the lock driver pins from the key pins, aligning them. He turned the key and the lock opened.

Avakian yanked his bump key out and went through the door. And was immediately confronted by three of Volkov's bodyguards, big Russians with steroid bodies, barely-suppressed steroid rage, and the look of mixed martial arts fighters: five o'clock stubble haircuts, cauliflower ears and all.

"I remember you from the last time," Avakian said in Russian.

That threw them off track for a moment, saving him from getting thrown into the stone wall at high velocity. The Russians looked back in the direction of the house at Payne-Best's security man, the regimental sergeant major type with the moustache. He'd been hurrying across the lawn to see what the trouble was. Catching sight of Avakian, he nodded to the Russians that it was all right.

"Go ahead," said one of the Russians in heavily-accented English.

"The last time," Avakian told them confidentially in Russian, "the Nigerian said his bodyguards thought you were all cowardly little bitches. They said if you were in jail they'd be giving it to you in the ass."

Leaving it at that, he continued across the lawn.

The regimental sergeant major hurried up to him. "Colonel, how did you come to have a key to that door?"

"I didn't," said Avakian, without pausing to chat further. He would have suggested a bolt for the door, a little free security advice, but he might want to come in that way again.

The Nigerian bodyguard contingent were gathered at a neutral corner on the opposite side of the lawn, near the pool. Avakian walked up to them, stopped, and looked them over. They gave it back to him, half cautious because he was one of the principals, half puffing up over his challenging eye.

"You guys look plenty tough to me," Avakian mentioned in English.

"We are, man," one of the Nigerians said.

Avakian shrugged lightly. "Well, it's just that I was asking those Russians what all the commotion was the last time, and they were telling me they made you cry like little girls. They said if you were in jail they'd be giving it to you in the ass."

His outside work done, Avakian walked alongside the empty pool, crossed the patio, and knocked at the door to Payne-Best's study.

De Wet opened it. "Where the fuck did you come from?"

"Not the front door, that's for sure," said Avakian.

It was the same as before. Payne-Best, Volkov, Okong.

"What's wrong?" Payne-Best asked De Wet.

"Something," De Wet replied.

"We ready to start the meeting?" Avakian asked.

"Yes, of course," said Payne-Best, still puzzled.

"Great," said Avakian, taking his place among them. "Then I'd like to begin with a simple question. Who's been running their fucking mouth?"

As expected, the way he spat out the question captured the full attention of everyone in the study. Henry Okong compressed his fat face until his eyes were two little piggy suspicious slits. Volkov was giving him a uniquely Russian laser blast of pure distrust. De Wet had that look of every military officer who sensed that someone was about to make his life much, much more complicated.

Payne-Best was merely puzzled. "Whatever are you talking about?"

"That's it exactly," said Avakian. "Talking. Who's been talking?"

"No one has been talking!" Payne-Best thundered.

"Really?" said Avakian. "That's not the impression I get."

"Perhaps you tell us your impressions?" Volkov suggested coldly.

"Love to," said Avakian. "I've got CIA officers trying to talk to me in Cape Town. I've got Chinese intelligence officers trying to kill me in Cotonou. Now, I'm no Stephen Hawking, but I'm thinking this operation is totally compromised."

Everyone starting talking then, but De Wet immediately growled, "Just a bloody minute." That silenced them, and he turned to Avakian. "Let's take this step by step, mate. Start with the CIA."

When in doubt, Avakian thought, don't defend—attack. "I'm out in town shopping and this American comes up to me, all buddy-buddy. You know, expatriates in a foreign land. Invites me to lunch and I blow him off. Then I follow *his* ass back to the U.S. Consulate. Now that does say CIA to you?"

Muttering from the assembly.

"Next," said Avakian. "I'm having dinner and this blond sits down at my table and asks if she can join me. And no, she's not a hooker. She's a U.S. diplomat, a little homesick, wants to touch base with a fellow countryman. And in case you're thinking about trying to rationalize it, she picked up the check. Know any woman who would do that, who wasn't CIA?"

"The question seems," said Payne-Best, "do they know something, or are they just feeling about? What was the path of her inquiry?"

"This was just the get-to-know," said Avakian. "Lots of questions about me, wanted to have dinner again."

"Did you?" said Payne-Best.

"I gave it much less thought than I gave to you guys shooting me in the head if I did it," said Avakian.

"Might be a good idea," Payne-Best mused. "Get a sense of the situation."

"It might be a good idea to slam my balls in your desk drawer," said Avakian. "But I won't be doing that, either."

"So this accounts for your arrival through my back wall," said Payne-Best.

"Oh, almost forgot," said Avakian. "A reporter shows up at my hotel, wants to ask me a few questions. And I have to send her packing, too."

"The reporter's name?" said Payne-Best.

Avakian held up a hand. "Oh, no." He pointed one finger back toward himself. "*I'll* handle the reporter. Things are getting complicated enough without leaving bodies around town."

"Sounds like you don't trust us, mate," said De Wet.

"I've definitely got some issues," said Avakian. "Wouldn't you?"

"All of this, it seems to be happening to you," said Volkov. "You are taking care of your security, yes?"

"*Da*," Avakian said emphatically in Russian. "But I

don't have six bodyguards sealing me off from the outside world. Maybe I'm the only one talking about it, who isn't afraid of screwing up the deal?"

As intended, that had Volkov and Okong eyeing Payne-Best and De Wet.

It was the first time Avakian had seen De Wet look nervous. He quickly said, "Now what's this about the Chinese and Benin?"

Avakian opened up his nylon briefcase and plopped four thick sheaves of paper, held together with binder clips, onto the table. Then four flash drives on top of them. "In case you're wondering, these are the only four copies. I printed them out myself, then I destroyed the laptop hard drive and the printer memory. Pictures and video on the flash drives. There's a page in the report about the Chinese." An edited page, that is. Avakian neglected to mention running into the delegation at the ministry, among other details. "The thumbnail sketch is that they put a bomb in my car."

"Yet you are still here," said Volkov.

"The day I don't have someone watching my car when I'm not around, I won't deserve to be," said Avakian. "I am still here. My interpreter and driver decided to play explosive ordnance disposal. They're not. As I was leaving the scene of the explosion, a Chinese jumped me on a dark street."

"What happened?" Okong rumbled.

No one could resist a war story. Avakian pulled back his shirt sleeve and the gauze to show them the fifteen stitches.

"Nice," said De Wet. "And the Chinese?"

"He joined his ancestors," said Avakian. Silence as

they digested that. He looked down at the table. "Too bad. It was one of the best recons I've ever done."

"What do you mean too bad?" said Payne-Best.

"The operation is blown," Avakian said in genuine surprise. "You can't be thinking about going ahead?"

"I am by all means," said Payne-Best. "The CIA is just poking about. By the time they are able to get a firm idea of our activities we shall be in Benin and they shall be presented with a *fait accompli*. You don't understand, old boy. Oil is more powerful than governments, more powerful than the CIA. Provide them oil and they'll be eating out of your hand. As far as the Chinese, I'm inclined to think that the source of your troubles was your own history with them, not your work for us. Even if that is not the case, there aren't enough Chinese in Benin to bother us upon our arrival. Afterward I'm sure they shall be happy to deal with the new government, as will everyone else."

Avakian was taken aback. He'd been sure his story would scupper the deal and send him back home with skin intact. But it seemed he hadn't given enough thought to one crucial detail. Payne-Best and De Wet had too much invested to weigh the risks rationally and fold their hands if the odds turned against them. They were plunging ahead no matter what. Volkov and Okong were only risking money, and it wasn't enough not to continue to gamble, considering the size of their bank accounts and the potential reward. So arguing wasn't going to do any good. So much for the best laid plans. "Suit yourselves. Why don't you all take a look at my report? Then I'll answer any questions."

"Fine idea," said Payne-Best.

They all settled into the club chairs and began

thumbing through the paperwork. Avakian went back to perusing Payne-Best's bookshelves.

"This hydrographic survey is lovely," said Payne-Best. "Is it the beach at the Presidential Palace?"

"No," said Avakian. "I would have gotten myself arrested on that beach. This is just a bit down the coast, but the gradient and sand are typical. There's no water obstacles at the Presidential Palace that would give a Zodiac any problems. And any intrusion sensors on the beach won't matter if you hit it in force. You can either breach the seaside wall, or blow the gate with a ladder charge."

"And this appreciation of Presidential Guard equipment and motivation is accurate?" said Payne-Best.

"Don't worry, no offense taken," Avakian said dryly. "You're not paying me for guesses, so I haven't made any. I had them pull me over so I could get a close look at them."

"You had the Presidential Guard pull your car over?" said Payne-Best.

"That's right," Avakian replied. "We parted friends, and all it cost *you* was a pack of cigarettes."

Okong chuckled.

"How the bloody hell were you able to diagram the *inside* of the Paracommando base?" De Wet demanded.

"Knocked on the door and asked for a tour," said Avakian. "They were very nice about it."

"You asked for a tour," said De Wet, as if he couldn't quite believe it.

"Yeah," said Avakian. "What would you have done? Put on your black cat suit, paint your face camouflage, and sneak over the wall?"

Volkov was laughing. "It seems you picked the right man," he said to Payne-Best. And then to Avakian, "You have balls, my friend."

It was always the case, not to mention the summation of Avakian's entire military career. Give your superiors what they wanted and all your other sins were forgiven.

"We may be able to make do with less than a battalion if we can transition from one objective to the other quickly enough," Payne-Best was saying to De Wet.

"Page 26," said Avakian.

They both looked up at him.

"There's a transportation company that serves the port," Avakian said. "They have a fenced-in vehicle park with enough trucks parked there at night to move two battalions, including their own fuel pump. The keys are in a locker in the office. It's less than a kilometer from the ocean."

"One group assaults the Presidential Palace directly, and the others make straight for the trucks," said Payne-Best.

De Wet nodded.

"Do you see any reason to modify the equipment list?" Payne-Best asked.

De Wet shook his head.

"Equipment list?" said Avakian.

Payne-Best crossed the room, removed a folder from his safe, and handed it to Avakian.

It was an inventory of weapons, enough to equip a battalion of troops. All Russian types. A thousand AK-47's. Twenty-eight PKM machineguns. Forty RPG-7 rocket launchers. Eight 82mm mortars. Enough ammunition to feed them all, with a substantial stock in reserve. And 10,000 hand grenades. At the bottom of the list it read 4 SA-14. Russian shoulder-fired heat-seeking anti-aircraft missiles.

"You know something about an air threat that I don't?" said Avakian.

"Better to be safe than sorry," Payne-Best replied.

And clever rather than dumb, Avakian quickly realized. After the coup any intervention by one of the great powers would have to come by either plane or helicopter. Even marines preferred helicopters over landing craft these days. A few photos leaked over the internet of the new regime's black soldiers standing around the airport with SA-14's on their shoulders would lower the odds of that intervention to about zero, considering Western armies' refusal to risk casualties. That's why they weren't worried about France. "Are you planning on pulling everything out of your stockpiles?" he asked Volkov.

"Fortunately or unfortunately, business has been too good lately," Volkov replied. "I do not have sufficient inventory in stocks. I will supply new equipment, from the factory."

"I know you must have a stack of end-users in your briefcase," said Avakian. An end user certificate was a document submitted with a weapons order. It said that the government of, for example, Nicaragua, required 1,000 AK-47's to equip a new border guard unit. And that these arms were for the sole use of Nicaragua and would not be transferred to any other party. Someone like Volkov obtained this document in exchange for a donation to the retirement fund of an official in the ministry of defense, or a defense attaché in an embassy. He then took the end user to one of the smaller countries that made AK's, like Hungary or

Pakistan or Egypt, who needed orders to keep their factories running and therefore weren't likely to ask a lot of questions as long as the paperwork was in order and the check was good. "But aren't you worried about putting in an order for a battalion-size weapons package? Other agencies might get interested."

"Is not a problem," said Volkov. "The weapons, they are new from the factory, but not from the factory. This…"

Pop. Avakian's brain immediately processed the sound as a 9mm handgun, from out by the pool. Could it be another bodyguard donnybrook, this time escalated to gunplay? Oh, no. However did that happen? Usually, where there was one gunshot…

Pop. Pop-pop-pop-pop.

Avakian dropped to one knee to place himself below window level.

"JESUS CHRIST!" De Wet bellowed, drawing his own handgun. "You BLOODY people!" He charged out the patio door.

Much more prudent, Volkov and Okong paused behind each side of the doorway and shouted, "Put down your guns!" in each of their respective languages before proceeding outside. Payne-Best trailed behind them.

Avakian didn't join the parade. He locked the door behind them and jammed a chair under the handle. The drapes were already closed for privacy. He also locked the house door, even though the missus was probably bolting herself into the panic room right about now.

Sometimes you had to create your own opportunities. He made a sprint across the room for the handheld thermal imager at the bottom of his briefcase.

Purchased for $8,000 of the mercenaries' expense money, a top of the line piece of industrial testing equipment with better than .05 K thermal resolution. He aimed the unit at the safe's keypad. The rubber keys still bore the traces of heat from Payne-Best's fingertips when he'd opened it. And through the LCD screen of the imager each one shined with a different intensity in the order he'd touched it, the last brighter than the first. Avakian tapped the keys in reverse order: 4-8-7-3-9, and twisted the locking handle. The safe opened right up.

He was careful to keep the folders in their original order as he flipped through them. There we go—like a good little bureaucrat, all the investors and the percentage of their cut. Wouldn't want anyone to get shorted. Avakian snapped photos with his BlackBerry. Nice—the payoff sheet, what the New York cops called the pad. Politicians, cops, and intelligence officers in South Africa. Politicians in Nigeria. A lot of people in Benin, including several military officers who must be ready to move up the food chain.

The outside doorknob rattled. Okay, folders back in place, safe shut, locked, and checked. Thermal camera back in the briefcase. House door unlocked. All done as they tried the key outside and found the door barred. He had the chair off just as they began yelling and pounding on it.

"What the hell?" De Wet demanded as he pushed past Avakian, standing there in the doorway with the chair in his hand.

"Hey, just a little precaution to keep the gunfight from migrating indoors," said Avakian.

"Many thanks for thinking of my house," said Payne-Best.

"I keep telling you guys," said Avakian. "I'm the only one around here who's not carrying, and I don't take my fists to a gunfight as long as there's a choice."

"Very wise, my friend," said Volkov. Right behind him came Okong, silent and flat-out furious. Probably his boys who either started it or got the worst of it. Or both.

"Anybody hurt?" Avakian asked. Pour a little gas on the fire and deflect everyone's attention away from him.

"Idiots were all wearing vests," De Wet said dourly. "Arms and legs. We weren't lucky enough for any of them to take one to the head."

"I'm assuming we need to get out of here before the police arrive," said Avakian.

"That would be a wise precaution, yes," said Payne-Best. "One never knows about the neighbors."

"You can go with Dmitri, talk about your trip to Bulgaria," De Wet told Avakian.

"Bulgaria?" said Avakian.

"We need you out of town, anyway," said De Wet. "Too many people want to make your acquaintance."

"Before we break, I'm going to need another 250,000 advance on my fee," said Avakian. He held out the arm with the stitches. "Call it hazardous duty pay." Sometimes the best insight into people's intentions was the amount of crap they were willing to take from you. He didn't think they'd pay him if they were planning on getting rid of him in Bulgaria. Come to think of it, they might even fire his ass right here and now.

A brief huddle. "Agreed," said Payne-Best.

Shit, Avakian thought.

Chapter Seventeen

AVAKIAN WAS JUST FINISHING up breakfast when Patience Mbatha came through the door of the restaurant.

She had a smile on her face. And it wasn't that *kind* of smile, so Avakian didn't figure he was going to get shot. Maybe all was forgiven. Or maybe he was finally going to hear what she really wanted. He stood up. Half out of politeness, and half to be ready in case he actually did need to defend himself.

In fact she went to give him a hug. Avakian held out a hand, which would have been in character if anyone was watching. "Please, Patience, let's hold off on the public displays of affection." Hmmm, he hadn't used that expression in a long time. He'd walked a lot of punishment tours at West Point for public display of affection. Bastard tactical officers used to hide in the bushes waiting for you to come back from the weekend and kiss your girlfriend goodbye in the parking lot, just so they could write you up.

Now she pouted and made an issue of scraping her

chair as she sat down. "Is it because you don't mind making love to a native girl, but you don't want to be seen embracing one in public?"

Avakian sighed. "Yes, that's it exactly. It has nothing at all to do with me getting killed if the wrong people see me hugging a reporter."

She didn't have a reply to that, so instead made an airy gesture and said, "Anyway, I'm here. Do you want me to leave?"

"I guess that would really depend on what you want."

She shrugged off that shot and exclaimed, "I found out some more information."

Lord help us, thought Avakian. He stood up, put on his coat, and set some money down on the table. "Let's walk you back to your car."

Fortunately Dolores the baker's husband worked the mornings, so she wouldn't be able to tell anyone asking that, oh yes, Mr. Avakian was here with the nice colored girl he had tea with before.

"There was no need to rush out," Patience said when they were on the street.

Avakian had pretty much embraced the futility of explanation.

"I think the coup will happen soon," she said, practically dancing around him. "Men are being recruited in Pomfret."

Pomfret was the former asbestos mining town in the desert where the South African government had exiled the former Angolan soldiers of 32 Battalion. About as much a hellhole as you'd imagine a former asbestos mining town in the desert to be. Avakian didn't find it surprising that Patience had contacts among the black mercenary side of the house.

Someone pissed off about not getting hired would always be willing to gossip with a sympathetic soul who bought the drinks.

"You're still nosing around," he said. It was a statement not a question. Damn he was glad he hadn't told her anything. She was definitely playing him. Just how much or how little was the question.

"I thought about what you said very carefully. The quicker I can publish my article, the quicker the authorities will be forced to do something about them."

Avakian considered that an unrealistically optimistic assumption. He suddenly stopped on the sidewalk. "Where are you parked, anyway?"

"The tennis center. I thought it would be more secret that way."

Avakian also decided not to mention that it was easier to follow someone on foot than in a car. He'd been watching carefully, but there was no close-in surveillance. Not that anyone with a pair of binoculars couldn't see them just fine. "I can't persuade you to get out of town, can I?"

"I was very frightened before, but you were so lovely to me. You gave me back my courage. I'm sorry I was angry and ran out. As soon as I left you I did not see the men outside my apartment any more, and I knew I had been foolishly imagining that people were following me. I will finish my work, and everything will be all right."

"Do you know anyone who drives a really beat up silver Honda?" Avakian asked suddenly.

"What?"

She would have turned around, but Avakian gently but firmly held her in place. "Wait a minute." He grabbed her upper arms and spun her about as if he was giving her a lecture. "See them?"

"I see them," she said shakily, the fear having returned. They had just entered the tennis center parking lot, and the car was slowly heading down the street outside.

"Anyone look familiar?"

"No. No, I don't recognize them."

"Okay, keep walking. Give me your car keys. *Without* a big show of ripping your purse open, please."

She handed him the keys.

"Where are you parked?" said Avakian.

Patience pointed to her car, then quickly brought her hand up to her mouth. "I'm sorry, was I not supposed to point?"

"It's okay," said Avakian, purposely keeping his voice calm. A reporter driving a Mercedes? Even a C-class. What was that all about? "Pick up your pace a bit, but don't run. When we reach the car get in the passenger side as quickly as you can and buckle your seatbelt."

Like most good plans, this one didn't survive contact with the enemy. The Honda zipped across the parking lot and came to a stop between them and Patience's car. It really was a piece of crap, paint flaking, dented all over, belching exhaust, the bumper held on by duct tape. The driver stayed behind the wheel and two black men in their twenties got out, one of them brandishing a pistol. Avakian didn't recognize them. Not from the streets, and not from Okong's bodyguard team.

Patience said something to them, and Avakian didn't have to speak Xhosa to know they were telling her to shut her mouth. He noted the opposition, their armament, the parking lot, the distances, and the angles. He had no play. Nothing to do but wait and see what was going to happen.

The one with the pistol motioned them toward the car. The first rule of personal survival was to never get into a vehicle with armed men. Problem was, Avakian didn't see any way around it.

The sound of a speeding engine, and everyone turned around to look at the pewter SUV that entered the parking lot and raced toward them. As it approached the leader stuck his gun hand inside his jacket. The SUV came to a screeching stop and the tinted passenger window powered down. Sitting there was the walrus-mustached Afrikaner regimental sergeant major type who handled Payne-Best's security. "Need a hand?" he asked Avakian.

Avakian turned his back to the black gunmen. "You equipped for it?" he asked, pantomiming a pistol with his hand in front of his chest.

"Of course," was the reply. The back seat window slid down.

The black leader pulled his hand out of the jacket and brandished the pistol. "Get the hell out of here, man!"

Avakian slid his arm around Patience's shoulders and violently yanked her down to the ground. Once they landed he rolled over on top of her.

There was a sound like two cap pistols being fired on full automatic. An instant later this was interspersed with the sound of grunts, the ping of metal on metal, and breaking glass.

When all that commotion stopped Avakian cautiously raised his head. The two gunmen were dead on the ground and the driver was slumped over the

Honda steering wheel, leaking blood all over it. The vehicle itself was riddled with the holes of bullets that hadn't struck the gunmen, along with a nice tight cluster in the center of the driver's door. A look in the other direction and the RSM and a black backseat passenger were reloading Uzi submachineguns with bulbous sound suppressors screwed onto the barrels.

"Get in," said the sergeant major, as the rear door opened.

"Her car is right here," said Avakian, regaining his feet.

The sergeant major made that an order. "Both you get in."

Once again Avakian didn't see any alternative. "Who were those guys?" he whispered fiercely to Patience.

"I don't know. I swear," she said.

"Don't give me that bullshit," he muttered.

As the SUV door closed behind them the sergeant major leaned over the front seat. "I brought my shooting glasses," he said to Avakian, holding them up before replacing them with a pair of sunglasses from the dashboard.

"Glad you did," Avakian said. "Thanks."

"Who were those sorry blokes?" the sergeant major demanded.

"No idea," said Avakian. "Though lately I've been magnetic north for every mugger on the whole continent."

"Young lady?" said the sergeant major.

Sitting with her arms folded across her chest, Patience just shook her head.

They stopped in front of Avakian's hotel.

"Here you go," said the sergeant major.

Avakian stepped out. The black mercenary in the back seat had a firm grip on Patience's arm.

"Pleasant journey," the sergeant major said to Avakian out the window. The SUV sped off with Patience Mbatha inside.

Chapter Eighteen

THE VIBRATION of the twin turboprop Antonov-26 beat its way right through Avakian's earplugs. Back during the Cold War the Russians designed their transport airplanes without a lot of superfluous bells and whistles like safety features and cabin silencing, which meant they could be built in large numbers by drunken factory workers and maintained by indifferent conscripts in rugged locations without a lot of high-tech repair facilities. If one fell out of the sky, for whatever reason, they just dragged a replacement out of the hanger.

Half the jump seats that folded down from the fuselage on both sides of the cargo area didn't fold down. A few of the windows seemed to be held in place with duct tape. There was a slow but steady drip of some sort of fluid from the cabin roof. And Avakian wondered how the pilots could see through the cockpit glass for all the cigarette smoke.

Fortunately the majority of their flight had been both commercial and first class. Avakian and his companions had only picked up the Antonov in Cyprus, where the Russians had a layover to do some banking. Greek Cyprus was a wonderful combination of European Union membership and the kind of no questions asked banking the Swiss had once pioneered but lately had become a bit squeamish about.

Avakian was accompanying a Volkov lieutenant named Andrei, no last name offered, and two bodyguards. The latter had of course been unarmed on the commercial flights, then mysteriously acquired pistols in Cyprus. Probably the reason for the Antonov. No metal detectors or security checks if you owned the plane.

Avakian would have preferred to go without bodyguards. When you arrived at a place bodyguards told people you were important, which wasn't always for the best. And the bigger the entourage, the less quickly you could move in an emergency.

He checked his watch. If the pilot was right—no sure thing there—they were almost at their destination. The two bodyguards were stretched out over four jump seats each, snoring louder than the aircraft engines. Andrei was another former Russian intelligence type in his late thirties with hair both the color and texture of straw, watery blue eyes, and a rubbery Slavic face that seemed to get by without either cheekbones or chin. By all evidence he spoke at least a bit of every language on earth, and had diligently spent the flight playing video games on his laptop, ramming in a succession of battery packs. When asked earlier if he wanted to play Avakian had to explain that people of his generation were physically unable to move their thumbs fast enough to be competitive. Andrei was now engrossed in some first person shooter whose gunfire and explosions Avakian occasionally heard over the engines and the snoring.

"Andrei!" Avakian shouted.

Andrei looked up from the screen. He'd been tickled to discover that Avakian spoke some Russian, then disappointed to discover just how bad it was.

Avakian raised his voice over the sound of the plane. "When are we going to talk about what we're about to do? We have to get our moves down."

"Moves?" Andrei shouted back. "No moves. Don't worry, Pyotr."

Avakian hated being the guy along for the ride.

About twenty minutes later they made their approach over the Black Sea. The pilot brought the Antonov down as if he was going to make a bombing run instead of a landing. Avakian hoped that all the juking was just because the crew was used to dodging antiaircraft fire, not because they were lousy flyers.

The wheels touched down with a thump but then the Antonov bounced back into the air. This caused both bodyguards to snap awake and even brought Andrei's eyes up off his computer screen. Avakian checked the inside of the cabin for any cracks that might indicate that the airplane was about to break into pieces. But the pilot slapped it back down onto the runway again, hard, and that was that.

The flight engineer eventually roused himself enough to open the hatch and kick down the air stairs. Avakian picked up his usual small carryon bag. He was a firm believer in packing light and moving fast. Two suits, one black and one dark blue. Wear one, pack one. Toilet kit, a couple of spare shirts and ties, and microfiber socks and underwear you could wash out in a hotel sink.

It was about 50 degrees and sunny, not bad for the beginning of winter in southeastern Bulgaria. There were three commercial jets on the tarmac. Bulgaria Air, Finnair, and Ural Airlines. A U.S. Air Force KC-135 tanker aircraft was parked off by itself, guarded by a Bulgarian police car with a sleeping cop inside. Probably there to refuel the streams of cargo planes traveling to and from the war zones.

Two black SUV's and an official airport vehicle drove right up to the plane. Avakian nearly laughed out loud at what came out of them. Two near perfect examples of the Slavic gangster. Power lifter builds, no necks, crew cuts, black leather jackets and turtlenecks, gold watches and neck chains. Unbelievable. Walking clichés.

They shook hands with Andrei, who conversed with them in Russian too fast for Avakian to follow easily. He said, "Pyotr," by way of introduction, and the two gorillas stuck out their hands.

Avakian knew what was coming, and they all had a little alpha male struggle for dominance in the form of a handshake competition that ended in a draw. No bones broken, but it would take a while for the feeling to return to everyone's hands.

"Your passport," said Andrei.

Avakian handed it over, and one of the Bulgarians took it to the airport vehicle.

"Something's wrong," he said privately to Andrei.

Andrei's response was only a slight eyebrow raise. "What is wrong?"

"These guys are all wrong," said Avakian.

Andrei was still the very picture of calm. "Perhaps you explain."

"If this was a routine pickup, they'd be bored,"

said Avakian. "If their boss told them to be nice to us or else, they'd be nervous. If they wanted to send the message that they were bad motherfuckers and we shouldn't even think about messing with them, they'd be displaying it, sizing us up with their hands on their hips and their elbows out. But take a good look. Their jackets are open, they're balanced and leaning forward, they keep looking at each other for reassurance and to make sure they keep track of where the other guy is. They're ready. Ready for something."

"Very interesting," said Andrei. "They are ready for us to do this deal."

"Your English is really excellent," said Avakian. "Did you happen to understand anything I just said?"

"You are nervous, it is natural," said Andrei.

"I'm telling you something is wrong with these guys."

"They are *mutri*, that is all."

"What the hell is *mutri*?" Avakian demanded.

Andrei took a moment to search through his card file for the correct translation. "Mugs."

"Mugs?" Avakian said in disbelief.

"No problem," said Andrei. "We do these deals all the time. Come. I go in one car, you in the other."

No problem. If there was one constant in Peter Avakian's life, it was that every time someone told him there was no problem, there was one. He took a long look around the airport, searching for an alternative. But there wasn't. This was why people in the business were control freaks. He climbed in the SUV with one of the Russian bodyguards and one of the Bulgarians, who handed him back his passport all stamped. It seemed they'd just cleared customs.

Andrei in the other vehicle meant there was some

business to be talked that he didn't need to be a party to. He checked the windows. Polycarbonate. The armored black SUV had just about supplanted the armored black limo in most circles.

They exited through an opening in the jet blast fencing. A sign said, in English:

Bourgas Airport. Welcome to Bulgaria.

Avakian had never been there, but during the NATO intervention into Kosovo, a little dance he'd attended, the U.S. had shipped a lot of equipment through Burgas. Or Bourgas. Go from the Cyrillic alphabet to the Latin and you could spell it both ways.

They turned onto a highway with the sea on their right and flat wetlands to the left. Low hills in the distance. The Bulgarian driver lit up a cigarette. One thing about armored windows—they didn't roll down. Avakian suffered in silence. It was the kind of crowd that would meet the request to put out a butt with derisive laughter.

Narrow canals cut under the highway and through the marsh. A lake came into view on the right. Big. Lots of birds. Not a lot of junk along the shore, which was not typical for Eastern Europe.

A few minutes later they entered the city. Avakian was surprised. Instead of the usual communist concrete nightmares you saw throughout the former eastern bloc, this was a city of pleasant 19th and early 20th century architecture. Well, the world wars probably hadn't rolled over it, and central planners were never known for building anything they didn't have to.

The lead SUV stopped at the port entrance so one of the Bulgarians could confer with the gate guard.

They were waved through and followed the signs to Terminal West and one of the smaller covered container warehouses. Two medium sized freighters were parked at the pier opposite. *MV Scorpio* and *MV Juno*. Okong's contributions to the operation. At least that part had gone right.

Two more Bulgarian hoods were waiting for them there. Another argument against bodyguards if you were traveling. If you brought two, the home team could always round up four, or six, or eight to set against them.

"Everything okay?" Avakian asked Andrei in English once they got out of the SUV's.

Andrei just gave a Russian shrug, like what was ever okay?

One of the no-necked Bulgarians unlocked the warehouse and snapped on the lights. If was filled with crates, because it took a lot of supplies to put a battalion in the field. Avakian had spent a solid week on the computer back in Cape Town, ordering gear with five different credit cards on the accounts of Chromium Futures, the shell company. The bank accounts were on Cyprus, St. Kitts and Nevis, and the British Virgin Islands. Banks that weren't likely to be forthcoming to routine inquiries.

The internet did make equipping your own mercenary unit a lot easier than in the past. Avakian had everything shipped from all over Europe to this warehouse in Bulgaria. Surplus French Army green battledress, because that's what the Benin Army wore. The old model U.S. military jungle boots, which were in ready supply. Socks, underwear, shaving kits, toothbrushes, towels. From canteens and first aid kits to Zodiac inflatable boats and fifty-five horsepower outboard motors. Fuel bladders. Cases of French Army combat rations, because he wouldn't wish U.S. Meals Ready to Eat on his worst enemy and the French made the best war chow bar none.

Nothing had been done in a single order. The Zodiacs had come from four different suppliers, each paid with a different credit card. Even the boots were bought from three different military surplus dealers. A lot of stuff, but not an unfamiliar process, as Payne-Best and De Wet had known very well when they hired him. It was what Special Forces did. Each 12-man A Team was supposed to be able to equip, train, and lead an indigenous battalion. And Avakian had equipped more than a few in his time. Except now came the part he always hated.

"Yeah, I know," he said to Andrei, who was looking at him. "We need to do an inventory and make sure everything's here. Okay, weapons first. Somebody better have a pry bar."

One of the Bulgarian hoods did. The wooden crates of weapons were sitting on pallets in front of the open and empty shipping containers they'd be loaded into.

Avakian dragged a crate from the middle of a pallet and broke it open. It was marked Arsenal, and filled with Bulgarian AR model AK-47's with black plastic stocks. Ten rifles to a case, each with four magazines, a magazine pouch, a sling, and a cleaning kit. He pulled one rifle out of its protective wrapping and detail disassembled it. The gummy metal protectant got all over his hands, but the rifle would fire. Rifles didn't work without ammunition magazines, and the magazines were useless without belt pouches to hold them. Rifles didn't shoot long without cleaning kits, cotton patches, solvent, and lubricant. The Bulgarians made AK's in sixteen different models and three different calibers, so it was important to make sure that the rifles, magazines, and ammunition were all compatible.

The ammunition crates were labeled Arcus, and there was a difference between rifle and machinegun ammo. The AK ammo was packed in green metal cans that looked like Spam and opened the same way. Inside those the individual rounds were in cardboard boxes. Twenty rounds to the box, seven hundred in the can, two cans to the case. Avakian wedged a round in between the slats of the crate and pried the bullet from the brass case, pouring out the gunpowder. Slipping inert drill ammunition into crates marked live ammo would allow someone to pocket a major price differential.

Two machineguns per case, plus accessories. Were the spare barrels there? Nine RPG-7 rocket launchers per case, plus sights, slings, cleaning gear and ammo bags for the rockets. Twenty five P-MO2 9mm pistols per case. These were crap, but it was easier for the mercenaries to buy all their gear in one place.

It wasn't that Avakian had changed his mind and wanted the coup to take place, but of all the possible ways he might get killed the silliest would be having the mercenaries chase him down later because he hadn't done his job and stuck them with defective weapons.

Twenty GHD-2 hand grenades to a case, and each grenade in a protective plastic cup that unscrewed in the middle to reveal the treasure inside. Avakian did just that.

"Is necessary?" Andrei asked, acting nervous for the first time.

"It is unless you want to explain why you accepted training grenades instead of the real thing," said Avakian.

"They are training grenades?" said Andrei, now concerned.

"No," said Avakian. "They're the real thing." He screwed the plastic cap back together and replaced it in the crate. But during their discussion he'd palmed the grenade and slipped it into his jacket pocket.

He was just taking random samples and counting crates. Otherwise they'd be there all week.

As he broke down the green and black painted hardware, working actions back and forth with those lovely precision spring-loaded snaps of metal on metal, it occurred to Avakian that at least a third of what attracted men to war was all that seductive lethal machinery. The rest was the camaraderie and the action. And lately, of course, the money.

A smaller pallet held a stack of long metal boxes like much larger versions of the cases hunting rifles were stored in. They snapped open like suitcases and revealed Russian SA-14 antiaircraft missiles. Very hard to come by these days. Governments kept a careful eye on them since they were equally suited to shooting down airliners as well as jet fighters and helicopters.

"You are satisfied?" said Andrei.

"No," Avakian replied. It was easy to determine if a mortar or RPG would work. Missiles were something different. He unpacked and checked the gripstock assembly that rested on your shoulder and snapped on one of the four and a half foot long missile tubes. Each one came with several battery/coolant units that looked like a black softball topped with the cap from a bottle of laundry detergent. He screwed one into the well on the underside of the missile body. Unsnapping the cap from the front of the tube to expose the missile seeker head, Avakian said, "Open the door."

Consternation from the Bulgarian side when Andrei translated the request. Avakian just repeated, "Open the goddamned door."

Eventually the Bulgarian guarding it did, cautiously. Avakian pointed the missile tube at the hot stack of the freighter outside and pulled the trigger back partway. This powered up the missile electronics, uncaged the seeker, and pumped coolant into the seeker head to make it more sensitive to infrared temperature differentials. About five seconds later the little light in the sight turned from red to green and an alarm in the gripstock buzzed to indicate that the missile was locked onto the stack. If Avakian pulled the trigger all the way back a charge would blow the missile out of the tube and send it on its way. Instead he released the trigger, replaced the cover on the missile tube, and drained the coolant back into the battery pack. That particular battery/coolant unit was now useless, but he knew the missile worked. And at $4,000 per gripstock and $13,000 per missile, it was nice to know they worked. "Now I'm satisfied," he said.

It took him two more hours to go through the rest of the supplies, and by then everyone else was completely bored out of their minds. This was about the time that, in the past, a large suitcase filled with currency would be exchanged. These days all it took was a cell phone call to execute a bank transfer.

Earlier one of the Russian bodyguards had been about to light up a cigarette and the Bulgarians had yelled at him, pointing to all the cases of ammo, in particular the pallet of TNT. This set off quite an argument. Avakian had been able to understand a bit, the Russians chiding the Bulgarians for being nervous Nellies. But after that the Russians had gone outside to smoke, usually accompanied by one of the Bulgarians.

Now Avakian noted that one of the Russians had not returned from his cigarette break. The other was sitting on a pallet yawning and hadn't noticed. Andrei was busy texting away on his cell phone. And the Bulgarians were giving each other little looks.

Avakian stuck his hand in his pocket and casually eased over to one of the pallets. He studiously paid no attention as one of the Bulgarians worked his way around behind him. Why oh why hadn't he listened to his gut instinct and just disappeared during the stop in Cyprus, flown home before the CIA put him on a blacklist, and kicked off a nice quiet retirement?

Someone shouted, "Hands up!" in Russian, and lo and behold the Bulgarians were pointing pistols. At Avakian, a very surprised Russian bodyguard, and at Andrei who, to his credit, didn't look all that shocked.

Avakian pulled his hand out of his pocket and yanked out the grenade pin, ostentatiously holding it up so everyone could see.

One of the Bulgarians yelled something that had to be grenade, and then all of them were shouting at him. Probably something along the lines of put that pin back in or we'll kill you.

"The only thing that's keeping this from going off is me holding down the spoon," Avakian announced to Andrei. "I get shot, the first thing I do is drop it. Tell them."

Andrei translated, and the Bulgarian hoods shouted even louder.

"They think you bluff," Andrei said in an even voice.

Avakian reached down into the open crate in front of him and jerked out a canvas bag with his left hand.

More shouting, and one of the Bulgarians closed on him fast, pistol pointed at his head.

"Tell him he takes one more step and not only do I drop the grenade, I drop it into this bag of TNT," Avakian said. The canvas bag was filled with ten one-kilogram blocks of Bulgarian military TNT. While Andrei translated again Avakian slung the carrying strap over his shoulder and plunged his grenade hand into the bag. "If they think anyone inside this warehouse might survive the explosion, tell them to go ahead and shoot."

"They say you not do it," Andrei reported back after a lot of yelling.

"If I've got a choice between taking all these assholes with me and getting shot and dumped in the harbor," said Avakian, "then I'm going out now and taking all these assholes with me."

More yelling.

"They say, what you do now?" said Andrei.

"I'm leaving," Avakian said calmly. He pointed to the Bulgarian with the pistol aimed at his head. "And if this asshole moves one millimeter we're all going up."

The asshole didn't move, but the other two hoods grabbed Andrei and the bodyguard and held pistols to their heads.

"They say we are not going with you," said Andrei.

"That's okay," said Avakian, backing toward the door and remembering to pick the pry bar up off the last pallet he'd opened. "They can keep you."

Andrei shouted for the first time. "WHAT?"

"Hey, you said no problem," Avakian told him. "So deal with it."

He opened the warehouse door with his left hand, bringing the grenade back into view because he expected to have to negotiate with more Bulgarians outside.

But there were no Bulgarians outside. No Russian bodyguard either. No one at all. As a matter of fact, this part of the pier was empty. Only a few workers milling around at the next warehouse down the way. Avakian closed the door and jammed the pry bar into it. That ought to slow them down some.

A sign from the universe that this was his lucky day would be a set of keys in the ignition of at least one of the SUVs. Otherwise it would be a swim across the quay. He didn't fancy a run down that long straight pier with people shooting at him. That harbor water looked really cold and really scummy.

"Mr. Avakian?" a voice from behind one of the SUVs said in Slavic-accented English.

Avakian whirled about. A head poked up over the roof of the SUV. It belonged to a man in his forties, wearing a business suit. And with him four compatriots wearing full police SWAT regalia. Blue jumpsuits with white police insignia, body armor, drop holsters, and helmets. All carrying AK-47's.

"I am Colonel Borisov of the Bulgarian Interior Ministry," the man in the suit announced. Then, after a short pause, "Is that a hand grenade you are holding?"

"It is," said Avakian.

"Am I correct that the pin has been removed?"

"It has," said Avakian.

Colonel Borisov said, "Could I persuade you to reinsert the pin?"

"No, not right now," Avakian replied.

A pounding from within the warehouse as someone tried to kick the door open.

The Colonel paused to speak a word of command into the walkie-talkie radio in his hand. Then back to Avakian as if nothing had happened, "And the bag at your side."

"Ten kilograms of TNT," Avakian said.

Colonel Borisov took that news with an unexpected degree of calm. It was one of those days when everyone seemed hard to rattle. "Would it help if I told you that you were not in any trouble?"

"You could tell me," said Avakian. "I just wouldn't believe it."

Two police vans came speeding around the side of the warehouse, flashing lights but no sirens.

Colonel Borisov glanced at them. "Then, since I have pressing business and I cannot allow you to leave and I do not wish for you to detonate your explosives, may I suggest that you rest yourself by this pier until we can continue our discussion?"

"All right," said Avakian.

"Good," said the Colonel. "You must excuse me now. If your hand becomes tired, you will please throw the grenade a safe distance into the water."

"Be careful, there's a lot of ordnance in there," said Avakian, indicating the warehouse. "It's crated, but watch where you shoot."

"You are very thoughtful," said the Colonel.

Just trying to reduce my sentence, Avakian thought. He pondered his options and took a seat at the edge of the pier. Bulgaria was a member of NATO, so the CIA should be able to get him out of prison. If they wanted to, that is.

The Bulgarian SWAT team lined up in a train formation beside the warehouse door, and the point man yanked out the pry bar. The door crashed open and the first pair of cops grabbed the Bulgarian who came flying out and threw him onto the ground, beating the living crap out of him with their rifle butts. The rest of the unit charged in, shouting what Avakian now recognized to be hands up in Bulgarian.

Avakian thought about jumping into the water, but with the port full of cops they'd be waiting for him on every shore long before he could swim there. Unless he died of hypothermia in the Black Sea first. Well, he'd always heard that prison was the best place to write your memoirs.

Unless someone fired a round into one of those crates of mortar shells, in which case all their troubles would be over.

But there was no shooting, and soon all the shouting died down. Much to Avakian's surprise Andrei was the first man to walk out the door. And without handcuffs.

He strolled over to Avakian and sat down on the pier with a tired grunt. "Tell me, Pyotr, are you familiar with the American film, *The Maltese Falcon*?"

Avakian nodded.

"Good. You are Samuel Spade, my friend. You are man of nice judgments and many resources. And ruthless. You leave me to my fate, yes?"

"Hey, Andrei, you didn't want to talk about how to deal with any problems, so when they came up I dealt with them myself."

"True. I must concede this. But as you have seen,

the problem would have been resolved without your interventions."

"Yeah, well, I didn't know that, did I?" Avakian stopped cold as the realization hit him. "You knew what was going to happen all along! You little prick!"

Andrei was puzzled. "Prick? Prick?"

Avakian translated it into Russian for him. His curse word vocabulary was pretty comprehensive.

"Ah, yes?" said Andrei. "I cannot blame you. Orders, Pyotr. I cannot tell."

"What about now? You going to tell me what's happening? My hand's getting a little tired."

Andrei glanced at the hand that was still resting inside the canvas satchel. "Yes. This group of *mutri*, they are what you call…" he thought about it some more. "Middlemen? Yes? Middlemen. The arms, they go from factory to warehouse. The *mutri*, they watch and protect. These *mutri*, they decide to take the arms. Sell themselves."

"And kill us," said Avakian.

"Very foolish, to try and cross our Volkov. But we know of this. No problem."

No problem again. "And the cops?"

"Cops?" said Andrei.

"Police," said Avakian.

"Ah. Minister of Interior, boss of cops? Big reformer. Clean up Bulgaria. What is the word? Bust. Bust the gangs of *mutri*." He nudged Avakian. "In actually, he bust only the *mutri* that do not work for him. Good man. Next President of Bulgaria, to be sure. Much money for campaign." Then a classically Russian shrug at the corrupt ways of the world.

"What if the *mutri* blew us away inside the warehouse while your Bulgarian cop friends were still waiting outside?"

Andrei gave a different kind of shrug. "My friend, in this game there are risks. Is why it pays so well. You see my phone? I text Colonel Borisov whole time, yes? You throw off timetable a bit, but all is well."

Avakian removed his hand from the bag. With his left, he fished around in his jacket pocket until he found the grenade pin. He looked at the grenade, then the pin. No, never a good idea. He stood up, turned, and heaved the grenade into the harbor. It plopped into the water, and about three seconds later there was a muffled thump of explosion. A concentric ring of shock wave spread outward, and the water boiled up briefly.

"You have another grenade in your pocket, perhaps?" said Andrei.

"Maybe," Avakian lied.

"You care to give to me?"

"No." Avakian handed over the bag of TNT. "You can have this."

Andrei took a quick peek inside and closed the flap. "A thousand thanks. No need to tell me if you blow us all up or not. I believe you then. The *mutri* do also."

A series of gunshots thudded through the walls of the warehouse.

"The competition being eliminated?" said Avakian.

"Bad men die in gunfight with police. Heroes. Show on television tonight. Rest of *mutri*, they see their fate. Smart ones fall into line."

"You mind telling me what's next?" said Avakian.

"Load crates into containers. Load containers into ships. Sail away."

"They'll need to be combat loaded," said Avakian.

"Everything spread between the two ships. Containers positioned so they can be opened in the hold. The first equipment they'll need should be the last loaded aboard."

"You tell them how you want," said Andrei. "Bulgarians do the work."

"You coming along?" said Avakian.

Andrei nodded. "You like vodka?"

"Only if there's nothing else to drink," said Avakian.

Chapter Nineteen

THE GANGWAY SWUNG OVER, and the dock workers who had tied the ship up secured it to the pier.

Peter Avakian was the first man off, carrying his hand bag. It was dusk. He'd been hoping for complete darkness, but had no intention of waiting aboard the ship for it. A lesson learned from his nighttime troubles in Benin had him wearing a black polo shirt with his black suit and hat instead of his usual white dress shirt.

They were tied up at the multipurpose terminal in Duncan Dock of the port of Cape Town. Avakian took out his South African prepaid cell phone and dialed the number Constance Springfield had given him. It was definitely time to call in some help.

The phone rang three times before she picked up. "Hello?"

"Hello," said Avakian. "This is the man from the no-fly list."

There was a pause, and the connection broke.

Avakian stared at his phone. Enough bars. What the hell? He dialed again.

It went to voice mail this time.

Something was very wrong, and it was no time to be standing around. Avakian passed a line of old tankers on the long walk down the quay to the Customs Gate. Following the building signs and the usual run around to Customs and Immigration, he put his bag up on the counter and handed over his passport.

Awaiting him was what he'd come to call from his time in South Africa the official pair. An older white man and a younger black man poised as his heir apparent. In this case a younger black woman.

Avakian ran the rule over the white revenue officer. Chubby. Tired. Near retirement. But probably seen it all. No fool. He'd invite you to treat him like one, but it would be your mistake.

"Welcome to South Africa, sir," the revenue officer said. "Anything to declare?"

"Nothing at all," said Avakian.

"Any fruits, vegetables, animals or animal products?"

"None," said Avakian.

The officer scanned Avakian's information into his computer, gazed intently at the screen, then at Avakian, and began thumbing through his passport. "You're quite a traveler, Mr. ..."

"Avakian."

"Avakian." He rolled his Dutch tongue over the correct pronunciation. "I see you've left and returned to South Africa quite often over the past month."

"I've been doing some business here in Cape Town," said Avakian. "It's required a lot of back and forth traveling."

"And what is your business?"

Avakian did not list it in his passport. He handed over his business card.

The officer read it carefully. "Security consultant. Sounds like interesting work."

"You'd be surprised how much of it is really boring," said Avakian.

"I see that your previous arrivals and departures were by air, not ship."

By this time his black partner was going through Avakian's bag.

"My clients are thinking about leasing the *Scorpio*," said Avakian. "So they wanted me to check out the ship and the route, particularly the Suez Canal to Cape Town. I joined the ship in Bulgaria and sailed down from there."

"Worried about pirates?" the officer said.

"It's the latest media craze," said Avakian.

"See any?"

"Not a one."

"Any stops?"

"None."

"How was Bulgaria?"

"Just spent a day there," said Avakian, knowing the man was following his passport stamps. "I'm sorry to say I didn't care for anyone I met."

"Unpleasant people?" said the officer.

"I'm not saying everyone," Avakian replied. "Just the ones I ran into."

"Would have thought so," the officer muttered. "Voyage pleasant, though?"

"A freighter isn't a cruise ship," said Avakian. "You can only watch so many Bollywood movies with the crew, and if you run out of books it gets a bit grim. I'd rather fly."

"The wife is always after me to take a cruise. What do you think?"

"A lot of people really enjoy them. As a security professional I'd warn you that cruise ship companies recruit crew in undeveloped countries, pay low wages, and aren't really diligent about background checks. Rape, theft, and assault aren't uncommon, and the companies are usually more concerned with sweeping nasty incidents under the rug than resolving them. You should also be aware that once a ship crosses territorial limits the only jurisdiction is the country of registry, and it's doubtful Liberia or Panama will do anything for you. That said, you could just as easily break your leg skiing."

The officer had been staring at him throughout the speech. "I think we'll just go to the beach." He stamped Avakian's passport. "Pleasant stay in South Africa, sir."

"Thanks," Avakian said. "Don't forget to use sunscreen."

A gentle rain was falling as he left the port area, and there didn't seem to be any cabs on the street. By all rights he ought to get under cover, call one, then right to the airport and the next direct flight to the States before anyone could do anything about it. Enough of all this nonsense. High time he followed his instincts. But he couldn't do that. He had to find out what happened to Patience Mbatha. Yeah, she got herself into it. Yeah, she was using him to get her story. But life was all about what you could live with, and what you couldn't. And he didn't think he could live with running out if there was a chance he could have helped her.

All this came to the fore when that familiar pewter

SUV turned the corner and headed toward him. Running would definitely be the smart thing to do right about now. Avakian stood his ground. The window rolled down and it was his old friend the Afrikaner regimental sergeant major.

"At least you're not wearing your shooting glasses," Avakian said.

"Not today," the RSM replied with a wan smile. "Get in."

"Got your Uzi handy?" Avakian inquired.

"It's where I can lay my hands on it. Get in— haven't got all day."

This was one of those momentous decisions that, unfortunately, life only gave you a few seconds to make. Avakian's gut was telling him not to get into the car. He got into the car.

Just the RSM and his black driver this time. The other black mercenary gunman was off doing something else.

They headed west, but not to Payne-Best's house at Bishopscourt. The trip proceeded in silence for a few minutes until the RSM said, "Don't you want to know where we're going?"

"Why" said Avakian. "So you can tell me I'll find out when we get there? I'll find out when we get there."

"You're a funny little bloke. No questions about your reporter friend?"

Expressing a burning interest wouldn't be the swiftest idea until he got a little better insight into what was what. "Not if it's going to make me an accessory after the fact."

The RSM showed him the face of every conventional army organization man who'd made rank by shiny boots and unquestioning obedience and were forever on their guard for clever bastards who thought they might be smarter than everyone else. "What's that supposed to mean?"

"It means I don't care," said Avakian.

The sun was just hitting the horizon as they skirted Table Mountain on the M3 highway, and this was the first time Avakian had seen the tablecloth phenomenon. A white cloud bank sat right atop the mountain, falling down over the face but never completely covering it. Really beautiful.

They kept going south into the Constantia Valley. Old farm and wine country. They turned off the highway and wound through narrow roads. Now they were entering a wine estate, acres of vineyards stretching out over the hills. Past the main buildings and onto a dirt road that ended at a small cottage. Very isolated. Avakian wondered whether he ought to make a move before it was too late to make a move. "Go ahead in," the RSM ordered.

North American winter was the beginning of summer in South Africa, and Pieter De Wet was relaxing in the tiny living room in T-shirt, shorts, and Teva sandals. One leg draped over the arm of the chair, holding his usual sundowner of a bottle of Castle Lager, watching rugby on TV like a good Afrikaner. Very simple furniture. Avakian hoped the cottage wasn't De Wet's, or he was the most Spartan son of a bitch on the planet. Not a single personal item was anywhere in view.

De Wet picked up the remote and turned the TV off. "Take a seat, mate."

Avakian said, "I guess Mrs. Payne-Best drew the

line at using her house for any more meetings after the last time."

"Pommy bitch. Care for a beer?"

"No thanks. Your place?"

"Friend's letting me use it. How was the trip?"

"Boring."

"See any pirates?"

Avakian shook his head. "Broke out one of the 12.7mm machineguns just in case, but they didn't oblige."

De Wet chuckled. "That would have been the surprise of their fucking lives. Everything all right with the ships?"

"Ready to go," said Avakian.

"Good. Heard about Bulgaria. Bloody Russian drama. Always has to be some intricate Machiavelli plot with those people. Can't just shoot the fucking competition and be done with it. Would have given my left ball to see you threatening to frag everyone in exchange for a clear route to the door."

"Wasn't all that funny at the time," said Avakian.

"'Never is, mate. But you have to admit, makes a gob-smacking story at the pub later. Never have to buy a drink. Sometimes I think that's why we do it."

"What about your end?"

"Men are all trained, ready to go. Plan—no problems. That's the easiest thing for me and Payne-Best. But I have to admit the rest had us stumped. CIA and what not."

"I can't believe Payne-Best couldn't come up with anything," said Avakian.

"Ah, irony," said De Wet. "Not much for it myself, but you do enjoy it, don't you? Old Herbert's a lovely bloke. Those old school manners? Charm your socks off. Brilliant at the cocktail party chat. Everyone's friend. You need that at the high end of this business, to make the deals. He puts a more pleasant face on it than a gruff old Boer like me. Good soldier too, don't get me wrong. Nothing more than battalion command, though. The Brits knew what they were doing. He certainly wasn't going to command Special Air Service, let alone a brigade. And I wouldn't care to tell you how much money he's pissed away trying to be the master businessman. One of the reasons we hired you. He wasn't up to the logistics. Not my cup of tea, either. Not general officer material."

"No?" said Avakian. This was the most talking he'd ever heard De Wet do, and that alone was making him nervous.

"Who knows? They weren't about to make a recce commando a general anyway, not in the new South Africa Defense Force. De Wet killed too many kaffirs to suit the kaffirs in charge."

Kaffir was to white South Africa what nigger was to white America. Avakian always thought it interesting to see someone's private face emerge.

"Anyway," said De Wet. "You've noticed I have no gift for diplomacy. And that's what a general is anyway, half uniformed politician and half uniformed diplomat. You're wondering about the CIA."

"Take your time," said Avakian.

"You're a good listener," said De Wet. "I never was. Right. As it happened, neither of us could figure out what to do. Out of our depth. Know who came up with the solution? Okong. Bloke doesn't say much, doesn't look like much, but there's a reason he's where he is. Bloody brilliant. And I'll admit it when I run across a brilliant kaffir, though God knows I haven't run into many in my time. You don't mind working for one like that."

"Big of you," Avakian mentioned.

"Man knows how the oil business works," said De Wet. "More important, he knows how government works. Know what his solution was? Go to an American oil company. We said, what? But he was firm on it. Didn't go to the top—that was the brilliant part. Regional manager, right here in Africa. Just like the army when you come to think of it. General sits behind the desk, spouts orders, has no bloody clue, and the lieutenant colonels on staff are the ones who actually run the whole show. So he talked to the American bloke, probably the same one who buys all that stolen Nigerian crude from him. Says, how would you like a big fucking oil lease and a sweetheart contract when the government of Benin changes hands? What's the man going to say? Of course it'll be yes, thanks very much. Business is business, after all."

"And Safoil?" said Avakian.

"That's the way it goes. The investors still get their cut, so they'll go away happy. Less happy, but still happy."

"And this solves your problem how?" said Avakian.

"You ought to know how it works, mate. That was Okong's genius. We don't have to deal with the CIA. We don't have to deal with the U.S. government. We just have to deal with the oil company. As soon as we hopped in bed with them all our troubles were over. They turned their lobbyists loose on your government, and you must know how that goes. Just learning myself. You don't need Presidents or cabinets. Those blokes only know what they're told. You go to all the ones with the smaller offices who make things run the way lieutenant colonels run the army. Talk to the ones who used to work for the oil companies and will again after government service. The ones who get paid to worry about where the oil and natural gas will come from. Tell them all they have to do is sit tight and they'll get a new pro-U.S. government. Oh, and it will be democratic and all. Free elections? Guaranteed. A future major oil supplier with U.S. contracts. No worries."

"No worries," said Avakian. He did know how it went.

"Have to say it worked like magic, and it didn't cost us a penny. Okong was the one who said it. Nothing a government loves more than getting what they want without having to get off their arse and do anything."

"That was it?" said Avakian. Though he knew very well that was really all it would take.

"Of course we didn't tell them who, or how, or when. Not that they wanted to know anyway—no one wanted to leave any fingerprints. Still, didn't care to put too much temptation in their path. But the contracts are signed. If we succeed then everyone makes a big pile of cash and you Yanks can keep driving your cars without it costing you too much. If we fuck up the oil company feeds our contracts into the shredder and it never happened. I tell you, mate, it's been an education. I'd venture to guess that if you *did* try and get in touch with the CIA now, you'd find they're not accepting your calls."

Funny he should say that. Well, that was one question answered. Without making a show of looking around, Avakian began contemplating escape routes. "So your way is clear."

"Absolutely. All we have to do is get ashore. Not that we couldn't take the crack Benin army with a half battalion of South African hairdressers anyway. But it'll be quick and clean, and all over in one night. Your friend Andrei the Russian has been texting Volkov in code every day. Can't say enough about you. Attention to detail, toothbrush for every man. Probably a lot better supply than some South African ops I've been on. You Yanks know how to do it. You've been a good soldier, mate. That's what makes this hard."

At that cue the RSM entered the room with his Uzi leveled at Avakian.

You didn't do anything when they were ready and waiting for you. "Does this mean I just lost my portfolio as the principle advisor to the Minister of Economic Development?" Avakian asked.

"Afraid so," said De Wet.

"I was thinking more along the lines of a wall plaque, a nice firm handshake, and the next flight home. But you can forget all that. Let's just make it the next flight home."

"Believe me, mate, nothing I'd love more. But there's just too many questions about you. God knows, you're smooth. You've got the right answer to every question under the sun. Usually before we even think to ask them. What better way to cover working for the CIA than to come right out and admit they tried to recruit you but you sent them packing? That way, even if we see you with them you're in the clear. Brilliant."

"For what it's worth," said Avakian. "I'm not working for them."

"Makes no difference. Too many questions. What were you doing in Payne-Best's study when you locked us out? I know, you were locking the bodyguard fight out. And Payne-Best swears his safe wasn't tampered with. But you are a clever bastard, aren't you? Benin.

Good job but what's all this about Chinese and cars blowing up? Make no mistake, I give you full credit. Screwed the arse off that cherrie reporter and she still has no proof you're working for us. Suspects it, of course, like everyone seems to suspect you of something. But hat's off. Man who can keep his mouth shut in bed, well, there's a man for you."

"So let me get this straight. You're pointing a gun at me *because* all my explanations check out?"

"Fucking unfair, but it dawned on everyone that you know an awful lot about an awful lot of things. All of us, Bulgaria, what have you. Sorry mate, too many questions. Okong and Volkov insisted."

"What happens when you get the job done and they insist on you?"

"We'll see about that then. No hard feelings." Said as a statement, not a question. "Just business. Nothing personal."

Avakian wondered if a business school had ever written up *The Godfather* as a business model. "That's what they say in the movie. But the book goes on to say that *everything* is personal."

"Suit yourself," said De Wet. "Stand up and put your hands behind your back."

Moving carefully to stay clear of the RSM's line of fire, De Wet snapped a pair of handcuffs onto Avakian's wrists, ratcheting them tight. That done, he gave him a frisk. "No weapons?"

"I keep telling you guys. I'm the only one around who doesn't go strapped."

"Your misfortune, that." De Wet rummaged through Avakian's pockets and relived him of everything in it: passport, wallet, loose change, and phones. He pulled the key ring out, looked at it for a moment, and took that too. So no tekko. "By the way, since we had your bank account and routing number, we went to get our money back. Seems your account is deposit only. Would you care to give me the procedure for making a withdrawal?"

"Let me think about it. No."

"Sure you won't reconsider? Can't take it with you, after all. Save yourself the headache?"

"It's a 20 digit PIN," said Avakian. "Symbols and numbers. It's written down in a safe deposit box back in the States. I made sure I wasn't going to remember it even if I wanted to."

"We'll have to see about that. Told them you'd be a contrary bastard, but the money men want their money back." Then, to the RSM, "March him out, Rob."

"You're not doing it?" said Avakian.

"Not my job, thanks," said De Wet. "I'd like to say *vaarwel* to you, but I rather think this is goodbye."

Chapter Twenty

"I DON'T SUPPOSE I could visit the bathroom real quick?" Avakian asked.

"Not on your life," the regimental sergeant major replied.

Out across the front of the cottage. There was a little garden off to one side. Night had now fallen completely. The air was utterly still. Not a sound but the insects buzzing. The overcast had cleared off and the stars were brilliant.

The RSM saw him trying to get his bearings. "Shout all you like," he said. "If it'll make you feel better."

It really wouldn't if no one was going to hear. When the SUV door was opened Avakian didn't wait to get kicked in. He scooted all the way across the seat so his right side was pressed up against the door. No one came over to put on his seat belt. Good.

The rear door stayed open and the driver didn't turn the engine on. Avakian wondered what they were waiting for. His question was answered. He heard the house screen door shut, and the RSM was leading a similarly-handcuffed Patience Mbatha to the SUV.

Avakian was enormously relieved to see her alive, even though they were heading from the frying pan into the fire. The point was probably moot at this late date, but he didn't want to express the concern he felt for her safety for fear of how it might be used against them both.

The RSM put a hand on her head and pushed her inside. She nearly fell on Avakian's lap. Then he grabbed her shoulder and straightened her up in the seat. The door slammed shut and both rear locks clicked.

Other than the expected amount of fear, it was also clear that she expected to see him alive. That was about all Avakian could read on her face. "Hello, Patience. It's good to see you."

"I thought you were dead," she said.

He still didn't think so. "Ditto."

The RSM got into the front seat. The driver started the engine and backed out into the street.

"Where are we going?" Patience asked.

Avakian sighed almost inaudibly. Everyone just had to ask that.

"You'll see," said the RSM.

Avakian had expected nothing less.

Patience turned to him and said, "They are going to kill us."

You think? But Avakian only shrugged. Not knowing how long the trip would take, he got started right away. His visit to the sex shop hadn't really been about handcuffs. It had been about handcuff keys. But you couldn't get one without the other. For the most part handcuff keys were universal. Which was how a cop or a jailer unlocked another cop's prisoner. One of the keys to the handcuffs he'd purchased was taped to the inside of his belt, directly at the small of his back. Alongside a small circular box cutter in case he happened to be tied up with cord or plastic zip ties. He hadn't been all that great in the anticipation department lately, but at least this was something. His only other ace in the hole was a miniature butane lighter taped under his belt buckle—that added after the near thing of being without a fire starter in Cotonou. That definitely seemed to be his karma lately, either a Molotov with no light or a light with no Molotov. Avakian slid his right forefinger under the belt and began picking up the edge of the tape with his nail.

Instead of driving back north they headed west. He had the edge of the tape up and was now peeling it away from the belt very slowly and carefully so no arm or body movement would give him away. It was absolutely imperative that he not jingle the handcuffs.

"Were you working with these people after all?" Patience demanded.

"Yup," Avakian replied.

"You lied to me."

"If it will make you feel better, I apologize unreservedly."

The RSM and the driver both laughed.

"You want to joke now?" she said, on the verge of tears.

"I wasn't joking," said Avakian.

She chewed that over a bit, then said, "I suppose you were working for the CIA, too?"

Where the hell did that come from? Probably her interrogation. No matter. He wasn't about to do anyone any favors. "Of course not." He had the piece of tape off the belt and was now peeling the key away from the tape.

"Did you lie to me about anything else?" she demanded.

Getting the handcuffs off was only the first in a very long chain of events that would have to be executed without the slightest hiccup. In case it didn't come off, Avakian didn't want to hurt anyone's feelings. "Not to my immediate recollection."

The RSM laughed again.

"I am very glad we are amusing you," Patience told him.

"You are," the RSM replied. "Keep it up."

That of course practically demanded that she be silent. But it didn't last long. "Aren't you going to ask if they hurt me?" she said to Avakian.

"If you were smart you told them everything they wanted to know before that happened," he replied. He balled up the tape and stuck it down the back of his trousers. Someone might notice if he left it on the seat.

The SUV ran over something in the highway, and that squishy off-road suspension gave them quite a bounce. Avakian dropped the key. Shit.

"What the hell?" the RSM exclaimed.

"Sorry, *baas*," said the driver.

"I don't like that," the RSM said in a warning tone.

"I couldn't get out of the way," the driver said quickly. "Car in the other lane."

The RSM said quietly, "Don't you ever run over a dog again, my son."

"Yes, *baas*," said the driver. "Sorry."

"Don't you care if they hurt me?" Patience asked Avakian again.

Avakian couldn't find the key. "Uh, of course. That's why I didn't want to ask." It wasn't under his butt. He stuck his fingers into the crack between the back of the seat and the bottom.

"But you don't think I'm very smart," Patience said.

Oh, yes. It was *just* the time for recriminations. Avakian pushed his fingers deeper into the crack. They brushed the key. He tried to put his finger down on it, but it only slid deeper into the crevice. God-dammit!

"Well?" she said.

Avakian tried to hook his finger around the key. "Let's put it this way. If you'd been a little more inclined to take advice you wouldn't be taking this drive right now."

"You are," she countered.

"Yeah, well, I'm not prepared to contest my own lack of intelligence." He got his finger around the key and began slowly sliding it back toward him.

"Do you think they might not kill us?" she said suddenly.

"I have no insight to offer," he replied.

"They said they would let us go if we gave them the information they wanted. Did you give it to them?"

Avakian had worked the key out to where he was able to get two fingers on it. Finally. Answer, dammit, he told himself. Any lag in the conversation would make them suspicious. "No, I didn't."

"What? You mean you didn't tell them?"

"No." He needed his right hand free, so he'd have to unlock the cuffs with his left. As he was transferring the key between hands the SUV hit a pothole or something in the road and he dropped it again. For crying out loud! He pressed the back of his hand onto the seat, and the key was sitting right there. Okay, thanks. Sorry about all that.

Patience had begun to cry. "Please tell them. Please."

"This is probably the last piece of advice I'll give you, Patience, and by all means feel free to ignore it like all the rest. Never believe everything that people with guns tell you."

"But what if they are telling the truth?" To the RSM, "You are telling the truth, aren't you?"

"Of course," the RSM replied.

"Then tell them," she said to Avakian.

He said gently, "I don't have the information they want, so it's useless."

They were passing through industrial flatlands. Matching the bearings with the map of Cape Town in his head, Avakian thought they were near the airport. Then, off to the right, the lights of an airliner on approach confirmed it.

Full blown crying now from Patience. "You never cared for me."

Avakian had a good grip on the key now. "Think what you like. You're going to anyway."

"How can you be so calm?"

Avakian located the lock hole with the tip of his forefinger. He tried but couldn't get the key in. Calm, that was a good one. His fingers were slick with perspiration. Don't lose your grip on it. Take your time, work it around.

A broken concrete wall bordered the highway on the left. The driver slowed and turned off, and all of a sudden it was like he was back in Benin.

Patience looked around, as if for the first time, and

gasped. "They've taken us to Nyanga," she said to Avakian.

"And Nyanga is?" Avakian inquired.

"A black township," she replied. "One of the worst."

Under apartheid non-whites who worked in Cape Town as servants or laborers were not allowed to live in the city with whites. The townships were at first labor camps for those people to reside in. All racially segregated, of course. Under apartheid even the slums were racially segregated. Outside the city limits but within commuting distance. The residents had to carry passes and be back in the township after dark. If they lost their job they lost their pass and had to return to their tribal homeland. Later women joined the workforce, people married, and families were raised. But the townships remained slums where white South Africa kept their underclass out of sight and supposedly under control. There was no racial apartheid now, but the black underclass still lived in the former townships because they couldn't afford to live anywhere else.

The government and European aid had put in street lights and electric lines, public toilets and water taps, but it still reminded Avakian of nothing else but those hut villages in the center of Cotonou. Except these single room shacks where whole families lived, slapped down within inches of each other, were made from the ramshackle detritus of the first world, not the third. Corrugated metal walls and roofs, some with obviously salvaged doors and windows. Avakian could see blue sheet plastic—that same blue sheet plastic he'd seen in every poor part of the world—drooping over the roofs of some of them to try and stop the leaks, anchored in place by rocks. As they passed down the narrow road some of the shacks had fences and a random flowerpot or two stuck down onto the bare sand ground. Those noble but pathetic attempts at normality were the only things that ever threatened to crack his composure. It occurred to him that he'd now made the full tour of Cape Town, from the mansions to the slums.

There were some prefabricated metal shacks, that could have passed for backyard garden sheds back in the States. And shipping containers that passed as homes and stores. A few actual cinder block and brick homes with real metal roofs, chain link fences around them and cars in makeshift driveways between structures. Local notables.

Laundry hung on lines in the narrow, jagged lanes between the rows of shacks. But rows was not the right word. Everything had been built piece by piece on whatever ground was available, leaving as much organization to the neighborhoods as there was to a mound of children's Lego's on a living room floor.

As they drove deeper into it Avakian noticed the change. The casual observer would only see the poverty, but he was seeing a layered defense. Kids and dogs prowled the streets. People were walking around. They were gathered at the neighborhood bars called shebeens, drinking and listening to music under naked light bulbs and the red Coca Cola signs that somehow made their way, even if nothing else did, into every godforsaken corner of the world. But as they drove down the streets they were being checked through. Nothing overt like roadblocks or checkpoints or requests for identification, but they were still being watched, and noted, and allowed to pass.

The townships had originally been designed with perimeter walls and road bridges for access so they could be easily sealed off and contained by a few South African police, but like every other slum in the world everything that happened inside had been left to those inside. It would have been a societal miracle if there *hadn't* been any gangs.

He knew he was running out of time. He put the nose of the key in the lock hole and twirled it around slowly. The key finally slid into the hole. He had no idea how loud the mechanism would be, and he needed something to cover any sound. "You wanted to know why I'm calm," he said to Patience. "When it comes your time to die, be not like those whose hearts are filled with fear of death, so that when their time comes they weep and pray for a little more time to live their lives over again a different way. Sing your death song and die like a hero going home."

The RSM turned around in his seat. "Who said that?"

"A native American chief. A Shawnee named Tecumseh."

"That's fucking good," the RSM said.

Avakian's right hand was free from the cuff. "Yeah, it is." All soldiers dug that quote.

"It's *stupid*," Patience said through tears. "Death is death."

Avakian had his aiming point marked out: the back of the RSM's fleshy neck, just below the base of the skull. He coiled up to throw the rabbit punch. One good shot and then choke the driver out before he could pull a piece. But they were slowing down. Shit.

He slowly returned his hand to the small of his back, slipping the handcuff ring back on but not locking it. His jacket sleeve and the darkness would cover it.

The RSM turned around again in his seat to address them. "In the old days you might have been dropped off in the bush and left for the hyena. But they've gotten a bit scarce, and the parks are a long drive away. So we'll feed you to these hyena instead."

Chapter Twenty-One

AS THE SUV edged down the narrow road there were now young black men with pistols out, and one with a shotgun. They stopped at a dead end. A medium sized moving van was backed up against a shipping container. Inside the container, illuminated by a hanging portable light, a couple of men were stacking what looked like one kilo bricks of vacuum-packed, plastic-wrapped marijuana into brown cardboard moving boxes.

"*Dagga* from Swaziland," the regimental sergeant major informed them. "If Okong didn't have that for trade he'd have to buy his cocaine from the Colombians with rand, and the middle class clubbies wouldn't be able to afford it anymore." He retrieved the Uzi submachinegun from under his seat. "Keep an eye on them," he ordered the driver.

As the RSM slammed the door Avakian coiled up for his chance. One punch, over the driver's seat and behind the wheel, and they'd be gone. But the driver rested a pistol on top of that seat, aimed straight at him. Avakian leaned back and took his eyes off the man, waiting for his attention to flag in any way.

Patience had gone totally silent. The RSM was casually holding the Uzi by his side, just in case, while he discussed business with the leader of the group outside.

Avakian waited, but the driver didn't relax his vigilance. This was getting really complicated. He hoped Patience was up to it.

Two gangsters in the container. Four outside in the immediate area. Maybe a few more farther down the road. Only one way out by vehicle, the route they'd come in.

The RSM returned to the SUV. He opened Avakian's door and said, "Time to go."

Avakian swung his feet out before his arms could be grabbed. From air conditioned, leather-seated comfort to a hot night on dusty road. A smog of charcoal smoke in the air—that was what the locals cooked with. The smells of hundreds of dinners. Thick cheap cologne coming off the two gang members who had taken up position on either side of him.

The RSM leaned into the SUV and unlocked Patience's handcuffs. He tossed them onto the seat.

That didn't compute at all. Avakian wondered what the hell was going on.

Patience rubbed her wrists. "I'm sorry, Pete, but I had to take care of myself. Just like you said."

The RSM slammed the door shut with a smile.

Avakian stood there with his mouth open. Totally blindsided. Hustled to the accompaniment of the musical beat called township funk, which was playing from someone's blaster nearby.

"I'd give them those bank codes, double quick,"

the RSM advised in lieu of farewell. And after a pause in response to Avakian's silence, "Aren't you going to threaten to kill me?"

Avakian gave a bit of a startled twitch and turned to him, actually grateful for having his focus restored. "I don't think I'm going to have the time."

The passenger door slammed shut and the SUV took quite a few points to turn around in the narrow road.

One of the gangsters gave Avakian a hard shove toward their leader. Who was arrogant and pleased with himself, his hands on his hips and an automatic pistol stuck in the front of his black jeans. Mid twenties with a pair of flashy chrome-framed sunglasses perched atop a black do-rag. Immaculate white top-of-the-line basketball sneaks. And a green t-shirt with some kind of motif that Avakian couldn't make out in the darkness.

Avakian didn't need to bother about acting stunned —he already had sufficient motivation, thank you very much. He measured off the distance as he approached the leader, flanked by the two drug runners. This was not the time to wait and see how the situation would develop. One thing was certain: the situation wouldn't be developing any better for him.

When he was about fifteen feet from the leader Avakian transitioned from a dejected trudging into a flat-out charge, taking his escorts by surprise and leaving them behind. The leader's expression changed just as abruptly from smirk to shock.

Avakian swung his hands out from behind his back, the still-handcuffed left in a wide arc to whip the metal cuffs across the leader's eyes. A yell as they struck him, and his hands instinctively went up to his eyes. As they collided and went down together Avakian grabbed for the pistol in the man's belt.

Nothing to do but see if South African gunmen kept their pistols loaded. Avakian jerked it out, thumbed the safety forward, aimed upward toward the heart, and pulled the trigger. The pistol fired, provoking a grunt of pain. The leader went limp.

Someone jumped onto his back. Avakian twisted around violently, catching the man in the side of the head with his left elbow at the same time he jammed the pistol into the ribcage and fired again. Another body leaped onto the pile and grabbed for the pistol. Pinned to the dirt by all the weight, Avakian kept the pistol tight against his side so it couldn't be pried away and threw a left-handed stiff arm at the head in front of him to try and gain a little separation. Avakian had him by the throat and the guy was clawing with his hands and trying to bite him on the wrist. The outstretched arm held his assailant just far enough away for Avakian to swing his gun hand around the dead body that lay between them and shoot him in the side. An, "*oof*," at the shot, but he was still fighting. Avakian stuck the pistol under the man's jaw and fired again. The muzzle blast scorched his fingers but that fight was over.

A lot more people were shooting now. Avakian pushed and kneed the bodies off himself but stayed on his belly and stayed behind them. They were his only cover in the middle of the road.

Flashes from at least two pistols farther down. Someone had turned off the work light in the container. This was no time to be getting into a fire-fight, not without even knowing how much ammunition remained in the pistol he was holding. Or crank off a couple of feel-good rounds whose muzzle flash would only pinpoint his location to everyone. He patted down the bodies in front of him and found a short barrel revolver. Could have been used to blow his head off, but it was amazing what people forgot all about in high-stress situations.

A figure ran right by him. Probably from the container. Unarmed and trying to get clear. The pistols farther down the road went to a faster rate of fire and the shotgun opened up, all shooting at *that* poor fool. Who went down in mid stride and crumpled onto the road.

While that was happening Avakian sprang up and ran for the moving truck parked in front of the cannabis storage container. He leaped onto the front bumper, scrambled across the hood, and continued up the windshield. He was atop the cab when the shotgun fired again. Two quick blasts and he heard the pellets thudding into the metal below him. If you didn't aim you could miss just as easily with a shotgun as anything else.

From the top of the cab Avakian vaulted onto the truck roof, sprinting down the length of it and leaping across the four foot gap onto the top of the container. In mid air someone inside the container took a shot at him and he felt the bullet pass through his jacket. He landed with an echoing bang of metal and was instantly back on his feet and running for the end of the container.

Standing on the edge, Avakian took a look down. A family courtyard behind a shack, the entire space about the size of a maximum security jail cell. He jumped and did a parachute landing fall onto the sand. Closed in by corrugated metal on all three sides, with a couple of beaten plastic lawn chairs stacked up in one corner. He tucked the pistol under his arm and fumbled around in his pocket for the handcuff key. It was good to finally get that dangling bracelet off his left wrist. The gunfire had dogs barking frantically all over the neighborhood.

Dropping the cuffs onto the sand, Avakian readied the pistol and kicked open the flimsy wooden back door of the shack. Total pitch darkness. He reached under his belt buckle and tore out the mini butane lighter he'd taped there. Holding it arm's length from his body in case it became someone's aiming point, he sparked up.

God. Dirt floor. Beds against every wall. Furniture hammered together from scrap shipping crates. The poor family was huddled up in the corner, Mom protectively out in front of the kids, trying to hide them from whatever danger he represented. Well, at least they were hiding instead of everyone attacking him with kitchen knives to protect the homestead. Avakian just held the pistol up to his lips for silence. Not saying a word, he picked his way across the shack to the front door.

Lighter off, he opened the door to reveal a much narrower lane. Foot traffic only. One thing about regular gunfire in a neighborhood, it kept the prudent indoors.

He eased the door shut behind him and crept down the lane, staying in the shadows close to the shacks. A streetlight poked up over the roofs a short distance away and he used that for orientation. Where there was a streetlight there as a street.

In a pool of light it cast he removed the magazine from his pistol and counted out the rounds inside.

Eleven in the magazine and one in the chamber. Only five in the revolver in his pocket.

At the end of the was a packed dirt street, wide enough for cars. Bunch of people hanging around. Well, run across and attract everyone's attention or walk across. He walked.

Three steps out into the street someone yelled what sounded like, "*Mlungu!*" More voices rose up, and then, "*Fumana! Fumana!*"

People came pouring out of the darkness, and Avakian ran for his life. He sprinted across the street and into the nearest lane he could see.

Yeah, they were criminal scumbags but the whole neighborhood would try to kill *him* because he was a stranger, and he was different. And that was just the way the world worked, no sense crying about it.

Avakian knew his best time in the sprint wouldn't outpace a bunch of teenage South African track stars. He skidded to a stop at the next bend and waited. Not long. The mob came pounding up only seconds later.

It was a little known fact that most soldiers were terrible pistol shots, as were most cops. As Avakian advanced through the ranks of the Army and found himself more frequently armed with only a pistol, he made sure he mastered the weapon. He shot in International Defensive Pistol Association matches whenever he was in the States, but he was a bit rusty lately.

The mob's point man was carrying a handgun. Avakian also saw a few pangas, African machetes. He leaned out over the corner and sprang his ambush, firing until the point man dropped. The mass of people came to a screeching halt, everyone falling over everyone else. Avakian fired continuously across the width of the lane, shifting from one target to another. By the time his ammunition ran out the stream of humanity had fled in the opposite direction, everyone in the back running for the lives and pulling the rest along with them.

Six bodies were splayed across the lane, some of them groaning. Avakian trotted up and retrieved another automatic pistol from the dirt, checking the chamber and magazine. This one was an issue South African military Beretta copy with a full 15-round magazine.

A couple of single pistol shots rang out behind him. Signal shots? That wasn't such a bad thing. Periodic gunfire would make it hard to zero in on him if he had to do some more shooting.

Don't dawdle, he told himself. He didn't know the neighborhood, and the only thing that would keep them from encircling him was continuous movement. The rules were pretty simple. Always move unexpectedly, and never in a straight line. Never try to hide—always keep moving. If you let yourself get halted or pinned down you're dead.

The lane ended in a corrugated metal fence. Avakian grabbed an open edge and yanked the sheet of metal off the post. He ducked through the gap and found himself in a slightly larger backyard than the first. A dark blur shot out of the darkness at him. Avakian fired instinctively and there was a loud yelp. Shit. The poor dog was just doing his job. A window curtain moved and Avakian dropped into a shooting crouch. A face appeared in the window. A little boy. Avakian let the muzzle fall. I'm sorry I shot your dog, son.

A new noise attracted his attention. At the far end

of the yard was a line of chicken coops, individual cages stacked one on top of the other. Cramped as the quarters the humans around here occupied. But at least there was only one chicken per cage, to keep them from pecking each other to death.

Avakian stuck the pistol in his pocket and climbed up the stack of cages. He had his hands on top and went to push himself up when one hand went right through the flimsy wood and down into the cage. The top row collapsed and he lost his footing. Terrified chickens came shooting out at him like feathery missiles, squalling hysterically.

He landed hard on the ground, spitting out chicken fluff and manure. The shack door opened and a man came rushing out, shouting and brandishing a shovel. Avakian fired a shot over his head. That made the chicken farmer think twice about things and he scrambled back inside.

Avakian took a run at the fence and used the collapsed coop to boost himself up. A couple of kicks and he was over and into another lane.

Move, move. He trotted down the lane. At the next turn he paused to peek around the corner. Nothing there, but he thought he heard footsteps behind him. He turned back to listen, but didn't hear anything more. He trotted forward again, then stopped abruptly, cocking his ears. Yes, a couple of footsteps behind, then silence. Someone was there. Following him. Pacing him.

As soon as Avakian started moving again a young boy's voice behind him shouted, "*Uyaba!*"

Avakian rushed back down the lane but the footsteps retreated away from him. More signal shots popped off in the distance.

Shit. Maybe he'd chased him off. He began to run. But behind him the boy's breathless voice continued. "*Uyaba! Uyaba!*"

Avakian stopped. Both the trailing footsteps and the shouting stopped. He was frantic for another solution, but there wasn't one. The bottoms of most of the shacks were lined with rocks. He grabbed one and sprinted for the next turn. The shouting resumed behind him. "*Uyaba! Uyaba! Uyaba!*"

As Avakian went around the corner he stopped but hurled the rock farther down the lane ahead. It clanged off a metal wall. He dropped to the ground and aimed the pistol around the corner. The footsteps behind him kept advancing and a moving shadow appeared down the lane before halting abruptly, perhaps sensing something. Before the shadow could disappear Avakian squeezed the trigger.

After the report of the shot died away there was the sound of a boy crying in pain. Avakian was instantly sick to his stomach. He pushed himself to his feet and ran away from the sound.

The lane ended in a wooden fence with a padlocked gate. Metal spike strips atop the fence. Avakian was preparing to shoot the lock off when he was stopped by the sound of a vehicle roaring down a nearby road. Lots of loud voices over the engine noise. Full of reinforcements?

He ran back down the lane and yanked a couple of pieces of laundry off a drying line. Winding them around his hands he leaped up on the fence and used the spike strips to pull himself up. Swinging up a leg, he wedged his shoe in between the spikes and threw himself over. On the way down his jacket caught on a spike. He dangled there for a few seconds, feet suspended a few embarrassing inches off the ground, before his weight ripped the cloth free.

Touching earth he threw the wraps off his hands and took up the pistol again. The wooden slat fence bordered the lane on both sides for about twenty feet before opening up onto another street.

Through the fence slats Avakian could see the intersection and a pickup truck just below the corner streetlight. The pickup was in fact full of armed men. Just stopped broadside to him and about to unload. He couldn't let them get spread out.

With one knee on the ground and the frame of the pistol braced against the side of the fence, Avakian sighted in carefully. Always shoot the guy yelling orders first.

A careful trigger squeeze and the pistol bounced in his hand. The guy yelling orders dropped to the ground and Avakian fired much faster into the bed of the pickup. They definitely weren't expecting this. Some fell, some ran.

He'd be out of ammo soon, so he quickly pulled the revolver out of his jacket pocket, stuck it in his waistband for a fast backup, and charged them.

Avakian advanced with both hands wrapped around the pistol, arms locked outstretched. As he came closer he could see from that new angle a gunman trying to drag another away. He shot them both. Another figure broke and ran. Avakian shot him in the back.

Approaching the front of the pickup a head popped up over the hood and Avakian snapped off a shot. His pistol slide locked back, the magazine empty. He dropped it and pulled the revolver from his waistband. There was no one in the cab. Facing the front of the pickup, he bent his torso to the right, briefly exposing himself to the other side of the vehicle. A terrified kid sitting next to the front wheel, holding his pistol sideways like in the movies, blazed away at him and of course missed. Avakian shot him in the head.

The tip of a shotgun barrel poked around the back of the pickup. Bad mistake. As soon as the owner's head showed Avakian squeezed the trigger. The hammer clicked—the cartridge didn't fire. The gunman swung around the back of the pickup, bringing his shotgun up. Avakian cycled the revolver trigger as fast as he could. *Click. Click.* The cylinder spun on the last round.

BANG! BOOM! The pistol fired—the shotgun fired. The gunman fell back and the shotgun blast hit the sand in front of Avakian's feet, throwing up a shower of dust. Avakian dashed forward through the cloud, prepared to club him to death with the empty pistol, but the gunman was stretched out on his back, staring sightlessly up at the stars.

Avakian's entire body was shaking involuntarily. Brazilian revolvers were notorious for light hammer hits, striking the cartridge primers too lightly to ignite them.

He knew from experience that the only thing that would stop the shaking was forcing himself to move, to do something. He began harvesting pistols from the ground, firing a couple of rounds to find two that worked and salvaging the ammunition from the rest. Fortunately South African gangbangers used 9mm automatics almost exclusively. The dead shotgunner had a few extra shells in his pocket. Avakian transferred them to his and tossed the sawed-off double barrel 12 gauge into the cab of the pickup.

Get out of here, he told himself. He abandoned his labors and jumped into the front seat of the pickup. Shit, no keys. Roaring under the adrenaline overdose that had set off the shaking in the first place, he was struck by indecision. Find something to rip open the steering column or frisk the bodies in the street for keys?

If he'd been able to watch himself he would have seen a man literally rocking back and forth in the front seat of a pickup as he tried to make up his mind. This little dance came to a halt when an automatic rifle opened up on him from across the street.

Chapter Twenty-Two

THE FIRE DROVE Avakian across the cab of the pickup, out the other door, and into the street. One of the tires blew and he was showered with pieces of door window glass.

The shakes were gone. It seemed counterintuitive, but sometimes getting shot at again brought you back together.

His trained ear identified the sound of the bullets passing overhead. Not an AK-47. He'd been shot at by enough of those to know. Probably a stolen South African army weapon.

He reached back in the open door and grabbed the shotgun off the seat. Right, one barrel had already been fired at him. He broke it open and replaced that spent shell with a fresh one.

A shotgun against an automatic rifle wasn't a good matchup. Avakian aimed it straight up in the air and fired. The streetlight blew out and the intersection was plunged into darkness. The next barrel was aimed a few feet over, into the transformer box on the light pole.

Right after that blast there was an eerie hum and then the box blew with an incredible shower of sparks. All the lights went out in the entire block. The same instant Avakian was on his feet and sprinting down the street. As he'd hoped, after that moment of surprise whoever was manning the automatic rifle picked himself up off the ground and resumed firing on the pickup truck.

Avakian ran down to the next intersection and paused to reload the shotgun and see if he was being chased. No one behind him. It was about time he had a little luck.

He clicked the shotgun action closed and began looking around for another lane when he had the sudden revelation that his strategy sucked. Sneaking around these dead-end lanes would not only take all night, it would give his pursuers more than enough time to get organized. Every time he had an unfortunate encounter with a local they could run a vehicle down a side street to cut him off, just like before. Not to mention that there was no guarantee he could continue to survive firefights and pick up new weapons all night long.

So think, he told himself. How would you make your way through South Central Los Angeles, a Manila *barrio*, or a Rio *favella*? Not by strolling along, that's for damn sure. You'd do it at a dead run with a shotgun in your hands. Anyone with half a brain would want to stay clear of a nut like that, white or black. Anyone who wanted to mess with him would have to catch him, and anyone who wanted to shoot at him would have to hit a moving target.

Well, it was worth a try. How fast can you run a mile, Avakian? Six minutes in street shoes? The word of his presence in the neighborhood would have to travel faster than that—he'd take those odds any day. As best as he could figure, the nearest main roads outside the township were south and east. So he'd go north. He found the Southern Cross up in the night sky for orientation. Okay, here we go.

So Avakian began to run through the streets of the township. He never stayed on any long street, instead turning left or right at the next intersection before continuing north again at the next one over. At each turn he stopped for an instant, scanning for slowly moving cars on the street before resuming his pace. Good thing it wasn't during the heat of the day—he was already feeling dehydrated.

He skirted some kind of recreation area, dead brown grass where barefoot kids were kicking soccer balls. He ran past people eating in tuck shops and drinking in shebeens. Some yelled when he ran by. A few mothers dashed off their fronts steps to snatch up children playing in the street. But no one chased him.

Down the long axis of a street he could see a main road with two lanes of cars. Drawing nearer he could see what was between him and the highway. The township cemetery.

Avakian ducked off the road and followed the line of shacks bordering the cemetery fence so he could get a closer look. He paused for a moment, the shotgun pointed down his back trail to make sure he hadn't been followed. No one there. He lay down on the ground next to the fence to get the lay of the land.

The cemetery seemed to be a long narrow rectangle about half a mile long and a few hundred yards wide. Several roads cut across it and one went right down the entire length, probably for hearses and mourners. A few isolated trees whose lower limbs had all been stripped away for firewood. And a gently rolling landscape studded with monuments.

Crossing an open area was dumb, but each side of the cemetery was jam-packed with shacks. Sometimes you had to take the less shitty choice.

He wouldn't be traveling the roads here, or going through the regular entrances. The fence wasn't very substantial, just enough to keep the shacks from spreading into the cemetery grounds. He followed it until he found one of the inevitable gaps kids always opened up as shortcuts.

Slipping through, Avakian transferred the pistols to the small of his back and crawled on his belly until he reached the first line of monuments. No manicured lawns and perpetual care here. Just uncut weeds and bare dirt. And if everything else in the townships didn't move you to tears, this was enough to make the hardest heart weep. The headstones and monuments were notable only by how few there were. There were many, many more pitiful nailed-together wooden crosses and propped up plates of scrap metal with the deceased's name, age, and date of death painted on them by brush, in freehand. Age five, age seven, age two days.

Avakian shook it off and opened up his senses. He scanned the entire area slowly. Looking for anything out of the ordinary, any telltale movement. Take your time, he told himself. Take your time or die quick.

There was something out there. He just plain felt it. And he was not about to move until he convinced himself otherwise. No matter how tantalizing that highway was, almost close enough to touch it. And the headlights of those damned cars messing with his night vision.

The wind shifted direction almost imperceptibly, and Avakian caught a whiff of marijuana. He pointed his nose directly into the faint evening breeze and sighted down it like a rifle barrel. He stared at the area with total concentration until he caught just the briefest orange bob of light as the joint was passed between two headstones. Directly on a little rise in the right center of the cemetery. Avakian didn't doubt that if he'd been a little closer he would have caught the murmur of conversation. They might be dumb about their light and noise discipline, but they'd definitely picked the key terrain that commanded the whole area.

Now the problem. He didn't doubt that he'd be able to stalk right up on whomever was out there. But then what? There was more than one so he'd definitely have to do some shooting. Maybe shoot a bunch of kids just sitting in the cemetery getting high. And even if they weren't innocent, all someone would have to do is draw a line through each pile of bodies he left behind and follow the path straight for the airport. These crazy gangster kids probably wouldn't think twice about rolling right into the terminal to have a nice little shootout there, cops and security be damned.

So what to do? He couldn't risk trying to sneak around them. If he was seen then the firefight would go down on their terms, something he wasn't willing to accept.

Okay, so think of something. Break it down. He needed a distraction. Maybe the shotgun. But how? While he was trying to work it out Avakian was absently rolling a couple of stalks of dead grass between his fingers. He stopped and gave that his full attention. Yeah. Boy Scout camp. He felt around in his pocket. The butane lighter was still there.

He crawled around the row of graves to see what was on hand. The bunches of now-dried flowers people had left there were tied with string. Soon he had enough to make the right length. Someone had sunk a broken-off car antenna into the ground as a miniature flag pole. The ANC flag tied to it was faded almost beyond recognition.

Avakian used his suit jacket to lash the shotgun to the arms of a substantial wooden cross, twisting the whole thing in minute adjustments until both barrels were pointed at the hill. He packed in dirt and rocks where he'd loosened the earth at the base, to keep the cross from moving. The antenna was plunged into the ground right behind the shotgun. He tied a sting to the tip and the other end to the base of the cross, bending the antenna down until it was compressed nearly to the shape of a U, the tip almost touching the ground. Then another string taut from the shotgun triggers to the tip of the antenna also.

His next step was to build a hollow pyramid, layering first dry grass then the bunches of dry flowers, directly under the string holding the antenna to the ground. He covered the pyramid with his pocket hand-kerchief, leaving a vent hole on top. As a final touch he scattered the extra shotgun shells and a few 9mm rounds throughout the pyramid at varying distances from the center.

One last check to make sure everything was right and he stuck his hand into the center of the pyramid and set fire to the dry grass with his lighter.

As soon as it caught Avakian was up and moving in

a bent-over lope down the row of monuments to put as much distance as possible between his mechanism and himself.

In Boy Scout camp they'd had to start a fire with a single match, and the first one that burned through a string suspended above the blaze was the winner. In this case when the string burned through the antenna would whip back up and, hopefully, pull the shotgun trigger. But if that didn't work the fire would eventually ignite the ammunition.

When he was a couple of hundred yards away from it Avakian began working his way toward the highway. Much more carefully. He crawled across the open spaces between the rows of graves and followed every dip in the terrain. He moved quickly only when he was shielded from view of the hill, which he knew when he couldn't see it himself.

He kept an eye on his watch. With luck it would take the fire a little extra time to burn through the handkerchief, which would hopefully keep the flame from being too visible too soon. If it went out he'd really be pissed. No, he could definitely see a little glow from the fire, though the guys on the hill hadn't yet. Smoking weed on ambush just wasn't tactically sound.

He was contemplating alternate moves when a sharp bang went off to this right rear. Damn that was great. He could have sworn he heard the pellets tinkling among the grave stones on the hill. At that range they wouldn't be traveling fast enough to do more than scare them, but that was the whole point.

Instantly four figures sprang up and opened fire in the direction of his booby trap. So they were kids smoking grass, but they weren't *just* kids smoking grass.

Another pop from behind as one of the rounds

he'd sprinkled in the campfire cooked off from the heat. The hill opened up with another few seconds of wild shooting. The old cartridge in the fire trick was a great distraction device, but not as good for making the sale as those shotgun pellets landing in their midst.

No doubt someone was on their cell phone calling for help. With their attention totally focused on the mock firefight Avakian was able to get up and move a lot quicker. Once he was behind them he went as fast as he dared without risking tripping over something and making a lot of noise.

By the time help arrived and everyone worked up the gumption to see what they'd been shooting at all they'd find was a small smoldering fire. In the darkness they might even miss the shotgun lashed to the cross.

Each time a round popped in the fire there was a new round of shooting that left a smile on Avakian's face.

He reached the wood and metal fence that was the cemetery's far border. Once again he worked his way down until he found a section that had been sliced away near a post. He slipped though and scrambled up a short rise to the highway.

Just in time for the latest shock of the night. It wasn't the highway. It was another township road, and there was another line of shacks directly before him in the darkness.

Chapter Twenty-Three

OKAY, don't panic, Avakian told himself. Keep the head and think this through. About five hundred yards away on his right the road intersected north. That north intersection *had* to run into the highway. As if on cue, a plane roared overhead. Okay, airport still on the right.

That was his way out, but he couldn't take the road. Someone was bound to be sitting on a township exit. Where was the nearest lane into the shacks? Fifty, seventy-five yards on his right. No other choice.

He slid back down into the depression next to the road and followed it east. The sound of a car approaching and he flattened out in the weeds. The headlights swept overhead and disappeared.

Moving again. He kept one eye on the road and the other eye back in the cemetery. No more gunfire. No lights of cars on the cemetery roads yet.

About fifty yards. Take a look. Avakian crawled back up to the road. Maybe another twenty yards to the lane. He slid down and covered that distance. Back up. Car coming down the road. He pressed his face into the dirt. Human eyes, like animal eyes, shined at night under direct light.

Two more cars coming. He'd need a completely clear road. When they passed he jumped up and sprinted across. The dirt median on the other side was full of footprints, so he didn't have to worry about that.

No signs of alarm had proceeded him, so it would be an ambush or nothing. Which would seem to rule out both running and creeping. That would just let someone know they had the right target. Other than the white guy in the black polo shirt and the hat, he thought ruefully. Well, let's see what happens.

Avakian walked down the lane. He heard the sounds of daily life coming from inside their shacks, which was good. Too much silence would be a tip-off. Footsteps coming toward him. He kept going. Two men passed him in the darkness, smelling heavily of beer. Avakian nodded politely. One of them did a double take. He said, "*Mlungu*," to his friend, and then something else in Xhosa. Their conversation continued back and forth, but they didn't turn around and follow him, they just kept going.

A few people crossed the lane in front of him, but their strides and body language were normal. Now he heard two things from up ahead. The sound of highway traffic, and music. One was good. The other might not be.

The lane made a long gentle curve, and as Avakian rounded it the space opened up a little wider.

Five men, ranging from their teens to their thirties, were hanging around the front steps of a shack. Drinking beer, listening to music, and loudly playing dice on the concrete steps. Not good, Avakian thought.

The youngest saw him first and elbowed one of the others. In a second or two they were all turned around and looking down the lane at him, talking quietly to each other. Avakian kept walking toward them.

Probably the middle among the age ranges, a tough looking kid in his mid twenties, got up and sauntered into the center of the lane. The others followed him, with varying degrees of enthusiasm. Which was typical of group behavior.

Avakian made his call. These guys weren't gangsters. Or at least they weren't the kind that had been chasing him around all night. They just weren't going to let an opportunity for fun or profit pass them by. He stopped about twenty feet from them. One said something in Xhosa, and the rest laughed.

Avakian reached around his back and slowly pulled out first one and then his second pistol, holding them by his side. Anyone who knew shooting knew that one pistol in two hands was a lot more dangerous than one in each, but the world spoke the language of movies so if that's how they were expecting to be impressed then that was what you had to give them.

Consternation from a couple of them, who started edging away. The tough twenty-something said something sharp, and they held their ground.

Avakian wasn't going to shoot unless someone went for a weapon. Or they didn't get out of his way. He knew the deal about not backing down. When you were poor sometimes all you had was your pride and your reputation, which made it all the more important to hang on to both. With no expression on his face, he made a show of loudly cocking back the hammer of first one and then the other pistol. C'mon now, who was going to be the voice of reason?

As usual, it was the one in his thirties. The oldest always had the most to lose. He quickly addressed the group. Avakian couldn't understand Xhosa, but he could always recognize the voice of reason.

The oldest had a hot argument with the tough guy, and then started pushing the rest back toward the steps. The tough guy stood his ground until the last, then allowed himself to be pulled out of the way.

Avakian resumed walking. As he passed them he didn't get into a staring contest but he also didn't take his eyes off them. Some fear, some neutrality. Some defiance. That was okay. Passing by he kept his front to them, turning and walking backward down the lane.

When they were out of sight and he was sure they weren't coming he allowed himself a couple of deep breaths and a feeling of quiet satisfaction at having finally handled something well.

The lane continued to curve and he saw passing headlights in the space between two shacks. That had to be the highway.

Chapter Twenty-Four

REACHING the end of the shacks Avakian dropped to one knee and checked out the area. Yes, that really was the highway. Finally. He'd probably only traveled a couple hundred yards from the cemetery through this group of shacks.

The highway crossed across his front, and just to his right was an underpass access road. That had to be the airport road.

No parked cars. No pedestrians. It looked clear. But don't get careless now. Stay away from that underpass.

Avakian flicked the safeties of both pistols to de-cock the hammers and returned them to his waist-band. Now he pulled the polo shirt up and over them for concealment.

He jogged across the grassy median and the town-ship access road that came off the highway. Up a sand and grass rise to the highway itself. Not too busy at this time of night. A sign told him it was the N2 highway. He was definitely going the right way. Waiting for an opening, he sprinted across the westbound lane and then the eastbound.

And there was the airport off to his right, the terminals maybe a mile away. Avakian supposed he owed at least a bit of gratitude to the white racists, for locating the townships where no one else would want to live.

He squatted down in the grass beside the highway to do some planning. Between him and the airport was the airport industrial area. He'd gotten a look at that both times he'd flown in. This close to the township there had to be razor wire fences, attack dogs, and security patrols, so going overland in that direction was an iffy proposition. Only a lunatic would pick up a hitchhiker in this locale. Walking on the road it would only be a matter of time before he was stopped by the cops, and he definitely didn't fancy a trip to the police station.

The best and safest thing to do would be to follow the road but stay off it. Yeah, that was it.

Avakian came down off the high ground the highway was built on. He'd just crossed the airport exit road when a set of lights turned off the highway. A taxi. Service light on, but no passengers. Heading for the airport to get in the taxi queue. What the hell, you probably needed to be crazy to be a South African cab driver.

Avakian stepped up to the side of the road, took off his hat, and waved it at the oncoming cab.

The front end wobbled a bit, as if the driver couldn't quite believe it. At first the cab was definitely not going to stop, but suddenly it slowed down to take a look at him. Avakian leaned down to be eye level with the driver. He knew if he rushed the window the cabbie would definitely take off.

The driver was black. "Hi, how are you?" Avakian called out in good American English. "My rental car broke down, and I really need to get to the airport."

The driver was incredulous. "Sir, are you aware of how dangerous it is here?"

"Well, what can I say?" Avakian replied. "My car broke down here."

"Did you call for help?"

"The rental company said it might take an hour to come get me. Would you mind taking me to the airport?"

The cab door locks popped up. "Get in. Get in, sir. Quickly, please."

"I really appreciate it," said Avakian.

As soon as he got in the locks snapped down and the driver pulled out fast. "It's a terribly dangerous area, sir. Did you know the townships were right over there?"

"Really?" said Avakian. "Well, I'm glad you came along."

"I cannot believe the rental company told you an hour, sir. That is so irresponsible."

"It's been nothing but setbacks today," said Avakian. "What's your name?"

"Daniel, sir."

"I'm John. I guess you saved me from the lion's den, Daniel."

The driver suddenly quoted, ""Then the king commanded, and they brought Daniel, and cast him into the den of lions. Now the king spake and said unto Daniel, Thy God whom thou servest continually, he will deliver thee." Book of Daniel, chapter six, sir."

"I'll say amen to that," Avakian replied. He'd noted the crucifix dangling from the rearview mirror. He leaned back in the seat and reached into the front of his trousers.

Anxious eyes in the rearview mirror. "Whatever are you doing, sir?"

"Oh, just getting my wallet out," said Avakian. "When I travel I always keep an old expired passport in my pocket, and a dummy wallet with a few dollars in it. So if I get my pocket picked or I'm held up it's no big hassle. I keep my real passport and wallet in a pocket I had tailored inside my pants, near the crotch. No one likes to go poking around there."

"That is a most excellent idea, sir," Daniel said.

"I definitely recommend it," said Avakian.

The turned into the airport. Avakian said, "You can drop me in front of the parking area."

"Not your rental agency, sir?"

"No, I don't want to deal with them anymore tonight. I'll just call and tell them to pick up the car."

"But what of your luggage, sir?"

"I've already sent it on ahead," said Avakian.

Daniel pulled up in front of the airport parking lot and flipped the meter. "A very good evening to you, sir."

Avakian passed a wad of folded cash through the security window. "Thanks a lot, Daniel."

As he shut the door the window rolled down. "Sir, wait! This is a thousand euros. This is much too much."

"No it's not," said Avakian. "After all, you saved my life."

Daniel was sitting there holding out the money in his fist, tears in his eyes. "God bless you, sir."

Avakian just waved as he passed across the front of the cab. Yeah, there were some good people in the world.

As he walked through the parking lots Avakian kept an eye on the security cameras. When he hit a blind spot he dropped between two cars and quickly broke both pistols down into their component parts. And as he made his way to the international terminal dropped the pieces into a succession of trash cans.

The new terminal had a glass front with a shallow V-shaped roof and V-shaped supporting struts. Avakian paused to brush himself off as best he could and tuck his polo shirt back in before crossing the passenger drop-off road.

The doors whisked shut behind him. The light was bright and the air was conditioned. Two policemen were stationed beside the terminal door. They gave him a quick once-over, but that was it. If you were going to be dirty and disheveled in a South African airport, definitely be white.

Avakian automatically reached for the BlackBerry that wasn't on his hip, shook his head, and went to check the terminal screens for departing flights. Yeah, that had to be it.

He went to the KLM counter and joined the line. It wasn't long. Most people went the automated check-in route.

The agent was blonde and blue eyed and tiny. Even a few inches shorter than him. "Yes, sir?"

"I hope you can help me," Avakian said. "I was at a barbecue with some friends tonight." He patted his clothes self-consciously. "I got a call that my mother is very ill. I need to get to her as soon as possible. Is there a seat available on your Flight 598, the direct to Amsterdam?"

"Let me check," she said, tapping on the computer. "Sir, we have one first class and one coach seat available."

"I'll take the first class," said Avakian, setting his passport and credit card on the counter. "One way."

"I'm afraid the fare is 47,671.4 rand, sir."

Avakian did the conversion in his head. Six thousand dollars or so. "That's fine."

"Would you like me to arrange connections to the United States, sir? Or any other location," she added.

Avakian thought about it. "No, thank you. I'll see about available connections after we land in Amsterdam tomorrow morning."

"Very good, sir. Will you be checking any luggage?"

"No, I didn't even take time to pack. I'll buy some clothes and toilet articles at the duty free mall."

She printed out his ticket. "You are all checked in, sir. Your flight departs at 12:20 AM." She handed him the ticket, his card, and his passport. "I wish your mother a speedy recovery."

"Thank you so much for your kindness," Avakian replied.

As the Boeing 777 taxied down the runway the German businessman turned to ask the bald American in the first class seat next to him what he did for a living. But Peter Avakian was sound asleep. Not the sleep of the just, or the virtuous, or the clear of conscience. The sleep of the utterly exhausted middle aged man.

Chapter Twenty-Five

AVAKIAN KNOCKED ON THE DOOR. Jeez it was cold. The snow drifts on either side of the walkway were taller than him.

The door opened. Doctor Judith Rose stood in the doorway looking at him. Winter complexion, and the girl was pale to begin with. She pushed the dark bangs off her forehead and stared him down with those enormous brown eyes. God she was beautiful.

Avakian stood there looking back at her. He didn't say a word.

"You said you were going to show up at my door," she said.

"I did," Avakian replied. All his rehearsal flew out the window, and he was almost afraid to say anything.

Another long pause. "Is that for me?" she said, referring to the small gift-wrapped box in his hand.

He handed it to her.

She opened the box. "Chocolate truffles?"

"I know you hate flowers," Avakian said.

She popped one into her mouth and chewed it

over, making him wait. "Did you bring me any presents from Africa?" she asked finally.

"Kind of," Avakian said.

"What do you mean, kind of?"

"They're in the car. I was kind of waiting to see if you jammed the truffles up my ass first."

She shook her head. "No one has balls as big as you, Pete. No one."

"That's why I have such an unusual walk," Avakian said.

Judy stepped down from the doorway onto the salt-covered step, bent forward slightly, and kissed him. She pulled him tight, and he hugged her tighter.

"Thank you," he said quietly when the kiss broke.

"For what?" she asked.

"For the outcome I'd been hoping for."

"You'd better come inside," she said. "You look like those balls are about to drop off."

"It has been a while since I've been this cold."

"Are you hungry?" she said.

"Can I take you out?"

"No," she said. "I'll cook something."

Chapter Twenty-Six

JUDY ROSE LAZILY SIFTED a handful of Maui beach sand through her fingers. "All right, I admit it. You can only do so much skiing."

Stretched out beside her on the towel, Avakian rolled on his side and eyed her from under his beach hat. "Sorry for dragging you away from the slopes and all those skiers with broken bones, but I just couldn't take that Colorado cold anymore. Too much time in the southern hemisphere."

She slapped the copy of Vanity Fair magazine down next to them. It was open to an article. The facing picture was of Herbert Payne-Best and Pieter De Wet being led off to court in handcuffs and leg irons by Benin gendarmes. The title was: **The Coup, by Patience Mbatha**. "I'm ready to ask questions now."

"Hang on a second," said Avakian. He reached into the cooler and popped open another beer. "Okay, I promised I'd answer them, fully and truthfully, whenever you were ready."

"I'm holding you to it. First of all, is this accurate?"

He took a sip of beer. "Sort of."

"This is not a good start, Pete. What do you mean, sort of?"

"Well, all the essential facts are correct. The truth, as always, is about what does or doesn't get left out."

"All right. We'll get to that. Next. How did you do this?"

"You're going to have to narrow that down a bit, honey."

"Fine. How did you arrange for all of them to be captured when they landed in Benin?"

"Oh, that part wasn't hard at all. When I landed in Amsterdam I took the shuttle to Paris. Dragged a friend of mine at the French Ministry of Defense out of a meeting, threw him in a cab, and drove him over to the Benin embassy for a talk with the ambassador. I knew that if I just talked to Benin they might be dumb enough to think they could stop the mercenaries all by themselves, and end up with half their army slaughtered."

"So there were...," she consulted the article, "two battalions of French paratroopers and marine commandos waiting for them as they landed. And two French destroyers stopping the ships out at sea."

"Yeah, that's why I put them on freighters," said Avakian.

Judy looked at him over her sunglasses. "You did what?"

"They were originally going to go in by plane," Avakian explained. "They might have made a couple of stops along the way that I knew nothing about. People think that fighter planes can intercept airliners without any problem, but it's not so easy. Not to mention a very real chance of the airport and a bunch of innocent travelers getting all shot up. Stick them on a freighter and everyone's all wrapped up in one nice little package. And freighters aren't outrunning naval warships."

"You planned that right from the beginning?" she said.

"Yeah. But, needless to say, that wasn't the argument I made when I talked them into going by ship."

Wordlessly, she held up the page with Payne-Best and De Wet being led away in handcuffs.

"Everyone was quoting from *The Godfather*, anyway," said Avakian. "Well, revenge is a dish best served cold. White mercenaries trying to take over a country? They'll be in the Benin prison system forever. And South Africa sure as hell ain't going to intervene for them. From what I've seen of Benin, I don't even want to think about what their prisons are like. I hope the boys enjoy rice gruel for the next twenty years."

"Is that what they serve in African prisons?" Judy asked.

"If they're lucky. And, of course, as many cockroaches and centipedes as they can catch. For the protein."

"Don't make me heave," she warned.

"Sorry."

Still holding up the article, Judy's impatient finger was tapping the name Patience Mbatha.

"To tell you the truth," said Avakian. "I expected her to be a better writer. But hell, a story like that sells itself."

"Pete, I'm not talking about the quality of her prose. She doesn't mention you at all."

"Well, that's what I was talking about, what you leave out."

"But you risked your life to stop them, and you're not even mentioned."

"That was the one real favor she did me," said Avakian. "But realistically, what was she going to do? Write that she sold me out to get chopped up by South African drug runners?"

"That's what I'm talking about!" Judy shouted. "She sold you out to get killed."

"It was the smart move," Avakian said.

"WHAT?"

"It was the smart move. She didn't really know me, she didn't know what was going to happen. She made a deal. To tell you the truth, it was just as well. I don't think I would have been able to get her through that township." He placed his hand on her thigh. "There's only one Judy Rose."

"Don't try to mollify me. She nearly got you killed. You could have escaped. You put yourself in danger to try and help her. You could have betrayed her, and you didn't."

"Yeah, but to be honest I really didn't go out of my way to keep her out of trouble. I did a hell of a lot of fancy dancing around that issue."

"You would be temperamentally incapable of doing what she did," Judy informed him.

"Yeah, meaning: not as smart."

"And how did she get away with it?" Judy demanded.

"I'm just guessing, of course, but Payne-Best probably liked the idea of someone writing an account of his brilliant exploits. He's just the kind of idiot who'd think it would be good for future business, and all that.

Nothing like the threat of death to help you in negotiating the parameters of an article with a reporter. And don't think that isn't done every day. Leave out Volkov and Okong and whatever we say, or we kill you. To which she replies: sure guys, whatever. Then they all go off to do their thing and they all end up in the bag. Now she can write whatever she wants, hale and healthy."

"Unbelievable," said Judy. "Do you know she sold the movie rights to the article for a fortune. She's going to write the screenplay."

"I never thought so before," Avakian mused. "But it seems you *can* bargain with the devil. And when you sell him your soul, he keeps his promises."

"You're taking this rather well," she said.

"I am enjoying the fact that I'm sitting with a beautiful woman on a beautiful beach instead of being dead. And the bad guys are paying for it. It would be kind of inappropriate to complain, wouldn't it?"

Judy smiled at him fondly and then looked out at the horizon. "Did you know I'd been beating myself up for being a complete and total bitch every single day from the moment I broke up with you?"

"Oh, don't take that to heart. I've never had to be the one who stayed at home and waited, and I can just imagine what it must have been like. Especially you just *knowing* I was in some kind of jam."

"And it was even worse that I imagined, by the way."

"If it means anything," said Avakian. "It was worse than anything *I* could have imagined, too."

"And yet you came back for me," she said.

"Well, I love you," he replied.

She rolled over on top of him and kissed him. "Still."

"I told you you'd have to tell me to get lost in person." He paused. "Sometimes all you can do is give a friend a chance to change their mind."

She kissed him again.

"Can I ask you a question?" he said.

Judy did a pushup off his chest and held herself there, suspended over him. "You?" she exclaimed, stunned. "The man who never asks questions. Amazing. Are you going to ask me if I was with anyone after I broke up with you?"

"No," he said. Mainly so she wouldn't ask him.

"You wouldn't, would you." She hit him on the shoulder. "Okay, go ahead."

"This is just something that I've been thinking about lately. When we first made love, you kind of jumped out at me without your clothes on. What was your rationale behind that?"

"Why do you want to know?"

"I've just been wondering. Was there something about me that led you take me by surprise like that?"

"You really want to know?" she said.

"That's why I asked."

Dropping back down on his chest, she paused, nose to nose with him, as if thinking it over. "Pete, you talk to women the exact same way you talk to men. I found that incredibly attractive—I think all women would. But it also comes off as total indifference on your part as to whether you sleep with a woman or not. That's also quite tantalizing. I wanted you, and no one wants to be rejected, so I arranged things so no heterosexual man would reject me."

"For the record, this heterosexual man had no intention of rejecting you," he said.

"That notwithstanding."

Avakian mulled it over. "Thanks, Judy. I appreciate that."

"You're welcome. Now I have some more questions."

He set the cold bottle of beer on the small of her back, making her yelp. "You don't say."

Judy struck him on the shoulder again. Then rolled off him and rummaged around in her beach bag, pulling out a copy of The Economist she'd been hoarding for the right moment. Flipping it open to the dog-eared page, she presented him with another article:

MLND Leader Arrested By Nigerian Secret Agents in the Congo.

"It would have to be The Economist, wouldn't it?" said Avakian. "No American media would cover a story like that. And they wonder why they're going out of business."

"Pete," said Judy.

"Oh, that was another deal they were working on," said Avakian. "Guns and drugs for the Congo militias. I found the document in Payne-Best's safe. Figured when the coup went south that Okong might run to Congo, so I called a general friend of mine in Nigeria. I owed him a solid anyway. Besides, I felt bad about having to break a promise to go shooting with him. Maybe Okong can worm his way out it eventually—it's the Nigerian government after all—but at least he's off the streets for now."

"And you did the Russian, too? How?"

"When we were aboard ship I took a look at my buddy Andrei's phone while he was sleeping. What a pain in the ass that was. My Russian has just gone to hell. I had to download a Russian-English dictionary on my satellite phone to read all those texts. Got a good idea of Volkov's future itinerary."

"But the DEA?" she said.

"I've got more friends in Drug Enforcement than I do in the CIA, that's for sure. Plus the fact that the DEA hates the CIA for turning a blind eye to warlords and drug dealers they happen to find useful. Turns out the DEA wanted Volkov for running guns to Colombian guerrillas in exchange for coke. They managed to coax him to Thailand and get him arrested. But that's not a done deal, either. He's got enough money and enough pull with the Russian government to make extradition from Thailand an iffy proposition. But at the present he and Okong are preoccupied with their own troubles and not looking for me."

At that moment Judy experienced a realization. "Is that why we're in Maui? Because someone might be looking for us in Denver?"

"Well, look at this as a really nice extended vacation," said Avakian. "And if a side effect is getting us away from our last known address, then so be it."

She just stared at him and shook her head. "You know, Pete, that whole Doctor Lecter thing you have going on sometimes can just get to be a little too much, you know?"

"I have no idea what you're talking about," Avakian replied.

Judy shook her head fondly, and happened to glance at her arm, which was laying across his. She held it up as if by way of comparison. "This is an absolute disgrace."

"Okay, I now have another question," said Avakian. "What are you talking about?"

"This," she said, shaking her forearm at him. "You tan more under a beach umbrella than I would on the surface of the sun."

"You know, doctor, there's this little thing called skin cancer," Avakian said reprovingly.

"Yes, yes, I know all that," she said impatiently. "But it still would be nice to know what it's like to be tan. As opposed to freckled."

"It's overrated, I assure you," said Avakian. He held up a plastic bottle. "How about if I apply some more sunscreen to your glorious body?"

"You're just concerned about the UV rays, right?"

"Safety first, that's me."

"Right. That's exactly what I think of when I think of you."

"I'll have you know that the first thing they taught me in the Army was never volunteer for anything, but for you I am willing to make an exception."

She laughed and rolled over on her back. "Yup, it's all about the public service with you, Pete."

"I'm just glad you realize it."

He squeezed some sunscreen into his open palm and was poised over her back when she suddenly whirled about. "But what about all the other guilty parties? What about the oil companies, those bastards? What about the CIA?"

"Don't leave me hanging with a hand full of sunscreen," said Avakian.

"All right, all right," she said, settling back onto the towel. "But you can talk while you're doing that."

"You don't want me to lose focus, do you?"

"You can multitask," she said into the towel. "Talk."

He did just that while he rubbed her back. "Benin bought themselves some protection. They signed an oil exploration contract with a French company, for services rendered. And then a bigger one with the same U.S. oil company that was backing the mercs."

"That is so wrong," Judy said. "Just like they were a candy store in Brooklyn."

"Just like," Avakian agreed. "But what do they care? Whoever finds oil, Benin gets paid. Or should I say the ruling class. And now the President doesn't have to sleep with one eye open. It's the best kind of anti-coup insurance."

"Despicable."

"Honey, that's the way the world works. It's just not what they teach kids in social studies. Look at it this way. What is government, after all? The original protection racket. You pay them taxes: they provide security, enforce contracts, and resolve disputes. When government doesn't do their job, someone else steps in to provide those essential services. For a price."

"The world as *The Godfather, Part II*?" she said.

"You're being ironic, but you're not being wrong. The U.S. government has taken out more than a few Tattaglia families over the years, because they were messing with our business. These days the so-called great powers are totally spineless. They don't want to get their hands dirty or their soldiers killed. They're not doing their job. Other forces fill the void. So we have a new age of piracy. Pirates pop up in the spaces governments don't police. Pirates, and private armies that don't mind fighting dirty little wars. For a price.

After all, India was first conquered by The East India Company, a corporation. Should we be surprised that oil companies are securing markets the hard way? This is a big game played on a big table."

"Yes, what *about* the oil companies, Pete?"

"De Wet said it to me. Americans drive their cars. And they don't much care what it takes to keep gas under three dollars a gallon. What do you think the answer would be if you asked most of our politicians and fellow citizens if they cared about a coup in Benin, as long as gas stayed under three dollars a gallon? And all they had to do was sit still for it? What do you think they'd say?"

"I say I'm buying a hybrid as soon as we get back home," Judy said. "But what I meant was, you had your Sicilian revenge on everyone else. What about the oil companies?"

Avakian shook his head. "Too big, too powerful. No government's willing to take them on. I'm certainly not."

"So they get a free pass?" she said.

"Wait a minute," said Avakian. He paused from his sunscreen work with one hand on each of her buttocks, while he thought it over. "Tom Sizemore in *Heat*, right?"

"That is kind of what I was thinking about," she admitted.

"I love it when you get outraged," he said, moving down to her legs. "But the oil companies are a luxury. Sorry, but I'm not going to war on the streets with them."

"Then what about the CIA?"

"Oh, they're probably frantically shredding and burning everything that links them to this little debacle.

I don't think I'm going to have any trouble from them, they'll be too busy covering their ass. Besides, I recorded all the conversations I had with my case officer. Just in case. You like that pun?"

"Very funny," Judy said. "It would have been nice if you'd settled all the family business."

"I think I did pretty well, considering."

"I guess you did at that. Sorry, didn't mean to sound as if I was disappointed, but I've come to expect all kinds of nefarious stuff from you."

"Thanks. I think."

Judy rolled back onto her side and pushed her sunglasses up on her head to give him the old face to face. "You know, you didn't have to tell me you were retiring to keep me. I just want you to know that."

"I appreciate that, honey, but I'm done," Avakian said flatly.

"You say that now," she said.

"No, I'm done. Even if I don't wind up on a no-fly list." He slid over on the blanket so they were face to face again. "Judy, my judgment on this one just plain sucked, from beginning to end. I hurt a lot of poor people who not only didn't deserve to be hurt, they couldn't afford to be hurt. Just to save my own worthless skin. And anything I could do, like giving mercenary money to charity, isn't going to begin to pay that back."

"You did what you had to," she said.

"When the mojo is gone, you have to hang it up," he said as if he hadn't heard her. "You can't be like the old western gunfighter with failing eyes who's staying alive just on his reputation. I'm done."

"You'll change your mind," she said.

"No, I don't think so."

"I want you to know, it's all right with me if you do."

It took a lot to put a dent in Avakian's composure, but that did it. "What?"

She nodded her head and patted him on the cheek. "It's just that the next time, I'm going with you."

RELENTLESSLY VIOLENT AND HUMOROUSLY REALISTIC—A HISTORICAL ESPIONAGE THRILLER AT ITS FINEST.

"Heroism is having to do something drastic to keep from getting killed."

That's what security consultant Pete Avakian tells his dinner date, Dr. Judy Rose, on a night out in Beijing. Little does he know, his words are about to play out in graphic detail.

Just as they are starting to get comfortable with each other, chaos erupts in the street. China has launched missiles at Taiwan—a long history of tension given way to war. Suddenly, Pete and Judy are confronted by hostile youths, and an act of self-defense puts them on the run from the authorities in a country crazed by war.

Pursued by the Chinese police, the Americans race toward the Mongolian border. But Pete and Judy's only chance of survival is to work together to escape a country gone mad… even if that means taking drastic action.

AVAILABLE NOW

About the Author

William Christie was born in Massachusetts. He graduated from the University of Pennsylvania with a Bachelor of Arts degree in Political Science. He then joined the United States Marine Corps and served as an infantry officer.

After leaving the Marine Corps he began writing. His first novel, *The Warriors of God*, was published in January 1992. He has published nine novels.